ary

98284

April 2008

Berkley Prime Crime Titles by Jimmie Ruth Evans

FLAMINGO FATALE
MURDER OVER EASY
BEST SERVED COLD
BRING YOUR OWN POISON

Bring Your Own Poison

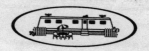

Jimmie Ruth Evans

BERKLEY PRIME CRIME, NEW YORK

THE BERKLEY PUBLISHING GROUP
Published by the Penguin Group
Penguin Group (USA) Inc.
375 Hudson Street, New York, New York 10014, USA
Penguin Group (Canada), 90 Eglinton Avenue East, Suite 700, Toronto, Ontario M4P 2Y3, Canada
(a division of Pearson Penguin Canada Inc.)
Penguin Books Ltd., 80 Strand, London WC2R 0RL, England
Penguin Group Ireland, 25 St. Stephen's Green, Dublin 2, Ireland (a division of Penguin Books Ltd.)
Penguin Group (Australia), 250 Camberwell Road, Camberwell, Victoria 3124, Australia
(a division of Pearson Australia Group Pty. Ltd.)
Penguin Books India Pvt. Ltd., 11 Community Centre, Panchsheel Park, New Delhi—110 017, India
Penguin Group (NZ), 67 Apollo Drive, Rosedale, North Shore 0632, New Zealand
(a division of Pearson New Zealand Ltd.)
Penguin Books (South Africa) (Pty.) Ltd., 24 Sturdee Avenue, Rosebank, Johannesburg 2196,
South Africa

Penguin Books Ltd., Registered Offices: 80 Strand, London WC2R 0RL, England

This is a work of fiction. Names, characters, places, and incidents either are the product of the author's
imagination or are used fictitiously, and any resemblance to actual persons, living or dead, business
establishments, events, or locales is entirely coincidental. The publisher does not have any control over
and does not assume any responsibility for author or third-party websites or their content.

PUBLISHER'S NOTE: The recipes contained in this book are to be followed exactly as written. The
publisher is not responsible for your specific health or allergy needs that may require medical super-
vision. The publisher is not responsible for any adverse reactions to the recipes contained in this book.

BRING YOUR OWN POISON

A Berkley Prime Crime Book / published by arrangement with the author

PRINTING HISTORY
Berkley Prime Crime mass-market edition / January 2008

Copyright © 2008 by Dean James.
Cover art by Paul Slater.
Cover design by Judith Lagerman.
Interior text design by Kristin del Rosario.

ISBN: 978-0-425-21905-8

BERKLEY® PRIME CRIME
Berkley Prime Crime Books are published by The Berkley Publishing Group,
a division of Penguin Group (USA) Inc.,
375 Hudson Street, New York, New York 10014.
The name BERKLEY PRIME CRIME and the BERKLEY PRIME CRIME design
are trademarks belonging to Penguin Group (USA) Inc.

PRINTED IN THE UNITED STATES OF AMERICA

10 9 8 7 6 5 4 3 2 1

*This book is dedicated
with great affection, admiration, and respect
to Doris Helen Cate,
who could teach Wanda Nell a thing or two
about being a strong, independent woman.*

Acknowledgments

Sergeant Wayne A. Wells of the Madison County, Mississippi, Sheriff's Department cheerfully answered questions about law enforcement personnel and procedures in Mississippi. Any errors in this book are mine, certainly not his. (I would like to say a special thanks to my cousin Vanissa who very thoughtfully married Wayne so I would have such a handy source of information. Aren't family members wonderful?)

My editor, Michelle Vega, continues to offer her enthusiasm, energy, and encouragement, and Wanda Nell and her family couldn't ask for a better sponsor. (Ernie says hi, by the way.)

My usual support team also offered encouragement and enthusiasm as needed: Julie Wray Herman, Patricia Orr, and Tejas Englesmith. I can't imagine trying to write a book without them egging me on.

One

"Miranda, Teddy's here," Wanda Nell Culpepper called down the hall to her older daughter. "He just drove up."

"Tell him I'll be out in a minute," Miranda yelled back.

Wanda Nell headed for the front door of her double-wide trailer. Dogging her every step and dragging his ragged bunny behind him, her grandson, Lavon, chattered nonstop. Wanda Nell listened to him with half an ear, smiling indulgently. At the moment, he was regaling her with a story about an imaginary adventure he and the bunny had the day before. At twenty-six months, Lavon had a robust imagination and tireless vocal chords.

"That's wonderful, sweetie," Wanda Nell told him as she opened the door to admit Miranda's boyfriend, Teddy Bolton. "Come on in, Teddy. Miranda will be ready in a minute."

"Afternoon, Miz Culpepper," Teddy said. He stepped into the trailer, and Wanda Nell shut the door behind him.

Lavon held his bunny up to Teddy, telling him the bunny was saying hello. Smiling, Teddy squatted down until his eyes were almost on a level with Lavon's. He patted the boy and his bunny on the head in turn, and said, "Hello, Mr. Bunny, nice to see you."

Lavon giggled, and Teddy picked the boy up in his arms and swung him back and forth. Lavon giggled even more.

Wanda Nell watched them with a smile. When she had first met Teddy several months before, she had been wary of him, worried that he would be a bad influence on Miranda. He was twenty-three, tall, muscular, and extensively tattooed. He had joined the Marines right out of high school, and he met Miranda three months after he left the corps. The tattoos made Wanda Nell nervous, because she thought at first he was a Hell's Angel or something equally terrifying.

Teddy had quickly won her trust, however, because he treated Miranda with care and respect. He adored Lavon, and the boy had already started calling him "Daddy." Miranda blossomed under his influence, though she still had moments in which she reverted to her old behavior in front of him. Teddy would gently shake his head, a slight frown on his face, and Miranda would stop doing whatever it was she was doing.

Marveling that Teddy had accomplished what she had not been able to in eighteen years as Miranda's mother, Wanda Nell welcomed him into the family. Teddy had extensive family of his own, mostly from around Water Valley. He had one sister who lived in Tullahoma, and for the moment he was staying with her. He had a good job as a mechanic at one of the car dealerships in town, and he was saving up to buy a house. He had confided all this to Wanda Nell not long after he and Miranda started dating, and Wanda Nell took this as a good sign as far as Miranda and Lavon were concerned.

"Here I am," Miranda announced.

Before she turned to face her daughter, Wanda Nell saw the look in Teddy's eyes when they came to rest on Miranda. He was very much in love, and Miranda was, too. She now confided in her mother more than she ever had, and Wanda Nell relished this closer relationship with her difficult middle child.

Wanda Nell stepped out of the way, and Teddy advanced to meet Miranda. One arm open, the other holding Lavon and the bunny, Teddy embraced Miranda before giving her a quick kiss.

"Where's Juliet?" Miranda asked.

"In her room, on the computer," Wanda Nell said. "I'll tell her you're ready." She headed down the hall to Juliet's bedroom.

The door stood ajar, but Wanda Nell knocked on it before entering. Juliet sat in front of the computer monitor, staring intently at something on the screen. She looked up when her mother cleared her throat.

"Hi, Mama," Juliet said. Her hand tightened on the mouse, and Wanda Nell heard rapid clicking. "I guess Teddy's here."

"He is, and they're ready to go," Wanda Nell said. She frowned at the computer. Lately, Juliet had been spending more and more time with the darn thing, and Wanda Nell was getting slightly worried. She had heard those stories in the news about Internet predators, and she feared Juliet might be a target for one of them.

She had sat Juliet down a couple weeks ago, and they had talked about it. Juliet assured her mother that she was always careful about who she talked to online, and Wanda Nell had to believe that. Juliet had always been the good child, the one who had never cost her mother any sleep, unlike T.J. and Miranda. The problem was, Juliet was very shy, and at an age when girls were usually running around in packs and hunting boys, Juliet preferred to spend time in her room, occasionally going to a movie with her best friend, Jennalee Hill. For a pretty fifteen-year-old, that was not much of a social life.

Juliet hugged her mother when she stood up. "Don't worry, Mama," she said with a smile. "I'm fine, really."

Startled that Juliet had read her mind so easily, Wanda Nell smiled uncertainly back. "I know, honey." She gave Juliet a little push. "Go on, now, they're waiting for you."

Wanda Nell followed Juliet down the hall.

"Hey, Juliet," Teddy said. "Ready to go?"

"Yes," Juliet said. "Miranda, do you have Lavon's bag?"

"Dang," Miranda said. "Be right back."

Teddy and Juliet shared a grin as Miranda scurried down the other hall to the room she shared with Lavon. Some things about Miranda hadn't changed and probably never would.

"Come on, let's go get this guy in his car seat," Teddy said, jiggling Lavon in his arms. He dropped the bunny, and Juliet stooped to pick it up. "We'll see you later, Miz Culpepper."

"Y'all have a good time," Wanda Nell said, following them to the door. They were going to have lunch with old Mrs. Culpepper, the girls' grandmother, and her companion, her cousin Belle Meriwether. T.J., their older brother, and his partner, Hamilton "Tuck" Tucker, would be there as well. Wanda Nell had been invited, but she wanted some time to herself. She had to work a private party at the Kountry Kitchen tonight, and she needed a nap. She knew from experience how tiring these bachelor parties could be, and this one surely wouldn't be any different.

Miranda joined her mother at the door and rested her

head for a moment against her mother's shoulder. "He's really wonderful, isn't he, Mama?"

"He's a good man," Wanda Nell said, slipping her arm around Miranda.

"I'm so lucky," Miranda said. "And Lavon, too. Teddy loves him like he was his own baby."

"Teddy's pretty lucky, too," Wanda Nell said.

"Thank you, Mama," Miranda said. "I wish Daddy could be here. I think he'd like Teddy, don't you?"

Wanda Nell heard the sadness in her daughter's voice, and her heart ached for the girl. Bobby Ray Culpepper hadn't deserved being murdered, and Wanda Nell still missed him sometimes, despite all the pain and distress he had caused her over the years. She'd had to divorce him and move on with her life, but for their children's sake, she wished he was still around. It was hard to believe that a year had passed since he was killed.

"Yes, honey, I think he would like Teddy a lot." Wanda Nell hugged Miranda once more before giving her a slight push. "Go on, now, they're waiting."

Wanda Nell watched from the doorway until the car pulled out of sight. She was about to close the door and head to her bedroom for a nap when the door of the trailer across from hers opened.

Mayrene Lancaster stuck her head out. "Hey, girl, you got a minute?"

Wanda Nell didn't have the heart to tell her best friend she really wanted to sleep, so she said, "Sure, you want me to come over there?"

"Naw, I'll be over in a jiff." Mayrene's head disappeared into her trailer, and the door shut.

Wanda Nell went to the couch and sat down. Suppressing a yawn, she waited for Mayrene. She wondered what

Mayrene wanted to talk about. Her best friend had been acting funny lately, and Wanda Nell was pretty sure she knew why. It must have something to do with the new man in Mayrene's life. So far she hadn't told Wanda Nell who he was, and maybe she was finally going to talk about him.

Wanda Nell perked up a little. This could be worth losing some nap time over.

Mayrene appeared about five minutes later, just when Wanda Nell started to nod off right there on the couch. "Wake up, honey," Mayrene said. "I know you're tired, but I promise I won't keep you up long."

Wanda Nell grinned, awake again, and patted the couch beside her. "Sit on down and talk to me."

About a dozen years older than Wanda Nell, who was forty-one, Mayrene was generously proportioned. She insisted there were plenty of men around who preferred women they could hold on to. If a man wanted a stick for a girlfriend, she had once told Wanda Nell, then he could go to the store and buy himself a broom and be done with it. She didn't hold much with dieting.

Air whooshed out of the cushion as Mayrene dropped down on the couch. "Well, you know I been dating somebody, and I reckon we could be getting serious about one another."

Wanda Nell nodded. "Yeah, I know the signs."

Mayrene's eyes narrowed. "What do you mean, 'signs'?"

Keeping a straight face, Wanda Nell replied, "For one thing, you get real secretive, and another thing, you start humming. I guess you don't realize it, but you hum a lot when you've got a new man on the line."

"Yeah, I guess so," Mayrene said, thinking about it for a moment. "I guess I do hum more than usual."

Wanda Nell decided not to mention the fact that

Mayrene's humming was decidedly off-key. Instead she said, "The other thing is that you change your hair every other day. I never know from one day to the next what you're gonna look like."

Mayrene was a beautician, and a very good one. She was by far the most popular stylist at the beauty shop where she worked. Her own hair was always perfectly done, and she rarely varied the style—except when she was dating. Then she just couldn't seem to leave her own head alone. Wanda Nell stared at the mass of blond ringlets Mayrene wore today. Shirley Temple she was not, but Wanda Nell couldn't tell her that.

Laughing, Mayrene said, "You got me on that one, honey."

"Enough of that," Wanda Nell said. "Tell me who this new man is. I been dying of curiosity."

Mayrene's expression turned coy. "Well, you know I've always liked a man in uniform."

"Yeah," Wanda Nell said, trying not to get impatient. She knew from experience that Mayrene would draw this out as long as she could.

"I've had my eye on this one for a long time," Mayrene continued. "We almost had a thing going a few years ago, but he was going through a real messy divorce at the time. I just couldn't deal with that, and we stopped seeing one another."

Wanda Nell cast her mind back. That must have been before she moved into the trailer park, about six years ago. The first person she met was Mayrene, who lived in the next trailer. From the beginning, they got on real well, and ever since they had been as close as sisters.

"No, that was before we met," Mayrene said, like she had just read Wanda Nell's mind. "But not too long before, as I recall." She shrugged. "Anyway, we parted company. Then his wife got real sick. She had cancer in her ovaries, and it was real bad. So they ended up not getting a divorce after all. He took care of her until she died."

"I see," Wanda Nell said. "He sounds like a good man. If it had been me and Bobby Ray, who knows what he might've done. He didn't like being around sick people."

"He is a good man," Mayrene said. "He did the right thing. But we didn't run into each other much there for a while, and when we did, well, I guess we both felt maybe it was too late or something."

"But obviously something changed your minds," Wanda Nell said.

Mayrene nodded. "Yeah, I ran into him at a dance out at the VFW about three weeks ago. Him and me got to talking and, well, I guess you could say we kinda picked up where we left off." She smiled broadly.

"Maybe this time it's the right time," Wanda Nell said, happy for her friend, but still a little wary. Mayrene had consistently bad luck when it came to men, and Wanda Nell hated to see her hurt yet again.

"That's what I'm thinking," Mayrene said. "I really do think it is."

"You still haven't told me who he is," Wanda Nell reminded her with a poke in the arm.

Mayrene laughed. "No, I guess I hadn't got around to that yet."

Wanda Nell rolled her eyes. "Honestly, Mayrene, you could be a politician, it takes you so long to get to the point."

Mayrene had another laugh at that. "Okay, okay, I get it." She leaned a little closer to Wanda Nell. "His name is Dixon Vance, and he's a policeman."

The name rang a faint bell with Wanda Nell, and she thought about it, trying to put a face with the name. "Oh yeah," she said, nodding when the memory surfaced, "I know him. He used to come in the Kountry Kitchen, but the cops hang out at the Holiday Inn these days. We don't see them that much."

From what Wanda Nell could remember, Dixon Vance was Mayrene's age, give or take a couple of years. Good looking, in a tough-cop kind of way. Gray hair, stocky but muscular, and tall.

"Yeah," Wanda Nell continued, "he's a nice-looking man."

"He sure is," Mayrene said, grinning salaciously. "I just love that uniform and the way he fills it out. He's in real good shape, if you know what I mean."

Wanda Nell laughed. "You are terrible, Mayrene. You sure move fast."

"Ain't nothing holding me back," Mayrene said smugly. "I'm old enough to know what I want, and what I'm willing to share." She laughed. "What about you and Jack? When are you going to start sharing with him? You can't tell me he's not getting frustrated."

This was the last thing Wanda Nell wanted to talk about right now. She and Jack Pemberton had been dating for several months. Jack had already told her he loved her and that he wanted to marry her, but Wanda Nell just couldn't make up her mind. They hadn't even been to bed together yet. Wanda Nell's two jobs kept her on the run, and her schedule and Jack's didn't give them that many opportunities. Jack taught English at the county high school, where Juliet had been one of his students. He often came by the Kountry Kitchen for his evening meal, but the only time they really had together was Sundays. There was no way she was going to jump into bed with him at her place, not with her daughters and her grandson anywhere around. That just wouldn't be right, and she would never do it.

They could have been together at Jack's house, but Wanda Nell felt funny about that, too. It would feel too much like shacking up with somebody while she left her girls and Lavon on their own, and that wasn't her way. She knew Jack was frustrated by the situation, and she was getting increasingly that way herself. She had finally admitted to herself that she really loved Jack, and it was only natural for them to take their relationship to the next level. Marriage was still a little further down the road.

"Don't mind me, honey," Mayrene said as the silence between them lengthened. "I know you don't really want to talk about it, and I shouldn't aggravate you by asking like that."

"Oh, it's okay," Wanda Nell said with a rueful smile. "It's almost funny, it's so ridiculous."

"No, it isn't," Mayrene said. "I know how you feel. You can't turn your back on your responsibilities to your family just to make things easier for you and Jack. You wouldn't be *you* if you did that." She patted Wanda Nell's shoulder.

"Thanks," Wanda Nell said. "But it's getting real frustrating, I can tell you."

"You don't have to tell me," Mayrene said, her laugh booming out, startling Wanda Nell. "I know how I get when I'm in a dry spell, if you know what I mean."

Wanda Nell couldn't help but grin at that, even though inside she wanted to yell. Her dry spell had pretty much lasted since she divorced Bobby Ray nearly twelve years ago.

"What we got to do is figure out a way for you and Jack to spend more time together," Mayrene said. "You need more time to yourselves without family hanging around."

"Yeah, but how?" Wanda Nell asked. "Which job should I give up? And who would be here with the girls? Mostly Juliet, these days, and even though she's fifteen, I just don't like her being here by herself."

"No, I know," Mayrene said. "You know you can always call on me."

"Yeah," Wanda Nell said, "and I thank you for that, but you have your own life. You can't always be running over here helping me out all the time."

"It'll work out, somehow," Mayrene said. "But I better stop all this jabbering, and let you get some rest. What time do you have to be at the Kountry Kitchen?"

"Not till five," Wanda Nell said, glancing at the clock. "That gives me time for about a four-hour nap, and I'm sure going to need it tonight."

Mayrene got up from the couch. "What's so special about tonight?"

"Oh, we've got this bachelor party," Wanda Nell said, frowning in distaste. "They reserved the back room from seven o'clock until. You know how those things are. Grown men acting like idiots."

"Yeah," Mayrene said. "You reckon they're going to have one of those big cakes, with some woman hopping out of it?" She had an odd look on her face.

Wanda Nell laughed. "Who knows? They're sure spending a lot of money on this."

"Dixon told me he's got something to do tonight," Mayrene said slowly, "something that he couldn't take me to, he said. Just some of the guys. He sure didn't tell me it was a bachelor party. I figured they'd be playing poker or something."

"That doesn't mean he's going to be at this party," Wanda Nell pointed out.

"Yeah," Mayrene said, her face darkening, "but what you want to bet that's exactly where he will be? Who's this party for?"

As Mayrene asked that question, Wanda Nell realized that Mayrene's new boyfriend probably would be there. "It's for some guy named Travis Blakeley. He's getting married next week, to this girl T.J. knew in high school. He's a policeman, too."

"Travis Blakeley," Mayrene said, her voice suddenly harsh. "I wouldn't let any child of mine anywhere near him. Who'd be crazy enough to marry him?"

"What on earth are you talking about?" Wanda Nell asked. She didn't know Travis Blakeley from Adam, but Mayrene seemed to. Whatever she knew, it obviously wasn't too good.

"He's been married twice already," Mayrene said, her face set in grim lines. "Both his wives died within a year or two of getting married in so-called *accidents*. Would you want one of your girls to marry a man like that?"

Two

Wanda Nell shivered. Something like that happening to one of her daughters didn't bear thinking about.

"No, I don't know much about him," she said. "How do you know all this?"

"His first wife was a girl from down around Winona," Mayrene said, "I knew her mama and daddy, Betty and Jack Treadwell. It liked to have killed them when she died."

"What happened?"

"She was home by herself one night—asleep, or so they said—and the house caught on fire," Mayrene said, her face dark with anger. "The smoke got to her before she could get out of the house."

"How did the fire start?" Wanda Nell asked, trying not to picture the girl's death in her mind.

"Some kind of explosive," Mayrene said. "They never did find out who set it. A lot of people thought it was Travis because of the insurance settlement he got. They couldn't ever prove anything, though."

"If it wasn't him," Wanda Nell said, "then who else could have done it?"

"Travis claimed it was somebody who'd threatened him," Mayrene said, and the scorn in her voice indicated what she thought of that idea. "He helped get some pretty nasty guys sent to the state pen at Parchman, or so he said. He claimed they said they'd come after him when they got out and make him sorry."

"Seems like that could have happened," Wanda Nell said.

"Maybe," Mayrene conceded, "but right after he got hold of that insurance money, he bought himself a fancy sports car. And he was courting some other girls less than three months after his first wife died."

"That's pretty tacky," Wanda Nell said, wrinkling her nose.

"It gets worse," Mayrene said. "A couple years after his first wife died in that fire, he got married again. To one of the girls he started running around with right after his wife was killed." She snorted. "Some say he was running around with them even *before* poor Jeanie Treadwell died."

"And something happened to the second wife, too?"

"You bet it did," Mayrene said. "The house they were living in burned down, too. Another explosive device, but this time the wife wasn't home."

"Creepy," Wanda Nell said. She was terrified of house fires.

"You got that right," Mayrene replied. "Well, a couple months after *that* house burned down, the second wife was driving home late one night. They were living out in the country, and somebody ran her off the road into a steep ditch. Her car rolled over several times, and she died."

"That's horrible," Wanda Nell said. It was all too easy to picture. A country road late at night, no lights other than car lights—or moonlight if you were lucky. Wanda Nell shivered at the thought. It was bad enough driving around Tullahoma late at night with streetlights.

"It was," Mayrene said, "because it turned out she was two months pregnant." She paused for a moment. "Travis had a big insurance policy on her, too."

"Didn't anybody try to investigate him that time?" Wanda Nell had thought Mayrene was maybe exaggerating at first, but the more she heard about this man, the more she was inclined to believe her friend.

Mayrene shrugged. "They might have, but what were they gonna do? He's a policeman, and the police department stood up for him. Travis claimed it was probably one of those same guys that threatened him that ran her off the road."

"So you're telling me they didn't really investigate it?"

Shrugging again, Mayrene said, "I think they probably did some kind of half-assed poking around, but it didn't amount to a hill of beans." She snorted in disgust. "So much for our police department."

"If you feel that way," Wanda Nell said, not certain how her friend would take this question, "then why are you going out with one of them?"

"I know, I know." Mayrene got a real sheepish look on her face. "I don't think they're *all* bad. Dixon's a good man, otherwise I wouldn't give him the time of day. If I find out he's not, then he's gonna rue the day he ever crossed my path."

Most women who uttered threats like that were just talking, but with Mayrene, it was probably the truth. Wanda Nell knew her friend well, and Mayrene never made idle threats.

"I just hope for your sake he's as good a man as you think he is," Wanda Nell said. "You deserve a good one."

"Don't we all, honey, don't we all," Mayrene said, grinning. She got up. "I'm going home and let you get some sleep."

Wanda Nell nodded, sagging a little against the couch. "I'm not gonna argue with you."

"I'll lock the door behind me," Mayrene said. "You just get on to bed."

The trailer was suddenly too quiet once Mayrene was gone. Without her daughters and grandson nearby, Wanda Nell felt oddly dislocated. She so rarely spent time alone in the trailer, the situation unnerved her a little bit.

Shaking away this unaccustomed twinge of nerves, Wanda Nell got up from the couch and went down the hall to her bedroom. Stripping off her clothes and slipping into bed in her bra and panties, she pulled the covers around her and made herself comfortable. Grimacing, she sat up and reached for the alarm clock. Sure as she didn't set it, she'd oversleep.

That task accomplished, she snuggled down in bed and willed herself to relax. For a few minutes, all she could think about was what Mayrene had told her about Travis Blakeley. She hadn't been looking forward to this bachelor party to begin with, and now she really didn't want to work it. She wasn't sure she wanted anything to do with a man like that.

She shouldn't be quick to judge, she knew, but the story Mayrene had told her was pretty compelling. Too many co-incidences for there not to be some truth to it. Yawning, she made another effort to banish these thoughts so she could sleep.

When the alarm sounded at four-thirty, Wanda Nell came out of a deep sleep. She had been dreaming about a girl trapped in a burning house, and the images from the dream lingered in her mind while she struggled to wake up completely. She sat up and shut off the alarm clock.

For a few minutes she stayed in bed, the covers bunched up around her. The dream had frightened her, and she couldn't seem to shake it.

The phone rang, startling her. Reaching out a trembling hand, she picked up the phone from her bedside table.

"Hello."

"Hey, darling, it's me." Jack Pemberton's voice, warm and comforting, brought her back to reality. "I was just calling to make sure you were up. I know you hate to oversleep."

"Thanks, sweetie," she said, smiling. Jack was thoughtful and caring, always doing little things to show how he felt about her. "I remembered to set the alarm, but getting a phone call from you is a lot better."

"Glad to oblige," Jack said. "I just wish . . . well, you know." His voice trailed off.

"I know," Wanda Nell said, her voice soft. She wished it, too, and maybe one of these days he wouldn't have to call her on the phone to wake her up.

"Are you coming by for supper tonight?" Wanda Nell said after a brief pause. "If you are, I'll make sure to save you some apple pie."

Jack groaned into the phone. "Honey, I'm gonna be about as big as the broad side of a barn if you keep on feeding me like that."

Wanda Nell laughed. Jack did sometimes eat a lot, but he more than compensated for it by regular exercise. He had a lean, fit body and . . . well, she'd better not go down that road. Thinking like that led her into visualizing too many distracting images. She laughed again softly, this time at herself.

"What was that?" Jack said. "Are you laughing at me?" He pretended to be outraged.

"No, honey, just at myself," Wanda Nell said. "Look, this party I've got to work is supposed to start around seven-thirty, so make sure you get there earlier than that. Otherwise I won't be able to spend much time with you."

"I'll be there around six-thirty," Jack said, "and I'll make sure you have time for me, if I have to bribe Melvin to do it."

Wanda Nell laughed again. Melvin Arbuckle, her boss at the Kountry Kitchen, liked Jack, and the two men got along well. That was a good thing, because Melvin had more than once expressed interest in Wanda Nell himself. Not since Jack had entered the picture, though, and Wanda Nell was grateful for that. Melvin had been a good friend to her, and she would hate to lose that friendship, not to mention her job.

"I'll see you then," she said. "Now I better be getting up and into the shower, or I'll be late."

"Okay, darling," Jack said. "Love you. Drive carefully."

"I will," Wanda Nell promised. She cleared her throat. "Love you, too." She hung up the phone.

She still had trouble sometimes saying those words to Jack. They came more easily to him, but for her they were so loaded with meaning she couldn't say them any old time. She knew it all had to do with commitment, and she was trying to be better about it. She had a hard time relying on a man after the years of marriage to Bobby Ray Culpepper, when she could never count on him for much of anything. She was used to relying on herself, and that was a hard habit to break. She had to keep reminding herself that Jack was very different from Bobby Ray, and that was a good thing.

A good thing she was determined to hang on to, Lord willing. She got out of bed and was soon in the shower.

By five o'clock she was dressed, her makeup done, and heading out the door to her car. The girls and Lavon wouldn't be home for a little while yet. After having lunch at old Mrs. Culpepper's house on Main Street, they were going to a movie.

Wanda Nell opened the door of her little red Chevy Cavalier and slid inside. The weather was still cool, but the warm April sun had heated up the interior of her car. She rolled her window halfway down before she headed out.

The Kozy Kove Trailer Park, where Wanda Nell lived, was situated close to the lake, and as she drove toward town, Wanda Nell passed a fair amount of traffic headed that way. It would be a nice night for a picnic or a barbecue at the lake, and suddenly Wanda Nell was envious. She'd much rather be doing that than going in to work tonight.

Shaking her head, Wanda Nell concentrated on driving to work. Nothing was far from anything else in Tullahoma, and it took her only about ten minutes to get to the Kountry Kitchen. She parked her car, grabbed her purse, and headed into the restaurant.

Melvin Arbuckle looked up from the cash register as she came through the front door. He smiled in welcome. "You're a little early," he said, glancing at his watch. "It's not even five-fifteen yet."

"Just couldn't wait to get here, I guess," Wanda Nell said. She slipped behind the counter and passed him on her way to the room in the back where the waitresses had space to keep their purses and other personal belongings.

"Glad to hear it," Melvin said.

"Hi, Ruby," Wanda Nell said, pausing to greet the other waitress.

"Hey, Wanda Nell," Ruby Garner said, her young face breaking into a wide smile. She was a sweet, smart girl, and Wanda Nell was very fond of her. She was attending the local junior college and working at the Kountry Kitchen to pay her way through.

"I'll be right back," Wanda Nell said. She paused in the kitchen to speak to the cook and the dishwasher before dropping off her purse down the hall. She made a last quick check of her makeup in the mirror there. Deciding that she looked fine, she returned to the front of the restaurant. She paused behind the counter to survey the room.

Only a couple tables and three stools at the counter were occupied, and Ruby obviously had everything under control up front. "What do I need to do for the party?" Wanda Nell asked Melvin.

"Not much," Melvin said. "It's been pretty slow this afternoon, so I think I've done everything that needed doing. You can double-check me, though."

Wanda Nell nodded. Melvin was thorough, but sometimes he missed a few things. She might as well have a look.

She paused near the end of the counter to speak to one of the regulars. "Hey, Junior, how're you doing?"

Junior Farley, his plump face creased into a grin, said, "Howdy, Wanda Nell. I'm doing about as well as can be expected, I guess. How're you?"

"I'm fine," Wanda Nell said. "You need anything?"

"Naw, I'm okay," Junior said. "Little Miss Ruby there'll take care of me if I need something." He beamed at the girl who blushed and turned away.

Suppressing a smile, Wanda Nell continued on her way to the restaurant's back room. Junior was pretty shy with women. He had been dating someone for a while, but

Wanda Nell heard the woman had dumped him. Now it looked like Junior was mooning over Ruby. He was a nice man, but he was a bit too old for Ruby, Wanda Nell thought. Junior had to be her age, if not older, and Ruby was barely twenty. She was smart enough to handle the situation, though, and Wanda Nell wasn't going to interfere. Junior would probably be too chicken to do anything anyway.

Melvin had shut off the back room and tacked a notice on the door that the room was reserved for a private party from seven-thirty until ten. Wanda Nell opened the door and slipped through.

Melvin had rearranged the tables and chairs to form a big square in the middle of the room. She counted twenty-five chairs there. This was going to be a pretty good–size party. Next she inspected the bar setup Melvin had provided. He had hired a bartender for the night, and the guy should be arriving around seven to get ready.

As Wanda Nell examined the rest of the room, she discovered the only thing Melvin had forgotten. There were no ashtrays on the tables, and Wanda Nell knew they would be needed. At every other bachelor party she had ever worked, the room quickly turned smoky. She went back up front to find ashtrays and to remind Melvin to take care of ventilating the room as much as he could.

Business remained slow for the next hour, and Wanda Nell relieved Ruby for a while. She would be working the front while Wanda Nell took care of the party. Ruby had offered to help her, but Wanda Nell didn't want the girl having to deal with rowdy men who had been drinking more than was good for them. She could handle them just fine, and Melvin would never be far away if she needed him.

At six-thirty on the dot, Wanda Nell looked toward the front door to see Jack Pemberton coming into the restaurant.

She moved forward with a smile to greet him, but she halted when she saw the expression on his face.

Her heart did a flip-flop. Something bad had happened, and Jack was coming to tell her about it. For a moment she couldn't breathe.

Jack came up to her and reached out a hand. "What's wrong, honey? Are you okay?"

"Why are you asking me?" Wanda Nell demanded. "What's wrong with you? Did something happen to one of the girls? Or T.J.?" Her heart thudded in her chest.

Jack shook his head. "No, they're all fine. Sorry if I scared you."

Breathing more easily, Wanda Nell said, "Then what on earth is wrong? The look on your face about scared me to death."

Jack scowled. "It's my cousin, Lisa," he said. "The guy who was stalking her in Meridian has found her here."

Three

"Oh, no," Wanda Nell said. "How did he find her?"

"Somebody at the hospital where she used to work." Jack's face was set in grim lines. "When Lisa started getting phone calls again, she said she called around at the hospital in Meridian and found out a cop had been asking questions about her. She figures somebody told him she'd moved to Tullahoma."

"Didn't she tell them that the guy stalking her is a cop?"

Jack shrugged. "She only told a couple of people at the hospital where she was moving. One of them must have slipped up somehow."

"Come on and sit down," Wanda Nell said, leading Jack to the counter. The few tables in the open part of the restaurant were occupied. "Let me get you some ice tea."

"I could use a stiff shot of bourbon," Jack said as he followed Wanda Nell and sat down. "I'm so angry about all this."

"Actually, I can get you some if you really want it," Wanda Nell said. She could raid the liquor stash set aside for the party.

Jack shook his head, smiling briefly. "No, really, tea is fine. I was just talking."

"What's Lisa going to do?" Wanda Nell said as she poured tea into an ice-filled glass. She set it in front of Jack. "Is she going to move again?"

"No," Jack said after a sip of his tea. "At least, not for a while, anyway. She doesn't want to run anymore. At this rate, she'd have to move to the other side of the country to get away from this jerk, and she doesn't want to do that."

"I don't blame her," Wanda Nell said. "She should be able to live where she wants to and not have to worry about some piece of slime like that." She shook her head. "I don't know what's worse, a guy like that stalking a poor girl, or marrying her and killing her for the insurance."

"What on earth are you talking about?" Jack stared at her.

Wanda Nell could have kicked herself. She couldn't believe she'd let that slip out. She glanced around. No one was sitting close to Jack. She leaned forward and spoke in a low tone. "It's this guy they're having the bachelor party for. Mayrene told me he was married twice before, and both his wives died in accidents." She snorted. "Except nobody really thinks they were accidents."

"And this guy is a cop?" Jack asked.

"Yeah," Wanda Nell said. "Can you believe it?"

"I would have said it was hard to believe, before I heard about what Lisa was going through because of a cop. But now I'm willing to believe just about anything." Jack's right hand tightened around his tea glass.

"When did this happen?"

"Just an hour ago," Jack said. "I've been with Lisa, trying to calm her down, since not long after I called you to make sure you were up."

"Where is she now?"

"At my house," Jack said. "She'll be okay there for now, but it probably won't take the guy long to find her. I don't know what we're going to do. I think she should call the police, but right now there's just no talking to her. Maybe when she calms down she'll be more willing to listen to me."

Wanda Nell placed a hand over his fist. "I know it's rough on you, honey, because you're trying to help her. You've just got to be patient with her. I think what we need to do right now is get Lisa to a safe place, somewhere this guy wouldn't think of looking for her. That will make her feel better."

"But where?" Jack asked. "Out of town somewhere? She has to work."

"I know," Wanda Nell said. She surveyed the room again. It was a wonder Ruby wasn't hollering at her, because she sure hadn't been much help since Jack walked in the door. Ruby seemed to have everything under control, though. She smiled at Wanda Nell as she poured tea at one of the tables.

"There's a couple of possibilities," Wanda Nell said. "But I think the best one's probably Mayrene."

"I'm sure Lisa doesn't want to put anyone else in harm's way," Jack said. "I don't know if she'd go for that, even if Mayrene was willing."

"Lisa may not have much choice," Wanda Nell said. "Besides, can you imagine some jerk like that getting the better of Mayrene and Old Reliable?"

Jack had to grin at that. "I guess you've got a point. Do you think Mayrene would help out?"

"Only one way to know," Wanda Nell said. "I'll be back in a minute. I'll order you something when I go through the kitchen. You think you can eat right now?"

Jack nodded. "I guess so."

"Right," Wanda Nell said. She paused in the kitchen long enough to order a chicken-fried steak dinner for Jack before heading to Melvin's office. She wanted some privacy when she called Mayrene, otherwise she would have used the pay phone out front.

Melvin was just leaving his office when Wanda Nell neared it. "Something wrong?" he asked.

"I need to use your phone a minute," Wanda Nell said.

"Sure," Melvin said. After one look at her face he evidently decided not to ask questions. "I'll be out front."

Wanda Nell shut the office door before going to the phone. She punched in Mayrene's number, hoping she was at home.

Mayrene picked up after three rings. "Hello."

"Honey, it's me," Wanda Nell said. Without giving her friend a chance to respond, she rushed on, "We need your help. That guy who was stalking Lisa, Jack's cousin, has found her again. We need to find her a place to stay where he wouldn't think of looking for her."

Mayrene had a few choice words for the stalker. When she finished, she said simply, "She can stay with me. He won't find her here, but if he does, he may be going back to Meridian with less than he came with."

"Thanks, I knew we could count on you," Wanda Nell said, relieved. "You sure about this?"

"I'm not gonna sit by twiddling my thumbs while some jackass is bothering that poor girl," Mayrene said. "I just want to see him try something while she's with me."

"We haven't talked to Lisa yet about this," Wanda Nell said. "She may not agree to it."

"Y'all just get her to come over here," Mayrene said. "I'll do the rest. That poor girl."

"Okay, then," Wanda Nell said. "I'll tell Jack, and he can talk to Lisa. He might bring her over there tonight."

"I'll be ready," Mayrene said. "I ain't going nowhere."

Wanda Nell thanked her again before putting down the phone. On her way back out front she mulled over another idea. Finding Lisa a safe place to stay was the first priority, but after that, she was going to need a permanent solution to the problem. Lisa needed a good lawyer, Wanda Nell decided, and thankfully they didn't have to look very far to find one. There was a lawyer in the family now, and there wasn't anybody better.

Hamilton "Tuck" Tucker had helped her family out of more than one mess, and now he and Wanda Nell's son, T.J., were living together. Wanda Nell worried about them, afraid they would be attacked because of the nature of their relationship, but both men refused to be intimidated. They were discreet, but they didn't hide their relationship either. Wanda Nell loved them both and was happy her son had finally settled down and was making a good life for himself. She just prayed that someone else didn't take it all away from him out of hatred and fear.

Wanda Nell paused at the counter. The front of the restaurant had just about cleared out, and Ruby and Melvin were bussing a couple of the tables. "I'll be right back," she said.

"No rush," Melvin said.

Ruby just smiled. She didn't begrudge Wanda Nell any of the time she spent with Jack at work.

"Mayrene said she'd be happy to have Lisa stay with her," Wanda Nell told Jack, slipping onto the stool beside him.

"She's a good friend," Jack said.

"None better," Wanda Nell agreed.

"Now I just have to make Lisa see that she needs to do

this," Jack said. "She's terrified, but she also doesn't want anybody else to get hurt if this guy suddenly gets violent."

"Mayrene can handle herself," Wanda Nell said. She had great confidence in her friend, but she knew the situation was potentially a pretty dangerous one.

"Lisa took some kind of sleeping pill," Jack said. "She fell asleep before I left to come over here. She'll probably sleep the night through, so I'll talk to her about it in the morning."

"Make her see sense," Wanda Nell said. She stood up. "Your order's probably ready by now. Be right back."

Jack's food was sitting in the window, and Wanda Nell brought it back to the counter. "Dig in, honey," she said, placing the plate in front of him, along with a basket of dinner rolls.

"Looks good, as usual," Jack said, eyeing the plate of chicken-fried steak, mashed potatoes, gravy, and green beans. "If things are a bit calmer tomorrow," he said, "you think maybe we can get away for a little while? Maybe take in a movie or something?"

"I'd like that," Wanda Nell said. She bent to give him a quick kiss on the lips. "Now eat your dinner, and I'll get you some pie for dessert when you're done."

Jack laughed. "I'm going to skip the pie tonight, honey. Either that or I jog home." He patted his stomach. "You're fattening me up."

Wanda Nell eyed him with a smile. "I got to slow you down so I can keep up with you," she said. "Can't have you running away from me."

"I'd never do that," Jack said. For a moment his eyes locked with hers, practically glowing behind his rimless glasses, and Wanda Nell had to take a deep breath. She put a hand on the counter to steady herself.

"I know," Wanda Nell said, her voice soft. "I know." She tore her gaze away from Jack's. "I'd better get to work now."

It was just as well that the party guests started arriving a few minutes later. Otherwise Wanda Nell might have had to grab Jack, take him to a dark corner somewhere, and have her way with him. She grinned at the mental image. *Slow down, girl*, she admonished herself. *When the time's right, it will all work out.*

The bartender, an older man named Wade Hemphill, turned up along with the first three guests. Wanda Nell had worked a few private parties with him before this, and she knew he didn't need any instructions from her. He greeted her politely before getting right to work behind the bar.

Tullahoma County was dry, and that meant nobody could sell liquor publicly. The way around that was, if you belonged to a private club, the club could sell liquor. For parties like this, the Kountry Kitchen became a private club for a little while, and whoever attended the party had to pay the "membership fee." In this case, that was three bucks a head. They paid for what they drank and ate on top of that.

Over the next twenty minutes, more men arrived for the bachelor party. A few of the tables in front had diners, but it was probably going to be a slow night out there. The main action would be in the back room, Wanda Nell knew. Jack left then, too, after giving Wanda Nell a quick kiss and a promise to call her if anything came up.

Wanda Nell and Melvin were busy for a while, bringing trays of food from the kitchen to the back room. Melvin had set the food up buffet-style, and that made it a lot easier. Wanda Nell just had to keep an eye out to make sure the food didn't run out, occasionally pick up discarded plates and glasses, and dodge a few roaming hands once the alcohol started flowing.

She recognized a number of the men attending the party. One of them, she knew, was Mayrene's new guy, Dixon Vance. She saw him in earnest conversation with another cop, a man she didn't know. Most of the partygoers were in their late thirties and older, but one guest was about T.J.'s age. In fact, Wanda Nell decided, he had been one of her son's classmates at Tullahoma High School.

What was his name? She puzzled over it, trying to dredge the name out of her memory. She thought this young man and T.J. had been buddies at some point in high school, probably before T.J. started running wild and getting into all kinds of trouble. This boy looked like the type who never did anything wrong, though. His name would probably come to her later.

At the moment he was busy drinking and talking to an older man Wanda Nell didn't recognize. She studied the older man for a moment out of curiosity. He wasn't very tall, maybe a couple inches under six feet, and his brown hair was thinning. He had a big bald spot on the crown of his head. He was dressed in a suit, and he sported a couple of expensive-looking gold rings, one of them a wedding ring. From the way he held himself, Wanda Nell figured he must be important, or at least he thought he was.

Dismissing him from her mind, she continued to look around and tick off the names of the other men she recognized. There was young Dr. Tony Crowell, the son of old Dr. Crowell, who had been her mother's doctor. Wanda Nell spotted the elder man in another part of the room. She would have to make a point of speaking to him. He had done everything he could for Wanda Nell's mother before her death, and Wanda Nell was grateful to him for that. He had also been her own doctor for many years before he retired.

She saw several other men she vaguely recognized as

cops, and there were at least two men she knew from the sheriff's department. There was some tension between the city police and the county deputies, and they didn't always socialize like this. Thinking of the sheriff's department brought to mind her nemesis, Chief Deputy Elmer Lee Johnson, who had been named acting sheriff a few months ago. He would fill in until the next election. She wasn't too surprised he wasn't here tonight. She couldn't see him as the bachelor party type.

Someone had brought a box of cigars, and several of the men were smoking them. Wanda Nell sniffed the air appreciatively. Her daddy had been a cigar smoker, and the smell of cigar smoke always reminded her of him.

The air was growing thick with smoke, because more of the men had discovered the cigar box and were lighting up. Wanda Nell had quit smoking over two years ago, before her grandson was born. Having the cigar smoke closing in around her only made her want a cigarette. She went to turn on one of the fans Melvin had put in the room. The resulting circulation of air cleared some of the smoke away.

Next Wanda Nell went to the kitchen for more roast beef and ham, and when she returned to the back room, she saw a few of the men gathered around a newcomer. They took turns thumping him on the back.

The guest of honor, Travis Blakeley, had finally arrived.

Wanda Nell glanced at her watch as she set down the tray of meats on the buffet. He was only fifteen minutes late to his own party.

From her vantage point behind the buffet table she examined him. No one was paying attention to her, so it didn't matter if she stared, she decided.

Blakeley was a big man, at least six-foot-three, she figured. He wore highly polished cowboy boots, tight jeans, and a sport shirt that strained across his broad shoulders. The sleeves of the shirt had been rolled up to expose his bulging biceps. His upper arms bore tattoos, but from this distance, Wanda Nell couldn't make out the designs. He had jet black hair, and when he turned in her direction and looked right at her, Wanda Nell discovered he had the coldest eyes she had ever seen.

He examined her for a moment, his lower lip twisting in a knowing smirk, before he turned back to talk to the men around him.

Wanda Nell shivered. Now that she'd had a good look at the man's face, she had no trouble believing the stories about him.

"Pipe down," someone yelled. The person yelled again, and suddenly the noise faded away.

The man who had called for quiet was Dixon Vance, Wanda Nell noted. He was good looking, she decided, and she could see why Mayrene was attracted to him.

"Time for a toast," Vance said. "Ol' Travis here's about to get hitched, and I reckon we better party while we can. After next Sunday, he's gonna be too busy with that young wife of his to wanna spend any time with us."

Wanda Nell did her best to block out the lewd words and suggestions that followed Vance's little speech. Men could be such pigs, especially when the booze had been flowing as freely as it had so far tonight.

The men raised their glasses to Travis Blakeley and drank. Blakeley stood there smirking. So far, Wanda Nell hadn't seen him drink anything.

"Come on, now, Travis," someone called out. "Speech!"

Blakeley smirked a bit more. He stepped over to a nearby table and picked up a glass, full of what looked like bourbon. "Y'all have seen Tiffany," he said, "so I reckon you know what I'll be doing on the honeymoon." He made a few very explicit remarks, and some of the men laughed with him. Wanda Nell could feel her face burning.

Of the ones who didn't laugh, one was the young man who seemed familiar to Wanda Nell. Another was the older man she didn't know, who still talking to the younger one. Even Dixon Vance, who had started it all, looked a little taken aback at Travis Blakeley's crudity. While she watched, the young man pushed his way to the front of the group to stand in front of Blakeley.

"Don't talk like that about her." His voice was loud and slurred. "She's a nice girl, and you talk like she's some slut."

"All women are, once you start giving them what they want," Blakeley said, with a derisory laugh. "Man like me, they start begging for it. It ain't my fault, Gerald, you ain't got what it takes."

The young man launched himself at Blakeley and managed to get in a punch to the bigger man's gut before Blakeley could react. The blow didn't appear to faze him that much, Wanda Nell noticed. She wished the younger man had knocked him cold. The name Gerald finally registered with her. He was Gerald Blakeley, and he must be Travis's brother.

Blakeley just shook his head at the younger man, now being held back by two of the cops. "Little man, you don't want me to pound you into the floor like I did when we were kids. Take a chill pill, or get your ass out of here."

The two cops hustled Gerald into a chair several feet away from his brother, and he slumped into it, muttering and holding his head.

Wanda Nell shook her head. Men never changed. Or, at least, most of them. She couldn't imagine Jack acting like this.

The men started laughing and talking again, and after a moment, Gerald Blakeley got up from his chair and went to the bar. Wanda Nell watched him with concern. Maybe she ought to talk to him, try to get him out of here.

Travis spoke again, claiming her attention, and this time Wanda Nell knew enough to clap her hands over her ears as the first few words left his mouth. He was disgusting, and she hummed softly to block out the rest of what he had to say about his bride and their honeymoon. Gerald didn't react. When Wanda Nell looked for him, he was back in his chair, nursing a drink. He glared at his brother, but he remained silent.

After a moment, Blakeley shut up, and Wanda Nell took her hands away from her ears. Travis picked up his glass, full again, from a table behind him. He held it out in front of him, inviting everyone to raise their glasses. Then Blakeley put the glass to his lips and knocked the contents back in one gulp.

He swallowed, grinning broadly, and started to say something. His face contorted, and he dropped the glass to the floor, where it shattered. Clutching his throat and gasping for air, Blakeley stumbled against the table behind him. He went down, bringing the table with him.

As the horrified men and Wanda Nell watched, Blakeley's body twitched a few times, then stopped. He lay unmoving on the floor.

Four

For a moment, no one did anything. Then the room erupted in noise and movement. The younger Dr. Crowell pushed his way to the front of the group that had collected around the fallen man.

"Get back," he ordered, his voice loud. "Give me some room. Dad!"

The elder Dr. Crowell shambled forward, and the men stepped aside quickly to let him pass. The younger man knelt beside Blakeley, and from where Wanda Nell stood, she couldn't see what he was doing.

One of the cops had a cell phone out, and Wanda Nell figured he was calling for an ambulance. The hospital was only a few minutes away. Would they get there in time to save Travis Blakeley?

There was something odd about the whole thing, she thought. Why should Blakeley collapse after bolting down some bourbon? He had drunk at least one glass already without any visible effects. Why should this glass of bourbon affect him like that?

Wanda Nell didn't deliberate any longer. She slipped

out of the back room, around the counter, through the kitchen, and back to Melvin's office. She dialed a number she knew all too well, thanks to the events of the past year. When the dispatcher at the sheriff's department answered, she asked for the acting sheriff, Elmer Lee Johnson.

"And don't tell me he's busy," Wanda Nell snapped when the dispatcher started asking questions. "Tell him it's Wanda Nell, and that there's an emergency."

The dispatcher didn't argue. "I'll patch you through to him, ma'am."

Wanda Nell waited, precious seconds ticking by, and nearly a minute later Elmer Lee came on the line.

"What the hell do you want, Wanda Nell? Don't you know it's Saturday night? I'm trying to have a little peace and quiet here at home."

"Oh, put a plug in it, Elmer Lee," Wanda Nell said, her temper flaring from having to wait. "You get your scrawny butt over to the Kountry Kitchen, and do it now. Something bad just happened here, and you need to see to it."

"What the hell happened?" Elmer Lee breathed heavily into the phone.

Wanda Nell resisted the urge to slam the phone down. Lord, but the man could be frustrating at the best of times.

"A cop named Travis Blakeley just collapsed during his bachelor party, and I think maybe somebody poisoned him."

"Travis Blakeley?" Elmer Lee didn't wait for further confirmation. He muttered something that sounded like an obscenity before saying, "I'm on the way." The phone clicked loudly in Wanda Nell's ear.

Setting the receiver in its cradle, Wanda Nell stared down at the phone.

What if she had overreacted? What if Travis Blakeley just had a weak heart or something like that?

Was she completely out of her mind? How could some-body poison a man in a roomful of people like that?

Wanda Nell shook her head. No, she trusted her in-stincts. Something was definitely fishy, and she was willing to bet that, if he was indeed dead, Travis Blakeley had been murdered.

The sound of approaching sirens brought Wanda Nell out of her daze. She hurried from the office back to the scene. By this time the few diners in the front of the restau-rant were aware something was going on. The doors to the back room were wide open, and people were standing and staring.

As Wanda Nell slipped through to the back room, the front door opened. The emergency team had arrived.

Wanda Nell scuttled aside and turned to survey the room. The younger Dr. Crowell still knelt beside Travis Blakeley, but from what Wanda Nell could see, Blakeley wasn't moving, or even breathing. The elder Dr. Crowell stood a couple feet away, staring down at his son and the victim, an enigmatic look on his face.

Wanda Nell stiffened as someone stumbled against her. She turned slightly, frowning. Gerald Blakeley stared at her, his eyes blinking rapidly. He held out a hand. In it lay a glass vial.

"Whattaya think this is?" His words ran together, and from the fumes emanating from his mouth, Wanda Nell de-cided he was as drunk as Cooter Brown.

Without thinking, she reached out a hand to take the vial from him. Then she realized what she was about to do. Her hand dropped by her side.

"I don't know what it is," Wanda Nell said. "Gerald, where did you find it?"

"You know who I am?" The young man gave her a

drunken smile. "Everybody knows Travis, but nobody knows me."

"Where did you find that?" Wanda Nell said, her voice stern.

Gerald wobbled his head at her. "Not sure."

Sighing heavily, Wanda Nell grabbed a clean napkin from a nearby table. "Let me have it," she said.

"Why do you want it?" Gerald asked, turning sullen. "It's mine. I found it."

"I'm afraid you might drop it, and then it'll break all over the floor," Wanda Nell said, hanging on to her patience by a mere thread. She held the napkin in her hand, ready for the vial. Before Gerald could react, she grabbed the vial out of his open hand, wrapping the napkin around it.

Gerald frowned at her as he swayed a bit. "Thass not nice."

"We'll worry about that later," Wanda Nell said. "I think we need to get you some coffee." She pulled him over to a chair and pushed him down into it. "You sit there, and don't get up."

The bartender had a carafe of coffee behind the bar, and Wanda Nell asked him for a cup, black. Without a word, he did as she asked and handed her the cup.

Wanda Nell turned back to Gerald Blakeley. He sat in the chair, staring off into space, a few tears trickling down his face. Wanda Nell touched his shoulder, and he tried to focus on her. She reached for a napkin and gave it to him. He wiped his face, but then his hand fell to his lap.

"You need to drink this," Wanda Nell said, her voice gentle. She picked up his right hand and placed the cup in it. "Come on, now, start drinking the coffee for me."

Gerald blinked up at her, but he did as she told him. He raised the cup to his face and started sipping. Wanda Nell watched him for a moment, and once she was satisfied he would be okay with the coffee, she stepped away to give him some space.

All the time she had been dealing with Gerald Blakeley, Wanda Nell heard the commotion continue over the supine body of Travis Blakeley. There was an oxygen mask on his face, but from what Wanda Nell could see, Blakeley wasn't responding.

As Wanda Nell watched, the EMTs bundled Blakeley onto a gurney and started moving him out of the room. The younger Dr. Crowell went with them. His father had found a chair and was sitting, staring into space.

"What the hell is going on here?" Melvin strode up to Wanda Nell and spoke in an urgent undertone. She started to reply, but before she could say anything, one of the cops spoke.

"Everybody stay calm," Dixon Vance said, his voice carrying through the restaurant. He waited a moment, until all conversation had ceased.

The sirens sounded again, and Wanda Nell shivered. She doubted there was any help for Travis Blakeley now. He looked dead to her. Melvin slipped a comforting arm around her shoulders, and Wanda Nell leaned against him, grateful for the warmth.

"We're not sure what just happened here," Vance continued, "but I need everybody to stay where they are. We're gonna have to start asking some questions, so y'all just be patient. We'll try to get you out of here before too long."

"What happened?" Melvin whispered in Wanda Nell's ear.

She pulled away and looked up at him. "I think somebody murdered Travis Blakeley."

Melvin's face twisted into a fierce scowl. He muttered something, shook his head, and strode away.

The buzz of conversation resumed. Wanda Nell glanced around the back room, examining the faces of the men attending the bachelor party. Most of them looked a bit stunned by what had happened, but none of them appeared to be really upset. The faces of Blakeley's fellow police officers revealed nothing. Most of them continued to smoke, but Wanda Nell noticed nobody was drinking now.

Elmer Lee ought to be here any second. He lived only a few blocks from the Kountry Kitchen, and for once, Wanda Nell would be glad to see him.

Right on cue, Elmer Lee walked into the back room. He stopped and looked around. His eyes raked over Wanda Nell, and she would have sworn he rolled them at her. Then his attention focused on Dixon Vance. He jerked his head, and Vance ambled over to him. The men began talking, but they were too far away for Wanda Nell to hear what they were saying.

Around them, the other men in the room had clustered in knots of three or four. There was a low buzz of conversation, and Wanda Nell could feel the tension in the room. She wished Elmer Lee would just get on with it, or she might start yelling. She couldn't take much more of this inaction.

A few moments later, Elmer Lee addressed the group. "I'm going to have to ask everybody to take a seat. I know this is inconvenient, but we're going to need to question everybody. We'll be as quick as we can, but this is going to take some time." He glanced briefly over at Wanda Nell. "I'm sure if anybody wants some coffee"—his eyes skittered over the bar in the corner—"Miz Culpepper over there will be glad to make sure you have some."

Wanda Nell nodded. The shock of what had happened to Travis Blakeley had sobered up a lot of the men, but some black coffee sure wouldn't hurt.

Elmer Lee's cell phone rang. He held up a hand to forestall the questions some of the men had begun firing at him, and the room went silent except for the chirping of the phone. Elmer Lee punched a button and spoke briefly. His face tightened as he listened.

He clicked the phone off and stuck it back in his uniform pocket. "Now, like I said, everybody just take a seat, and be calm. We'll get on with things in a minute. I'm waiting for an officer from the state police. He'll be conducting the investigation with my assistance."

Wanda Nell was surprised. She had figured Elmer Lee would be in charge, but when she thought about it, having the state police investigate made sense. She knew they had a district office in Tullahoma, but she tended to forget about it most of the time. She wasn't even sure who the officer in charge was.

Moments later, that question was answered. A tall, blond man, dressed in a dark suit, walked into the back room. He had *cop* written all over him, and Wanda Nell would have known what he was right away.

"Sheriff Johnson," he said, his voice deep and raspy.

Elmer Lee turned to face him. "Warren."

"What's going on here?" the state cop asked. He and Elmer Lee moved a few feet away and conferred, their heads bent together.

Wanda Nell was staring at Warren. She hadn't seen him in over twenty years, but as soon as she realized who he was, her heart fluttered in her chest.

Back in high school, before Wanda Nell had fallen so hard for Bobby Ray Culpepper, she had briefly dated a nice boy in her class. That boy's name was Bill Warren. At the time he had been a nice-looking guy—tall, thin, a bit awkward, but cute in a goofy kind of way. Wanda Nell's parents had liked him, but her interest in him waned once she caught Bobby Ray's eye. She broke up with Bill and started dating Bobby Ray. Not the best decision she had ever made, she told herself ruefully.

So Bill Warren was a cop now. As she watched him and Elmer Lee, she couldn't help noticing that Bill was no longer thin and awkward. He had filled out nicely, and he stood with an ease and confidence he had lacked as a teenager. After Wanda Nell broke up with him, she lost track of him. She vaguely remembered that he had gone off to college, maybe Mississippi State, and after that she hadn't a clue what he had done.

Now he was a state police officer, and he was back in Tullahoma. She shook her head over the coincidence.

Warren and Elmer Lee turned to face the group. Warren spoke. "Gentlemen." He glanced in Wanda Nell's direction, and his eyes widened in recognition. "And lady." He nodded slightly at Wanda Nell. "Sheriff Johnson and I'll be conducting this investigation. It's my sad duty to inform you that Officer Blakeley is dead." He paused a moment for the words to sink in. No one spoke.

"Because of the circumstances, we are treating this as a suspicious death," Warren continued. "We appreciate your cooperation, and we'll try to get you out of here as soon as possible. For the moment, we're going to ask you all to move to the front of the restaurant so we can begin the investigation back here."

The partygoers started moving out of the back room. Warren and Elmer Lee stood aside, as did Dixon Vance and the other police officers. Wanda Nell stayed where she was for the moment, keeping an eye on Gerald Blakeley. He hadn't moved from his chair, still nursing his cup of coffee. Wanda Nell didn't think he was aware of anything going on around him.

Elmer Lee came over to Wanda Nell. "You need to clear the room, too, Wanda Nell. We've got work to do back here, and we can't have you standing around in the way."

"Nice to see you, too, Elmer Lee," Wanda Nell said, giving him a sweet smile. She nodded toward Gerald Blakeley. "But I think somebody needs to look after him."

Elmer Lee turned to stare at the young man. "Gerald." He put his hand on Blakeley's shoulder. "I'm sure sorry about your brother."

Gerald stared up at him. "What do you mean?"

Elmer Lee squeezed his shoulder. "I'm afraid your brother died. They couldn't save him."

Gerald didn't respond for a moment. He fixed his eyes on the cup in his hands. He nodded.

"We need to clear the room." Bill Warren had come up behind Elmer Lee.

"Wanda Nell," Bill said. He stared down at her. "You're looking good." He paused. "It's been a long time."

Wanda Nell nodded. "It sure has." Bill had been really upset when she broke it off with him, and even now she felt a bit guilty just thinking about it. At the time, she hadn't given much thought to the way he felt.

At the moment, though, she could read nothing in his eyes. He had a disconcerting, noncommital stare, and she dropped her gaze.

Wanda Nell remembered the glass vial. She stepped a few feet away from Gerald Blakeley and motioned for Bill and Elmer Lee to follow her.

"What is it?" Elmer Lee demanded.

Wanda Nell pulled the napkin-covered vial from her pocket. "This," she said, holding it out for the men.

Bill took it gingerly in his big hand. He opened the napkin, and he and Elmer Lee stared down at the glass tube. They exchanged a brief glance.

"Where did you get this?" Bill asked.

"From Gerald," Wanda Nell said. "He showed it to me, and when I asked him where he found it, he said he wasn't sure." She frowned. "He was pretty drunk at the time."

Bill cautiously lifted the vial to his nose and sniffed. His eyes narrowed. He folded the napkin over the tube again before handing it to Elmer Lee. Startled, Elmer Lee almost dropped it.

Bill stepped around Elmer Lee and strode over to Gerald Blakeley, still sitting quietly in his chair.

Placing a hand on the young man's shoulder, Bill shook it roughly. "Gerald, look at me."

Startled out of his trance, Gerald stared up at the state cop.

"Did you kill your brother?" Bill asked, his voice harsh. He shook the younger man again when Gerald didn't respond. "Answer me."

Gerald still didn't answer. His head dropped, and he started sobbing.

Wanda Nell was getting angry with Bill. He shouldn't be treating the poor boy like this. She was about to say something to Elmer Lee about it when Bill yanked Gerald up out of the chair.

"Answer me, you little sonofabitch. Did you kill your brother?"

This time Gerald spoke, his words barely audible through the crying. "I don't know."

Five

Gerald Blakeley was such a miserable sight, standing there like a mouse in the clutches of a big cat, Wanda Nell felt sorry for him. Even if Bill Warren thought Gerald really killed his brother, he didn't need to treat him like this.

She opened her mouth to speak, but Elmer Lee forestalled her. "Warren, let go of him. Now!"

The state cop's body tensed, and at first Wanda Nell thought he was going to ignore Elmer Lee. His hand loosened on Gerald's shoulder, and he stepped back. Gerald sank down into his chair again, crying and shaking his head.

Warren turned to face Elmer Lee, and the hard set of his face unnerved Wanda Nell. This man was nothing like the sweet, easygoing boy she remembered. He looked mad, and he looked dangerous. Without realizing what she was doing, she took a step back.

Warren saw her do it, and for a moment his face softened as he looked at her. The next moment, he was all business again as he addressed Elmer Lee. "I want you to take him down to the jail for more questioning."

"We'll take care of that," Elmer Lee said, his voice firm.

"But first I think we need to start talking to everyone else, find out what they saw, if anything."

There was an edge to Elmer Lee's voice, one that Wanda Nell knew all too well. She knew better than to mess with him when he got that tone, and she was curious to see how Warren would react.

He backed down, and Wanda Nell relaxed. The tension between the two men had been making her nervous.

"Right," Warren said. "But I want someone keeping an eye on him at all times." He jerked his head toward Gerald.

"No problem," Elmer Lee said. "Now let's get out of the way so these men can do their jobs." He nodded at Wanda Nell. "You go on up front. We'll talk to you in a minute."

"Sure," Wanda Nell said, glad to get away from Warren and Elmer Lee, at least for a little while. She cast a worried glance at Gerald Blakeley, but there didn't seem to be much she could do for him at the moment.

Why was Bill Warren so sure Gerald had killed his brother? She shook her head over that as she walked behind the counter and toward the front of the restaurant where Melvin stood at the cash register. She wondered what motive Gerald might have to do such a thing. She would have to talk to T.J. about him, because he knew the boy far better than she did. She didn't know if T.J. had had much contact with him over the past year. T.J. had been gone from Tullahoma for a while, and since he'd been back he hadn't hung around with his old friends that much. Most of them were uncomfortable with T.J. being gay.

Thinking of T.J. brought her up short because she thought about Tuck, too. The way things looked at the moment, Gerald Blakeley was going to need a lawyer. Wanda Nell didn't like the way Bill Warren seemed so sure of the boy's guilt. She had faced that kind of prejudice herself when Bobby Ray got himself killed, and she wanted Gerald to have a fair shake, even if it turned out he was guilty.

Should she try to call Tuck now? What if Gerald didn't want a lawyer? She wavered, indecisive.

"What's going on back there?" Melvin asked her.

In a low voice, Wanda Nell told him what she knew.

Melvin frowned. "I just wish they'd get the hell out of my restaurant," he said. "Something like this may kill my business. Why did somebody have to choose tonight to kill the bastard?"

"Did you know him? Travis Blakeley, I mean?"

"Yeah, I did," Melvin said. "Didn't like him either. He was one cold sonofabitch, I can tell you that."

"Then why did you book that bachelor party?" Wanda Nell had to ask, but she already knew the answer.

"Couldn't turn down the business," Melvin said. He cut his eyes down at her. "You know how much we make on a party like that. Or at least, we usually do." He shrugged. "Who knows whether anybody'll pay for it now?"

Wanda Nell knew they both ought to feel more guilty about being so concerned with themselves, when a man had died in the back room of the restaurant. Probably murdered, too. But feeling sorry about Travis Blakeley's death wasn't going to pay her bills, or Melvin's either. That might be cold, but she couldn't help that. She had a family to look after. She tried not to think about the hefty tips she had lost tonight.

Some men from the sheriff's department had been questioning people in the restaurant, and from what Wanda Nell could see, they were letting anyone who hadn't been a party guest leave after taking down names and addresses. Pretty soon only the party guests remained, along with the cops and the restaurant staff.

One of Elmer Lee's men parked Gerald Blakeley on a stool toward the end of the counter. Wanda Nell kept an eye on them both, and when the deputy stepped away for a moment, she seized her chance.

Moving quickly down the counter to Gerald, she bent down and spoke quietly to him. "Gerald, do you have a lawyer?"

His eyes dull, he looked at her. He shook his head.

"I think you're going to need one," she said. "And I know a real good one." She watched the deputy's back as she spoke. He might turn around at any minute. "I can call him for you," she said.

Gerald frowned. "Don't I know you?"

Wanda Nell wanted to shake him. "Yes, I'm T.J. Culpepper's mama. Y'all were in school together."

"Yeah, I remember now," Gerald said. Then his eyes narrowed. "I heard T.J. was . . . well, you know."

"Yes, he is," Wanda Nell said, responding to the unspoken word.

"T.J.'s a good guy," Gerald said, surprising her.

"Thanks," Wanda Nell said. She glanced at the deputy, and he was starting to turn back in their direction. "Listen, you want me to call that lawyer for you?"

"I guess so," Gerald said, frowning. "My head hurts. I can't really think."

"I'll go call him right now," Wanda Nell said. She moved away from Gerald, trying not to attract any attention. She glanced over her shoulder, and the deputy had taken up his spot by Gerald again. He didn't appear to have seen her talking to the boy.

She hurried through the kitchen, back to Melvin's office where she could use the phone in private. She punched in the number of Tuck's cell phone and waited for an answer.

She was afraid the call was about to go to voice mail when she heard Tuck's voice.

"Tuck, it's me, Wanda Nell," she said.

"Hey there," Tuck said. "What's up?"

Wanda Nell explained the situation in as few words as possible. When she finished, Tuck didn't respond for a moment.

"Tuck? Can you be his lawyer?"

Tuck expelled a short breath into the phone. "I'll be glad to, Wanda Nell. I think he's going to need one."

"Do you know him at all?"

"A little," Tuck said. "I knew his brother better."

From the tone of his voice, Wanda Nell figured Tuck hadn't cared for Travis Blakeley all that much.

"You didn't like him either," she said.

"No," Tuck said. "He was the kind of man who should never have been allowed to wear a badge, and frankly, I'm not too sorry he's gone."

"That's what I've heard from several people, more or less."

"I don't think there'll be many people crying at his funeral," Tuck said. "More than likely, they'll be dancing on his grave. Look, I'd better get going. I'll be there in a few minutes."

Wanda Nell put the receiver down. She hadn't even asked Tuck what he was doing. He and T.J. were supposed to be going to the movies with Juliet, Miranda, and Teddy. If that's where they were, then Tuck could be here pretty fast.

She thought for a moment about what Tuck had said, that no one would be crying at Travis Blakeley's funeral. For the first time, she thought about the girl Blakeley had been going to marry. What about her? Wouldn't she be upset?

Wanda Nell felt sorry for the girl, but if everything people said about Travis Blakeley was true, maybe the girl was better off without him. She shivered. Who would want their daughter to marry a man like that?

When Wanda Nell came through the kitchen door, she found Elmer Lee standing at the counter, frowning.

"Where have you been?" he asked.

"I had to make a phone call," she said.

Elmer Lee's eyes narrowed in suspicion. "Did you call Tucker?"

Wanda Nell nodded.

"Probably not a bad idea," Elmer Lee said, surprising her. "That kid's going to need him."

Then he looked like he was sorry he had said anything. His expression hardened. "Come on over here," he said, jerking his head to the left. "We need to talk to you."

Wanda Nell walked around the counter and followed Elmer Lee to the back table in the front dining room. Bill Warren stood as they reached the table, and he motioned for Wanda Nell to take a seat.

There was activity all around them, but neither Elmer Lee nor Bill appeared to notice. All their attention focused on her. She sat down, took a deep breath, and folded her hands in her lap. She faced Bill Warren squarely.

"It's been a long time, Wanda Nell," he said.

"Yeah, it has," Wanda Nell said. "Twenty years or more." Now that they were this close together, she examined Warren as discreetly as she could. He had aged well. He was far more attractive now than he had been in high school. There was something about a confident man that Wanda Nell couldn't help responding to.

"About that long," Warren said. He examined her, not

discreetly at all. "Sorry you have to be involved in all this, but from what Johnson here tells me, it's not the first time."

Wanda Nell resisted the urge to pinch Elmer Lee. "No, it's not."

Warren raised one eyebrow, and Wanda Nell regretted her sharp tone. Baiting Elmer Lee was one thing, but Bill made her uncomfortable, and she wasn't sure why. She wasn't going to rile him if she could help it.

"Tell us about this evening," Warren said, ignoring her tone. "Tell us as much as you can remember, okay?"

Wanda Nell nodded. She paused for a moment before speaking to organize her thoughts. She started with the moment the bartender and the first guests arrived. She tried to picture it all in her mind as she spoke, and it was only when she reached the point of Travis Blakeley's collapse that she wavered. Remembering that made her a little bit nauseated. He might have been a terrible man, but watching anyone die was a nasty experience.

"That's good," Warren said. "You've given us a very clear picture."

"Yeah," Elmer Lee said. "Wanda Nell's usually a good witness."

Wanda Nell's eyes narrowed as Elmer Lee spoke, but she couldn't detect any irony in his voice.

His lips twitching slightly, Warren asked, "Did you see anybody put something in the victim's glass?"

"No," Wanda Nell said. "I didn't. The way they were all talking and laughing and carrying on, I don't think anybody would have noticed. There was too much going on."

When Warren didn't respond right away, Wanda Nell ventured a question. "Does that mean y'all think he really was poisoned?"

"I'm afraid I can't answer that," Warren said. "It's too early in the investigation for us to come to any conclusions."

Wanda Nell thought Elmer Lee muttered something, but she wasn't sure. Warren's eyes narrowed, and Wanda Nell felt a sudden chill. He had that dangerous look on his face again, and she didn't want to do anything to make him angry with her.

"Good evening, gentlemen."

Hearing Tuck's voice, Wanda Nell relaxed. With him here, she felt a lot better. He was more than capable of dealing with Bill Warren.

Warren and Elmer Lee stood up. Wanda Nell turned in her chair to watch.

"Tucker," Warren said, his voice flat. "I'm afraid you've missed the ambulance."

Only because she knew him so well did Wanda Nell see Tuck's reaction to such an obvious insult. Tuck didn't respond to Warren's words.

"I'm here to speak to my client," Tuck said. "Evening, Sheriff Johnson." He nodded at Elmer Lee.

"Evening, Tucker," Elmer Lee said. "Who's your client? Wanda Nell here?"

Tuck didn't appear amused at Elmer Lee's little sally. "I'm here for Gerald Blakeley. I'd like to speak to him. Now."

Tuck and Warren stared at each other. The cop was a bit taller and more muscular, but Tuck didn't appear the least bit intimidated. Wanda Nell was very proud of him.

"We're just about to take him down to the jail," Warren said. "You can talk to him there." He nodded at Elmer Lee. "Tell your man to take him in."

"Are you arresting him?" Tuck asked.

"No, but he's a material witness," Warren said. "I'm

going to have to question him at length, and I don't think this is the place to do it."

Tuck nodded. "Right. I'll meet him at the jail then, but I'm going to speak to him first."

Warren snorted. "Do you even know who he is? Who called you anyway?"

Tuck didn't respond. Instead, he turned and walked right over to Gerald and started talking to him.

Warren muttered an obscenity, just loud enough for Tuck to hear it. Wanda Nell saw red, and without even thinking about what she was doing, she jumped up from her chair. She drew back her hand and slapped Bill Warren so hard his head snapped back.

going to be to make that have a laugh. and I don't think this is the place to do it."

Pace nodded. "Right. I'll meet him at the jail then, but I'm gonna speak to him first."

Marion nodded. "He got even know who he's talking to anyway."

"See that you're there then," he turned and walked away, then rose to Casilda and started walking to him.

When a minute or so had passed, she got her ready for Pace Jr. and in hand and she out, and without even looking about what she was doing, she hugged up into her chair. She drew back her head and she put Bill with a snap of her head, snapped back at.

Six

Elmer Lee grabbed Wanda Nell by the arms and held her. "What the hell do you think you're doing?" His voice hissed in her ear.

There was dead silence in the restaurant. Everyone was watching to see what would happen next.

Wanda Nell shook loose from Elmer Lee. She looked straight up into Bill Warren's face. Warren was rubbing his cheek and glaring at her, but Wanda Nell didn't back down.

"Don't you *ever* let me hear you say such a thing, Bill Warren," Wanda Nell said. "You ought to be ashamed of yourself."

"You ought to be more careful about assaulting officers of the law," Warren said, scowling at her. "I've got half a mind to have you hauled down to that jail, too."

"You just go ahead and do that," Wanda Nell said, her temper still up. "And I'll be glad to tell whoever the hell I have to what you said. Don't think I'll let you get away with it. I'll go to the governor himself if I have to."

She waited a moment for Warren to respond. When he

remained silent, she said, "I have a witness, too. Right, Elmer Lee? You heard what he said."

Both Wanda Nell and Warren looked at Elmer Lee. He met both their gazes before exhaling. "Yeah, I heard it, Wanda Nell."

Satisfied that Elmer Lee would back her up, Wanda Nell folded her arms and waited for a response from the state cop.

"Why the hell should *you* care what I think of that jerk?" Warren said, his tone savage. "What's he got to do with you? You're not his type." He laughed.

"Don't start that crap again," Wanda Nell said. She was itching to slap him a second time.

Elmer Lee stepped between them. "Stop it, both of you," he said. Wanda Nell moved back a couple of paces. Elmer Lee faced Warren. "I think you owe Wanda Nell and Tucker both an apology."

Warren flushed. He pushed past Elmer Lee and went to talk to Dixon Vance. Wanda Nell watched him go, her stomach churning as her adrenalin rush faded. The hum of conversation resumed, now that the scene had ended. Many of the men still stared at Wanda Nell, though.

"Thank you, Elmer Lee," Wanda Nell said, holding out a shaky hand to him. "I appreciate your support."

Elmer Lee clasped her hand in his but let it go pretty quickly. "He was way out of line, and he knew it." Elmer Lee frowned. "But you're lucky he didn't have you hauled off to jail. Assaulting an officer's a serious offence, like he said. You can't do things like that, Wanda Nell."

Wanda Nell ignored that. She didn't think Bill Warren had the guts to make an issue of it, especially when she had a witness to back her up. "He was such a nice boy back in high school," she said. "What happened to him?"

Elmer Lee regarded her with an odd expression on his face. "How well did you know him back then?"

Wanda Nell shrugged. "We dated for a couple of months." She felt her face begin to redden. "And then I started going out with Bobby Ray."

Elmer Lee and Bobby Ray had been really close in high school and afterward. When Bobby Ray was murdered, Elmer Lee had been convinced, at least for a while, that Wanda Nell had done it. Back in high school he had acted like he couldn't stand to be around her, and over the years their relationship had been rocky, at best.

Averting his face, Elmer Lee said, "I see." Abruptly, he walked away, leaving Wanda Nell staring after him, puzzled by his behavior. She never would be able to figure him out, she decided, shaking her head.

"Thank you, Wanda Nell," Tuck said, placing a hand on her arm and giving it a little squeeze. "But be careful. Don't you get yourself in trouble for something like that. I'm used to men like Warren." He laughed, and the bitter sound of it tore at Wanda Nell's heart.

"That don't mean it's right," Wanda Nell said. "He shouldn't get away with talking like that."

Tuck smiled. "You certainly called him on it tonight." His smile faded. "Seriously, though, be careful around him. He's got a pretty tough reputation, and you don't want to be on his bad side."

"What do you mean?" Wanda Nell said. Tuck's words and his demeanor made her uneasy.

"We'll talk about it later," Tuck said. "Right now, I'd better get on down to the jail." He nodded in the direction of Gerald Blakeley. "They're taking him down there now, and I want to be on hand."

"I feel sorry for him, He needs a good lawyer." *Especially with Bill Warren acting like such a jackass*, she added to herself.

Tuck gave her arm another squeeze before he walked away. Wanda Nell walked behind the counter and approached Melvin and Ruby at the cash register.

Ruby's big green eyes were wide with admiration. "Wanda Nell, you were so brave to stand up to that man like that. I was afraid he was going to arrest you."

"You're lucky he didn't," Melvin said in a sour tone. "That temper of yours is gonna get you in big trouble one of these days if you don't watch out."

"I know, I know," Wanda Nell said, holding her hands up in a gesture of conciliation. "But he made me so mad, I reacted before I had time to think about it." She paused. "I would have done the same thing, probably, even if I *had* thought about it first. If you don't call people on things like that, you might as well say it yourself."

"Good point," Melvin said, smiling a little. "But my point is, you didn't necessarily have to knock his head off to get *your* point across."

Wanda Nell shrugged. Suddenly she was exhausted. With the adrenaline gone, she could feel the weariness creeping in. She just wanted to go home and climb into bed and try to forget about this night, at least until tomorrow.

"When do you think they'll let us go home?" Ruby asked, echoing Wanda Nell's thoughts.

"Soon, I think," Melvin said. "If they don't have any questions for you girls, y'all can go on home, and I'll close up."

"You sure?" Wanda Nell asked. "I don't mind staying if you want me to."

Melvin shook his head. "No, I think you need to get home and get some rest. Both of you. Wait here, and I'll go ask." He strode around the counter and approached Elmer Lee and Bill Warren, who were once again conferring.

As Wanda Nell watched Melvin talk to the two lawmen, Elmer Lee glanced at her and Ruby a couple of times. Bill Warren never looked their way, and that was fine with Wanda Nell. The less she had to do with him, the better. Until this case was solved, though, she knew she would probably have to talk to him again. She would face up to it when she had to. In the meantime she would do her best to block him and his hateful attitude from her mind.

"Do you think people will stop coming here?" Ruby asked, frowning. "What if this ruins business?"

Wanda Nell sighed. "As long as the cops don't shut us down for too long, I'll bet you anything we'll be so busy we won't know what hit us."

"Why?"

"People will be curious," Wanda Nell said. "It's like how people always slow down and look at a car wreck on the highway. They just can't help themselves."

"I guess you're right," Ruby said, "but that sure is pretty morbid. I'm just glad I wasn't back there to see it."

Wanda Nell put an arm around the younger woman's shoulders. "I'm glad you weren't either, honey. It was ugly."

"You gonna be okay?"

"Yeah," Wanda Nell said. "Don't you worry about me." She might have a few bad dreams, but she would just have to deal with that.

Melvin came back. "Y'all can go on home," he said.

"Are they going to close the restaurant for a few days?" Wanda Nell asked.

Melvin shook his head. "Naw. They think they'll have what they need tonight and tomorrow." The restaurant was closed on Sundays. "Monday we can go back to business as usual."

"Good," Wanda Nell said. "Okay, Ruby, come on and let's get our stuff." She headed to the back room for her purse.

A few minutes later she and Ruby were out in the parking lot, getting into their cars. Wanda Nell had avoided looking at Elmer Lee and Bill Warren when she left. They and their men were still interviewing the partygoers and examining the back room for evidence. Melvin would probably have to stay there for another couple of hours at least until they finished. She was glad she didn't have to stay.

She was surprised when she glanced at her dashboard clock. It was only a few minutes shy of nine-thirty. It sure seemed later than that. She yawned as she backed out of the parking lot and headed for home.

About ten minutes later she pulled her car into its covered parking space beside her double-wide trailer. T.J.'s pickup was parked nearby, and so was Jack's car. Though she was really tired and ready for bed, Wanda Nell was glad Jack was here.

The minute she opened the door to the trailer and stepped inside, Jack was waiting for her. She walked into his arms, and he wrapped her into a warm embrace. She rested her head against his shoulder, and he stroked her hair.

"You okay, honey?" he asked, his voice soft. "T.J. called me, so I thought I'd come over."

"I'm okay now," she said, pulling back a little so she could look into his face.

The light from a nearby lamp shone on his glasses, obscuring his eyes slightly. Wanda Nell could read the concern there, nevertheless.

"I wanted to call you," Jack said, "but I figured it would be impossible to talk to you."

"Yeah," Wanda Nell said. "So much was going on, I don't even know if anybody would've heard the phone, much less answered it."

"Come on and sit down," Jack said, leading her toward the couch.

T.J. walked out of the kitchen into the living room. "Mama, are you okay? Can I get you something to drink?"

"I'm fine, honey," Wanda Nell said, stretching up to kiss her son's cheek. "A glass of water sure would be nice."

T.J. gave her a quick hug. "Be right back with it."

Wanda Nell sat down on the couch next to Jack. He laid his arm across the back of the couch, and Wanda Nell snuggled up next to him. She closed her eyes for a moment and enjoyed the feeling of having the man she loved there with her.

T.J. came back with her water and set it down on the coffee table in front of her. Wanda Nell heard the clink of the glass as it touched the ceramic coaster, and she opened her eyes. "Thank you." She reached for the glass and drained most of the contents in one long swallow.

"Want some more?" T.J. stood over her, staring down at her.

"No, that's good," Wanda Nell said as she set the glass down again. "Sit down, or I'll get a crick in my neck looking up at you."

T.J. made himself comfortable in a nearby chair, leaning back and crossing one leg over the other. His highly polished cowboy boots shone in the lamplight.

"Are those new?" Wanda Nell asked, gesturing toward his feet.

"Yeah," T.J. said. "We did a little shopping when we were up in Memphis last weekend." He grinned.

Those boots looked expensive, but Wanda Nell didn't

say anything. T.J. and Tuck probably had at least ten pairs of boots apiece, but that didn't seem to stop them from buying more. It was their money, and they could spend it how they liked.

"Do you feel like talking about it?" Jack asked her. "We don't want to push you, but we're really curious."

"I guess so," Wanda Nell said. She gave them a quick rundown of the facts, but she did not tell them about the scene with Bill Warren and his insulting Tuck. If Tuck wanted to tell T.J. about that, she would leave that up to him. She might confide in Jack later, but for now she kept quiet about it.

"Pretty awful," Jack said. "I'm sorry you had to see that."

"Me too, Mama," T.J. said. "But I have to tell you, if anybody ever deserved killing, it was Travis Blakeley."

"Did you know him at all?" Jack asked.

"A little," T.J. said. "His brother, Gerald, and I used to be buddies back in high school, but Travis was a lot older. He always treated Gerald like a piece of, well, you know. Always beating up on him and everything."

"Didn't their parents do anything about it?" Wanda Nell asked. T.J. had never told her any of this.

"Naw," T.J. said. "Travis was all they cared about. Anything he did was okay by them. Gerald was an accident. At least, that's what his mama told him."

Appalled, Wanda Nell said, "That's an awful thing to tell a child."

"I can't believe a parent would do something like that," Jack said. "But unfortunately, I've seen worse with some of my students. It makes me think some people should be sterilized so they can't have children at all."

"Yeah, but by the time you know they're worthless as parents it's too late," T.J. said.

Now Wanda Nell felt even sorrier for Gerald Blakeley. If he had been so badly treated by his family, though, might that not make him hate his brother so much he could have killed him?

"I know what you're thinking, Mama," T.J. said. "That Gerald probably hated Travis enough to kill him."

"Yeah," Wanda Nell said. "You know him pretty well, or at least you used to. What do you think?"

T.J. shifted uncomfortably in his chair. "I don't think Gerald has it in him to hate somebody that much, even though Travis gave him plenty of reasons."

"But?" Jack asked. "I've got a feeling there's something else you know that you're not telling us."

T.J. nodded. "Yeah, you're right. The girl Travis was going to marry, Tiffany Farwell, was Gerald's high-school sweetheart. Travis took his girl away from him. I saw Gerald a few days ago, and he was going crazy. He wanted to stop that wedding, because he was afraid of what Travis might do to Tiffany after they were married."

Seven

"That's a pretty good motive for murder," Jack said. "Especially when you think about Travis Blakeley's reputation."

"The problem is, nobody could ever prove anything," T.J. said, shrugging. "From the way Gerald was talking the other day, though, he seemed pretty sure his brother was responsible for the deaths of his first two wives."

Wanda Nell nestled closer to Jack, feeling suddenly chilled. "Gerald must have been out of his mind worrying about that poor girl. I don't know what I would have done in that situation."

"Poisoning the guy at his bachelor party was a pretty desperate act," Jack said. "If that's what really happened."

Remembering the glass vial Gerald had shown her, Wanda Nell said, "I don't see what else it could be. Unless Blakeley had a really weak heart and just happened to have a heart attack at that very minute."

"Pretty big coincidence if he did," Jack said.

"Yeah," T.J. said, "and I don't believe that for a minute."

"No wonder Bill Warren was being so rough on Gerald," Wanda Nell said.

"Warren's about as big a jerk as Travis Blakeley was," T.J. said. "Plus I think him and Travis did some running around together."

"Have you had a run-in with Bill Warren?" Wanda Nell asked, her heart sinking.

"Tuck and I have seen him a few times around town," T.J. said, looking away. "He's made it real clear what he thinks of us."

"Sounds like a real prince," Jack said. "I'm sorry y'all have to deal with that kind of stupidity."

"I just can't get over the change in him," Wanda Nell said. "He was a really nice boy back in high school."

"You mean he's from around here?" Jack asked. "And you knew him in high school?"

"Yes, he grew up here," Wanda Nell said. She paused a moment. "Actually, he and I dated for a little while."

"You've got to be kidding!" T.J. said. "You and that ape?"

"It was about twenty-five years ago," Wanda Nell said, getting a bit irritated. "And I told you, he was nice. At least, I thought he was. But we didn't date for long, because I started seeing Bobby Ray."

Neither Jack nor T.J. said anything, and after a moment Wanda Nell went on. "With the way Bill's acting, Gerald really does need a good lawyer. I'm glad Tuck was willing to do it."

"Do you think he did it, T.J.?" Jack asked.

"I don't know," T.J. said. "I haven't been around Gerald all that much for about five years, and since I've been back in town I haven't talked to him more than two or three times. I probably wouldn't have those times either, except I ran into him down at the courthouse." T.J. worked in Tuck's office, and he spent a fair amount of time at the courthouse.

"What was Gerald doing in the courthouse?" Wanda Nell asked.

"He got a job a couple months ago in the county clerk's office," T.J. said. "Just the other day I had lunch with him in the cafeteria down there. That's when he told me how worried he was about Tiffany."

"Tiffany Farwell," Wanda Nell said. "Wasn't her daddy some kind of businessman?"

"Yeah," T.J. said. "He owned a big construction company, for one thing, plus I think he had a hand in a lot of other businesses all over northeast Mississippi. He was pretty loaded."

"I know who you're talking about," Jack said. "Didn't he die a couple of years ago?"

"Yes, he sure did," Wanda Nell said, sitting up. "And it was pretty embarrassing for the family. They tried to hush it up, but he had a heart attack in one of those strip clubs in Memphis and died right there."

"I think he and his wife were already divorced by that point," T.J. said. "It was bad enough, him dying in a place like that, but at least he wasn't still married."

"What happened to his money?" Jack asked.

"I think Tiffany got most of it, at least whatever her mother didn't get in the divorce," T.J. said. "I heard that Miz Farwell really took him to the cleaners."

"Sounds like he deserved it," Wanda Nell said, "if he went to places like that when he was married."

"He did," T.J. said. "At least that's what I always heard."

"Do you know Tiffany?" Wanda Nell asked.

"A little," T.J. answered. "But she didn't have much to do with me. She had her own little group, and they were too good for anybody who lived in a trailer park." He grinned.

"Sounds pretty stuck-up," Jack said. "I've got a few girls like her in my classes, I'm sorry to say."

"Yeah, she was stuck-up," T.J. said, "and about as smart as a dead rat." He laughed. "From what I heard, the only reason she made it into Ole Miss and was able to graduate was because her daddy gave them a *lot* of money."

"And this is the girl Gerald Blakeley is so in love with?" Wanda Nell just shook her head.

"She may be dumb," T.J. said, "but she's the most beautiful girl I've ever seen." He laughed again. "The trouble is, she knows it, but guys like Gerald don't care. She's not worth spit as a human being, but because of the way she looks, she's had guys slobbering all over her since she was twelve."

"And we know what they have on their tiny little minds," Wanda Nell said, poking Jack in the ribs.

"Hey, don't lump me in with that group," Jack said. "You know I love you for your mind. The fact that I think you're the most beautiful woman I've ever seen has nothing to do with it."

Wanda Nell couldn't help it—she fell out laughing. "You idiot," she said when she could catch her breath.

Jack pretended to be wounded. "Now, I really appreciate that. I really do. See how she treats me?" He appealed to T.J.

"You're not dragging me into this," he said, standing up. "I'd better get going. I don't know how long Tuck will be down at the jail, but I want to be home when he gets there."

"Good night, honey," Wanda Nell said, standing up to give him a good-bye hug. "Be careful."

"I will," he said. "Good night, Jack." He headed for the door, but he stopped with his hand on the knob. "Mama, I almost forgot. Juliet was coughing some today. I think she may be coming down with a cold."

"I'll check on her," Wanda Nell said, frowning. "It's probably just allergies. All kinds of stuff blooming right now, and she's allergic to some of it."

"Probably," T.J. said. "Good night."

As the door closed behind her son, Wanda Nell looked down at Jack. "Let me just go take a peek at Juliet, and I'll be right back." Jack nodded, and she headed down the hall toward her youngest child's bedroom.

Juliet's door stood ajar, and Wanda Nell pushed it open. Tiptoeing closer to the bed, she knelt over her sleeping daughter. She placed a hand gently on Juliet's forehead, hoping not to wake the girl. Her forehead was cool and dry, and Wanda Nell relaxed. No fever, at least. Juliet stirred in the bed, but her eyes remained closed.

Wanda Nell listened to the girl's breathing for a moment. She thought she detected a slight rasp to it, but nothing bad enough to worry much about tonight. She would keep an eye on Juliet the next couple days. Juliet sometimes had sinus infections, and Wanda Nell hoped she wasn't getting one now.

Back in the living room, Jack waited for her on the couch. "How is she?" he asked. He took off his glasses and set them on the coffee table. Wanda Nell smiled. She knew what that meant.

Resuming her place beside him, Wanda Nell said, "She seems okay now. No fever, but I'm going to have to watch her in case she's coming down with a sinus infection."

"Poor girl," Jack said. "I hope she isn't. They're so miserable."

"They sure are," Wanda Nell agreed. She laid her head on his shoulder again, and he hugged her closer to him.

Their lips met, and Wanda Nell enjoyed herself thoroughly for the next few minutes.

When Jack pulled away, Wanda Nell smiled at him. "You're getting pretty good at that," she teased.

"I'm willing to practice as often as you like," Jack said, his face solemn. "I like to be the best at anything I do."

Wanda Nell smiled. She let him practice a while longer, but finally she pulled away. She was so lucky, she reflected for the umpteenth time, that she had a good man like Jack, and not some psychopath after her.

Abruptly she sat up. She had forgotten all about Jack's cousin, Lisa, and her problems.

"I'm so sorry, honey," Wanda Nell said. "I just remembered about Lisa. Is she okay?"

"Relax, darling," Jack said, rubbing her arm. "I think you've got a pretty good reason for forgetting about her. She's okay. She's actually next door with Mayrene. Turned out that sleeping pill she took didn't work too well, so I was able to talk her into coming over here tonight."

"Good," Wanda Nell said, relaxing against the back of the couch again. "I was afraid she was going to be too stubborn to let us help."

"It took me a while," Jack said, frowning. "She kept saying that she didn't want to put anybody else in danger."

"Has the guy shown up in town yet?"

"I'm not sure. I think it's just phone calls so far," Jack said. "But Lisa thinks she might have spotted him yesterday, sitting in a car in the parking lot when she left work at the hospital."

"That's creepy," Wanda Nell said. "What did she do?"

"She went back inside for about half an hour and had something to eat at the cafeteria," Jack answered, "and when she came out again, the car was gone. She drove home, but a few minutes later her phone rang."

"And it was him?"

Jack nodded. "According to Lisa, he didn't say anything about being in Tullahoma, but she's convinced it was him in the parking lot."

"How do you stop something like that?" Wanda Nell asked.

"For one thing, Lisa needs to talk to a lawyer and see about getting some kind of restraining order. That's the first step. Once she's done that, she'll have a little more leverage with the police."

"I'm sure Tuck would help her," Wanda Nell said.

"I told her that," Jack replied, "but she's hesitating for some reason. I think she's so scared of him, she's afraid of doing anything, even trying to protect herself."

"Then we have to do it for her, I guess," Wanda Nell said. "We can't just sit by and let this guy terrorize her, or do something worse."

"I know," Jack said, "but she's so hard to deal with sometimes. I've been trying to help her without involving anyone else, but I'm about at my wits' end with her, I can tell you."

Wanda Nell squeezed his hand. "You're doing what you can, and maybe Mayrene and I can talk some sense into her. She can't hide from this guy for the rest of her life. There has to be some kind of solution, other than her moving away again."

"I sure hope so," Jack said. "Besides, even if she moved to California or Alaska, I'm not sure this guy would stop harassing her."

They sat in silence for a moment. Wanda Nell started

yawning, and with one look at her, Jack yawned, too. After a moment, he smiled at her. "I'd better get home and let you get some sleep."

She could read in his eyes that he didn't want to go, and she didn't want him to go either. She would have liked nothing better than to take him to her bedroom and spend the rest of the night with him. But she couldn't do that with Juliet asleep in the next room, and Miranda and Lavon at the other end of the trailer. It just wouldn't feel right to her. She even felt guilty about the kissing they had been doing earlier.

"I know," Jack said, his voice soft. He stood up. "Come on and lock the door behind me. Then you go on to bed. I'll talk to you in the morning." He moved toward the door, and Wanda Nell got up from the couch and followed him. They kissed once more before Jack left.

After she closed and locked the door behind Jack, Wanda Nell leaned against the door and closed her eyes. It was getting harder and harder to send Jack home alone, but what was she going to do about it? She wasn't sure she was ready for marriage just yet.

Sighing, she pushed herself away from the door. She moved quietly down toward the bedroom where Miranda and Lavon slept, and she pushed the door open to peek inside. Both her daughter and her grandson were sound asleep. Wanda Nell smiled at the sight of Lavon, his head resting on the body of his bunny.

She tiptoed away from their room toward her own. She couldn't resist one last check on Juliet. She checked her daughter's forehead again. No fever, but her breathing still had that little sound to it. Sighing, Wanda Nell left Juliet's room and went to her own to prepare for bed.

She was out of her clothes and into a nightgown in

record time. Her body ached as she slipped under the covers and pulled her pillow under her head. Getting comfortable, she willed herself to relax. She was determined not to think about the events of the evening. She wanted a peaceful night's sleep.

She woke up a couple times during the night, tossing and turning a bit before falling back asleep. By the time she woke on Sunday morning around eight, she felt good despite the interrupted sleep.

Leaving her bathroom several minutes later, Wanda Nell picked up a housecoat and slipped it on. She tied the belt loosely as she walked down the short hall toward the living room and kitchen.

Juliet sat at the table, toying with the cereal in her bowl. She looked up, her face wan, as her mother entered the room.

"Morning, Mama," she said.

"Good morning, sweetie," Wanda Nell said. "You don't sound like you feel too good. Are you getting sick?"

Juliet shrugged. "I guess so. I don't feel all that good." She grimaced. "My throat's a little sore this morning, and my nose is getting stuffy."

Wanda Nell felt her forehead. "You've got a little fever, too. Have you taken anything?"

"No, ma'am," Juliet said.

Wanda Nell went to the cabinet over the sink where she kept a few medications on hand. Selecting a bottle of liquid sinus medicine, she measured out a dose into the accompanying plastic cup and brought it to Juliet. "Drink this, honey."

Juliet made a face. "That stuff tastes awful." She took the cup, however, and drank down the contents. She made another face as she handed the empty cup back to her mother. "Yuck. It's even worse than I remembered."

"I know," said Wanda Nell, smiling in sympathy. "But it will help. You'll get sleepy soon, and resting will be good for you, too."

"I don't feel like doing anything anyway," Juliet said. She picked up her spoon and had a couple more mouthfuls of cereal. "That helps get rid of some of the bad taste." She dropped the spoon into the nearly empty bowl.

Wanda Nell picked it up and carried it over to the sink. She placed it in the sink and ran some water in the bowl. She was about to make coffee when the phone rang.

She reached for the receiver. "Hello."

"Hello. Wanda Nell, is that you?"

Wanda Nell started getting a headache the moment she recognized that voice. It was her former mother-in-law, Lucretia Culpepper. What on earth was she doing calling on a Sunday morning?

Suppressing a sigh, Wanda Nell said, "Yes, Miz Culpepper, it's me. Is there something I can do for you?"

"There certainly is. Maybe you can tell me why Tuck's car is parked in front of my house, and there's not a sign of him or that grandson of mine anywhere around." The old lady's voice was tart, but Wanda Nell could tell she was worried.

She was worried, too. What on earth could have happened to Tuck?

Eight

"Wanda Nell! Are you there?" Old Mrs. Culpepper's voice shrilled in her ear as Wanda Nell tried to keep from panicking.

"Now, Lucretia dear, don't you go getting poor Wanda Nell upset. I'm sure there's some logical explanation for this."

The new voice belonged to Mrs. Culpepper's spinster cousin, Belle Meriwether, who had moved in with her a few months ago to keep house for the older woman and serve as her companion. As she usually did, Belle had picked up another phone so she could join in on the conversation.

"Oh hush, Belle," Mrs. Culpepper said. "I'm sure Wanda Nell's not upset. Are you?"

"I'm okay," Wanda Nell said, exasperated with the old woman. "Tuck probably just had car trouble on the way home last night, and I guess in front of your house is where it happened."

"I sure didn't hear a thing," Mrs. Culpepper said. "Did you, Belle?"

"No, Lucretia, I sure didn't either," Belle replied. "But

you know how sound I sleep. Somebody will have to poke me with a stick, I reckon, when the angel Gabriel blows the trumpet to summon us all to glory. That's how sound I sleep. But is it the angel Gabriel? Maybe it's Michael, and is he an archangel? I'll have to go get my Bible and check."

The moment Belle paused for a breath, Wanda Nell spoke, cutting Mrs. Culpepper off at the same time. "Let me call Tuck and T.J. and find out what's going on. I'll call you back in a few minutes, Miz Culpepper. Okay?"

Mrs. Culpepper grumbled for a moment but then she agreed. Belle didn't say anything more. Wanda Nell figured she had put the phone down and gone off in search of her Bible.

If she hadn't been so worried she would have had a good laugh over Belle. That woman could talk the hind legs off a donkey, but at least she meant well. She wasn't malicious, the way Mrs. Culpepper could be when she had a mind to.

Her hand trembling slightly, Wanda punched in the number of T.J.'s cell phone. Her breath shallow, she waited, hoping he would answer quickly.

After four rings, Wanda Nell thought the call would go to voice mail, but then a sleepy voice spoke in her ear. "Hello, Mama. Is something wrong?"

"Honey, that's what I'm calling to ask you," Wanda Nell said, her heartbeat starting to slow down a bit. "Are you okay? And is Tuck okay?"

"We're both fine, Mama," T.J. said, more alert. "Tuck's sound asleep right here. Let me go in the other room. I don't want to wake him up."

Wanda Nell could hear the faint rustle of sheets as T.J. got out of bed. She waited as patiently as she could until he spoke again.

"Okay now," he said. "I'm in the kitchen. What's going on? Why are you so worried, Mama?"

"Your grandmother just called me, asking me if I knew what Tuck's car was doing on the street in front of her house. That's what I want to know, too. Did something happen last night?"

"Sorry, Mama, I guess I'm just not awake enough yet," T.J. said. She heard him yawn before he went on. "I'd forgotten about that. Yeah, Tuck had some car trouble on the way home last night. It happened while he was coming down Main Street, and he just happened to end up right there in front of Grandmother's house. He called me, and I went and picked him up. There wasn't anything we could do about his car last night, so we came on home. It was pretty late when we finally got to bed."

Somewhat relieved, Wanda Nell asked, "What was wrong with his car? It's only a couple of years old, isn't it?"

T.J. didn't answer right away, and that made Wanda Nell more anxious. "What was wrong with his car, T.J.? Tell me the truth now."

"Okay," T.J. said, expelling a long breath. "Something was wrong with his brakes. They started acting funny a few minutes after he left the jail. He thought he could make it home, but they gave out almost completely when he was coming down Main Street. He wasn't going very fast, thank goodness. He was able to stop the car without hurting himself, and he was in front of Grandmother's house when he stopped."

Mrs. Culpepper's house on Main Street was only about seven or eight blocks from the town square, where the courthouse and the county jail were located.

"Thank the Lord he's okay," Wanda Nell said. "But what was wrong with his brakes?"

Again, T.J. paused before answering. "We think somebody cut his brake line while he was at the jail."

Wanda Nell went cold all over. "Good Lord, what if he had been going fast? He might have been hurt real bad, or worse."

"I know, Mama," T.J. said. "I thought about that, too."

Wanda Nell heard the worry in his voice. "Has anything like this happened before?"

"Not exactly," T.J. said.

"What does that mean?"

T.J. sighed into the phone again. "Stuff has happened, but nothing as serious as this. Sugar in his gas tank a couple of times, his tires slashed three or four times. Just stupid stuff like that. Nothing really dangerous, just annoying as hell." He paused a moment. "They've done the same thing to my truck a few times, too."

"Oh my Lord," Wanda Nell said, appalled. "Who is doing this? Do y'all have any ideas?"

"It could be anybody, I guess," T.J. said, "but we figure it's got to be somebody connected with the courthouse, or maybe the police department or sheriff's department. Things usually seem to happen when our vehicles are downtown."

The building where Tuck had his office was on the square, just across the street from the jail and the courthouse. That meant anyone working around there had easy access to their vehicles.

"And I don't guess anybody would even think twice if they saw a cop or a deputy looking over somebody's car," Wanda Nell said.

"Nope," T.J. replied. "But it seems to happen most often when we've had to work late, after most everything else downtown is closed for the evening."

"I'd love to get my hands on whoever is doing this,"

Wanda Nell said. "I swear, if I had a gun, I'd go and shoot their you-know-whats off."

"I know how you feel," T.J. said. "And if I ever catch somebody in the act, well, I don't care who he is, I'm going to teach him a thing or two. Somebody may end up in the hospital, but it won't be me or Tuck, I can tell you that."

"Oh, honey, I hope it doesn't come to that," Wanda Nell said. T.J. in his wild teenage years had been in a lot of fights, but he had never been badly hurt. He had put a couple guys in the hospital, though, and that's how he ended up in jail. Wanda Nell hated even thinking about those days.

"Other than that," Wanda Nell said, "what can you do about this?"

"Tuck has been keeping a record of it all, and we've talked to Elmer Lee Johnson about it, too, so he's aware of what's going on."

"What did he say?"

"There wasn't much he could say. Until there's clear evidence of who's doing this, he can't do anything—the police either."

"Especially if it's somebody on the police force or in the sheriff's department who's behind it," Wanda Nell said. And as she said that, it hit her. "T.J., do you think Bill Warren had anything to do with what happened last night?"

"I don't know," T.J. said. "I sure wouldn't put it past him, but I doubt he'd do it himself. He'd put somebody else up to it. He wouldn't get his hands dirty."

"That creep," Wanda Nell said. "I'm glad I slapped him last night. I just wish I'd slapped him even harder a second time." As soon as the words were out of her mouth, she regretted them.

"What on earth are you talking about?" T.J. asked.

"What were you doing slapping a state cop?" He laughed. "I sure would love to have seen it, though."

"It was at the restaurant last night," Wanda Nell said. "He said something I didn't like, and before I thought about it, I let him have it. Elmer Lee was standing right there, and he backed me up, thank goodness. He heard what Bill said, too, and he didn't like it either."

"Did he insult you?" T.J. asked, his voice becoming heated. "That bastard."

"No, not me," Wanda Nell said. "And I'd rather not dwell on it anymore, okay? It's over and done with." She realized, however, that it wasn't. Maybe her defense of Tuck, and his defiance of Warren last night had caused Bill to retaliate by cutting Tuck's brake lines, or having them cut.

She hoped she did see Bill Warren again, and soon. She was going to tell him a thing or two, and by the time she finished with him, he was going to wish he had never come back to Tullahoma.

"Make sure you tell Elmer Lee about this latest thing," Wanda Nell said. "This is getting more serious, and maybe he can put a stop to it."

"We'll talk to him," T.J. said. "Tuck's going back to the jail this morning to check on Gerald anyway."

"Did they arrest him?"

"No, but they kept him overnight for questioning. You know they can hold him awhile without charging him with anything."

"Did Tuck say anything about it?"

"Not really," T.J. said. "He doesn't think they have much of a case, even if they find Gerald's fingerprints on that glass tube. They'd still have to prove it contained poison, if that's what really killed Travis, and they'd have to prove Gerald had access to it, or bought it somewhere."

"But if it wasn't Gerald, who could it have been?" Wanda Nell said. "It had to be somebody in the room last night."

"Yeah, that's what Tuck thinks, too," T.J. said. "We're going to start looking into just who was at that party and who might have a reason to want Travis Blakeley dead."

Wanda Nell heard him yawn again. "Look, honey, you get some rest, and you both be careful, you hear?"

"We will," T.J. said. "I think I am going back to bed for a while."

They said good-bye, and Wanda Nell hung up the phone.

It rang, startling her out of her reverie. She answered. "Hello."

"Wanda Nell, who have you been talking to all this time? When you didn't call back right away, I got even more worried. I've been calling and calling, but the line was busy."

Wanda Nell winced as Mrs. Culpepper's voice battered at her ear. "I'm sorry, Miz Culpepper, I was talking to T.J."

"Is he okay? And what about Tuck? Why did they leave that car out in front of my house?"

"Now, Lucretia, calm down, dear. If you don't, I'm going to have to give you an extra dose of your heart medicine, and you know you hate that." Belle Meriwether spoke in what she thought were soothing tones.

"Oh hush, woman," Mrs. Culpepper said. "I'm perfectly fine. I just need answers to my questions."

Wanda Nell looked around for something to snap in two with her free hand. Mrs. Culpepper was the most aggravating person she had ever known. "Both T.J. and Tuck are just fine. It was like I told you earlier, Tuck had some trouble with his car. He just happened to stop in front of your house. He'd been down at the jail with a client, and he was on his way home. They couldn't do anything about the car last night because it was so late, so he just called T.J. to come and get him. I'm sure they'll take care of the car sometime this morning if they can."

Amazed that she had been able to get in that many words without being interrupted by either Mrs. Culpepper or Belle, Wanda Nell paused for a deep breath.

Mrs. Culpepper sniffed into the phone. "Well, they should have called me first thing this morning to let me know what was going on. I wouldn't have worried so."

"Now, Lucretia," Belle said, "you heard Wanda Nell. It was real late last night when all this happened, and those poor boys were probably worn out. I'm sure T.J. would have called you otherwise, but they need their rest, just like you and me."

"When I was their age, I could dance at a party till three in the morning and still be up in time for breakfast with my daddy before he went to work," Mrs. Culpepper said, apparently still miffed.

Wanda Nell couldn't think of a thing to say. She was trying too hard to imagine Mrs. Culpepper as a young woman partying until the wee hours of the morning.

Belle chuckled. "Oh, Lucretia, you truly are something. They're only men, honey, and you know men don't have the stamina us women do."

"Well, that's true," Mrs. Culpepper said. "When I remember the things I used to do at that age, well, they couldn't keep up with me, I know that for a fact."

Wanda Nell seized her chance. "Ladies, it's been a pleasure chatting with you, but I need to see about some breakfast here. Y'all have a good day." She hung up the phone before either of the older women could start chattering again.

"Lord have mercy," Wanda Nell muttered. She finished getting the coffee on and then went to the refrigerator, intent on fixing breakfast for herself, Miranda, and Lavon. She glanced at the clock and frowned. It was almost eight-thirty. Miranda and Lavon were both usually up by now. She shut the refrigerator and went to check on them.

She found Miranda in the bathroom, on her knees, throwing up in the toilet.

"Honey, what on earth is wrong?" Wanda Nell soaked a washcloth in cold water, wrung it out, and held it to Miranda's forehead when she sat back from the toilet.

"I ate too much chocolate last night at the movies," Miranda said, looking away from her mother. "I knew better, but I just couldn't help myself."

"Oh, dear," Wanda Nell said. Miranda loved chocolate, but it sure didn't love her back. If she ate very much, she got sick to her stomach. "You must have really eaten a lot to make you throw up like this." Wanda Nell reached for the toilet handle and pulled it.

"I know," Miranda said, her voice weak. "I'll be more careful from now on."

Wanda Nell wiped her forehead and her mouth, just as she had done when Miranda was a child. "Can you get up now, sweetie?"

Miranda nodded. Putting her hands on the toilet seat, she braced herself and got up from the floor. "I think I'm done." She took a couple steps and leaned against the sink. "Maybe I ought to lie down for a few minutes."

"Sounds like a good idea," Wanda Nell said. She rinsed out the washcloth again and gave it to Miranda. "Take this with you, put it across your forehead, okay?"

Wanda Nell followed Miranda into her bedroom. Lavon was awake, playing happily in his crib with his toys. The minute he saw Wanda Nell, though, he started talking and demanding to be picked up.

Wanda Nell gave him a kiss and a hug, then picked him up and set him down on the floor. "Come on, sugar, let's go in the kitchen and we'll have some breakfast."

"I changed him before I got sick, Mama," Miranda said from the bed.

"Okay, honey. You call me if you need me," Wanda Nell said. She turned off the light and pulled the door halfway shut.

She followed Lavon back to the kitchen and gave him some milk to drink while she made his oatmeal. Once she had fed him, she prepared her own breakfast, some scrambled eggs and toast. Miranda appeared about half an hour later, and Wanda Nell gave her some ginger ale and a few crackers. That was all Miranda wanted.

The rest of the morning passed quietly. Juliet stayed in her room, sleeping thanks to the sinus medicine. Miranda eventually felt good enough to start getting herself and Lavon ready for church. Teddy arrived to pick them up, and Wanda Nell complimented him on his suit and tie. With all those tattoos covered up, he looked like a nice, clean-cut young man. She wondered if any of the people at Mrs. Culpepper's church had ever seen the ink on him.

"You're coming back here for lunch, aren't you?" Wanda Nell asked.

"I'm sorry, we promised to have lunch with my sister and her family today," Teddy said. "I hope you don't mind."

"That's okay," Wanda Nell said. "Give your sister my best, and I'll see y'all sometime this afternoon." She stood at the door, waving as they drove away.

She had better get started on lunch soon, she thought. Juliet probably wouldn't want to eat much, but she was expecting Jack. He would have a healthy appetite for sure.

She ought to invite Mayrene and Lisa over, too, she decided. She picked up the phone and punched in Mayrene's number.

"Good morning," she said when her friend answered. "Why don't you and Lisa come over and have lunch with me and Jack today?"

"Why that's terrible, honey," Mayrene said, and Wanda Nell almost dropped the phone in surprise. "I'll be right over to help you. You just hang on a minute." The phone clicked in her ear. She hung it up. What on earth was going on?

Moments later Mayrene knocked on her door. Wanda Nell had forgotten to lock it, and Mayrene opened it and walked in before Wanda Nell could get there.

Mayrene shut the door behind her and locked it.

"What is wrong with you?" Wanda Nell asked. "That was about the craziest talk I've ever heard. Did you even hear what I said?"

Mayrene glared at her. "You wanna talk crazy, honey? That girl over there is crazy as a Betsy bug, and I'm about to go nuts myself."

Nine

Wanda Nell couldn't remember a time when she had seen Mayrene this agitated. She took her friend by the arm and led her over to the couch.

"Sit down there, and tell me what on earth is going on," Wanda Nell said.

Mayrene stared at her. "That girl just won't stop *talking*. She follows me around everywhere. Last night I thought she was going to climb in bed with me and keep on talking. I finally had to practically shove her in the guest room and lock the door to make her leave me alone. And this morning, well, I heard her up about five o'clock, rambling around. She kept coming to my bedroom door, but I acted like I was sound asleep. She's like to drove me completely off my rocker."

She finally had to pause for breath, and Wanda Nell said, "Honey, I'm so sorry about all this. It's my fault, because I asked you to take her in. I had no idea she would act like that."

Her outburst over, Mayrene sat back on the couch and seemed to relax a little. She shook her head. "It's not your fault that girl has diarrhea of the mouth, Wanda Nell. I reckon she spends too much time alone, or something, and she's making up for it. And after I said I'd help out, I couldn't just shove her out the front door and lock it, no matter how tempted I was."

Wanda Nell shook her head in puzzlement. "I just don't get it. I've never heard her talk that much. The times I've been around her, it was the other way around. It's usually like pulling teeth to get her to say much."

"That's what I thought, too," Mayrene said. "I was expecting her to be real quiet, but something flipped her switch. I can't find a way to turn it off."

"I don't want you to have to put up with all that," Wanda Nell said. "Why don't you bring her over here, and maybe I can talk to her, get her to quiet down."

Mayrene sighed. "Thank you, honey. I appreciate it. I was just about to call you anyway when you called me. I spoke to Dixon this morning, and he's coming over in a little while to talk to her about this stalking thing. I thought maybe he could help her." She shook her head. "She's been talking at me so much I ain't even told her he's coming yet."

"Why don't you go get her, and you and me will try to calm her down until Mr. Vance gets here. He can talk to her here, and you can get some peace and quiet while he's doing it."

"Sounds like a good plan to me," Mayrene said, pushing herself up and off the couch.

"Wait a minute," Wanda Nell said. "Before I forget, did you hear about what happened last night?"

Mayrene nodded. "Dixon told me about it this morning." She frowned. "I can't say as I'm really sorry. It couldn't

have happened to a nicer guy. But I sure hate that you had to
see it."

"Yeah, it wasn't very nice," Wanda Nell said.

"You okay?" Mayrene asked.

Wanda Nell nodded. "I'll tell you about it later." She
stood. "Just give me five minutes to get dressed," she said,
glancing down at her housecoat. "I can't talk to a policeman dressed like this."

"I think I'll wait here while you're changing," Mayrene
said. "Then I'll go get her."

Wanda Nell tried not to laugh. She had never seen
Mayrene like this. Usually nothing fazed her. Wanda Nell
knew it wasn't that funny, though, and Mayrene sure
wouldn't appreciate it if she laughed at her.

She just nodded and went to her bedroom to change. A
few minutes later she was back, dressed in jeans and a
loose-fitting T-shirt.

"I'll be back in a minute," Mayrene said, heading out
the door.

Wanda Nell went to the kitchen for some coffee. Her
head ached a little, and she knew some caffeine would help
that. She had made a full pot of coffee without intending
to, so there would be enough if anyone else wanted any.
She poured herself a cup, added some milk and sugar, and
went back to the living room.

She had just sat down when the door opened, and Lisa
Pemberton walked in, followed by Mayrene.

"Good morning, Lisa," Wanda Nell said, standing up.
"How are you this morning?" She eyed the younger woman
closely for signs of stress and was faintly surprised to see
that Lisa appeared perfectly calm and happy.

"I'm doing fine, Wanda Nell," Lisa said with a friendly

smile. "Mayrene is just the nicest, kindest person. I can't tell you how much I appreciate you and your friend looking after me." She turned to Mayrene and startled her by wrapping her arms around her for a quick hug.

Mayrene, who was both heavier and taller than the petite Lisa, patted her awkwardly on the back. "Glad I could help out, honey."

"Would either of you like some coffee?" Wanda Nell asked. "Or something else?"

"I'm fine," Lisa said. "Mayrene fixed us a very nice breakfast."

"I'm okay, too," Mayrene said.

"Y'all sit down," Wanda Nell said, waving at the couch.

Lisa sat on the end of the couch nearest Wanda Nell's chair while Mayrene perched on the other end, as far away from Lisa as she could get.

"Mayrene's been telling me all about herself," Lisa said. "We've had a great time getting to know each other better." She beamed at her hostess.

Wanda Nell noted the odd expression on Mayrene's face as she gazed back at Lisa. From what Wanda Nell could tell, Mayrene was having trouble agreeing with Lisa's description of their time together. She was way too polite to say anything and contradict Lisa, however.

When Lisa turned back to face Wanda Nell, Mayrene rolled her eyes and shrugged. Wanda Nell tried not to laugh. This whole situation was getting odder by the minute.

"Mayrene just told me that her friend, Officer Vance, is coming over to talk to you about your situation," Wanda Nell said. She had almost used the word *stalker*, but she didn't want to upset Lisa if she didn't have to.

Lisa's pretty face clouded over. "I really hate talking about it, but I guess I have to."

Wanda Nell couldn't help but notice that Mayrene rolled her eyes once again.

Wanda Nell reached over and patted Lisa's arm. "I know, honey, it must be really scary for you. But we're going to have to put an end to it somehow. You can't live your life this way, always afraid."

Lisa hung her head. "No, I can't. It's awful." She was crying now.

"We'll figure something out," Wanda Nell said in bracing tones. "You'll see. Somehow we'll make sure you're safe and don't have to worry about this guy ever again."

Lisa raised a tear-stained face to Wanda Nell. "That would be so wonderful. It's been so long since I've had a sound night's sleep, I can't tell you."

Wanda Nell decided it was time to change the subject, at least until the policeman arrived. "How would you and Mayrene like to stay and have lunch with me and Jack? He'll be coming over in a couple of hours, and I know he'll be anxious to see you. And I'd love to have you both eat with us."

"Thank you," Lisa said, wiping her face with the back of one hand. "But I have to go to work a little later. I'm on the eleven-to-seven shift right now. Mayrene said she would take me and maybe Jack can pick me up later."

"I'm sorry you can't stay and eat with us, but maybe being at work will help take your mind off things." Wanda Nell picked up her coffee cup and sipped.

"Working does help," Lisa said. "And I feel pretty safe at the hospital, because there are always people around. Especially on a Sunday. Lots of people visit on Sundays."

"That's good," Wanda Nell replied.

They heard a car pulling up, and a moment later a door slamming.

"That's probably Dixon," Mayrene said, pushing up from the couch. "I'll go get him and bring him over here." She was out the door before Wanda Nell even had time to respond.

"Are you sure you don't mind him talking to me here?" Lisa had an anxious look on her face. "I'm sure you've got things to do, what with having to cook and everything."

"It's fine," Wanda Nell assured her. "I've got plenty of time. Besides, when Jack gets here, I'll just put him to work, too. He's pretty good in the kitchen." She smiled.

Lisa didn't say anything. Instead she sighed and stared down at her hands.

Mayrene came back in then, followed by Dixon Vance. Wanda Nell was a little surprised to see him in uniform. She had figured this would be a more informal talk. She stood up and extended her hand as the officer came forward.

"Good morning, Officer Vance," Wanda Nell said. "Thank you for coming this morning. I'm Wanda Nell Culpepper."

Vance grasped her hand and gave it a firm shake. "I'm glad to do it, Miz Culpepper." His eyes narrowed briefly. "You work at the Kountry Kitchen. You were there last night."

"Yes," Wanda Nell said. "It was a terrible thing."

"What happened last night?" Lisa asked, a puzzled look on her face.

"This is Lisa Pemberton, Officer," Wanda Nell said. "She's the one who needs to talk to you."

"Morning, ma'am," Vance said. "Mind if I sit here?" He indicated a spot on the couch near Lisa.

Lisa nodded. Before he sat down on the couch, though, Vance found a chair for Mayrene and made sure she was comfortable in it. Mayrene smiled up at him, and his gaze lingered on her for a long moment. Wanda Nell was delighted to see the rapport between the two of them.

When Vance turned back to face Lisa, he was all business. He sat down on the couch, giving her plenty of space. "Why don't you tell me about your problem, Miss Pemberton?"

"I will," Lisa said, "but first, won't somebody tell me what happened last night?"

Vance grimaced. "One of my fellow officers died last night during a bachelor party at the Kountry Kitchen."

"Oh, how awful," Lisa said, appalled. She turned to Wanda Nell. "And you were there, weren't you? I bet you saw everything."

Wanda Nell nodded. "Yes, I was. It was awful. The party was for him. He was supposed to be getting married in a few days."

"Who was he?" Lisa asked.

"Travis Blakeley," Vance said, his face darkening.

Wanda Nell expected him to say something about his fellow officer, but he didn't.

"I didn't know him," Lisa said, "but how terrible."

"Yes, ma'am," Vance said.

Vance proceeded to question Lisa, and Wanda Nell was gratified to observe how skillfully and gently he accomplished it. She hesitated over giving Vance the stalker's name, for some reason, but Vance persisted without pressuring her too hard. Finally she gave in. Vance jotted down details in a notebook, and when he was done he put it away.

"I promise you, Miss Pemberton, that we're going to take this seriously. We'll be on the lookout for this guy, and any time you think you see him in town, I want you to call us right away." He pulled his notebook out again for a moment and consulted it. "When I get a chance, I'll get in touch with the Meridian police and see what I can find out about this officer. Lester Biggs, right?"

Lisa nodded. "Thank you, Officer. I feel a lot better now."

"Good," Vance said. He stood up. "I've got to get going."

"Can you hold on just a few minutes?" Mayrene said as she stood up. "Let me take Lisa back over to my place so she can start getting ready for work, and I'll be right back. Okay?"

"Sure," Vance said, smiling as he looked at her. "I can hang on for a few minutes more."

"Come on, honey," Mayrene said, motioning for Lisa to get up and follow her. "You need to start getting ready for work."

Lisa got up and followed Mayrene to the door. Mayrene went out ahead of her, and Lisa paused in the doorway. "Thank you," she said. "Thank you both."

"Take care, Lisa," Wanda Nell said. Vance simply nodded.

Once Lisa was gone, Vance started moving toward the door. Wanda Nell called out his name, and he stopped and turned to face her.

"Yes, ma'am," he said. "Something I can do for you?"

Wanda Nell knew she probably shouldn't be asking him anything about the events of last night, but her curiosity was getting the better of her.

"Well, you know I was there last night," she began, and Vance nodded at her. "I just couldn't help wondering, do they know what happened? I mean, did somebody really poison him?"

Vance didn't respond for a moment, and Wanda Nell was about to apologize, thinking he was annoyed, when he surprised her with an answer. "They're pretty sure it was poison. They're not saying what just yet, but Doc Crowell—the young one, I mean—said he was pretty sure it was poison."

"So it's definitely a murder case," Wanda Nell said.

"I don't think it was suicide," Vance replied.

The flippant answer stymied her for a moment. Maybe it was just cop humor, she reckoned, but it seemed like an odd response to her. Ignoring it, she said, "Any idea yet who did it?"

Vance stared at her. "Why are you so interested?"

Wanda Nell shrugged. "I saw it happen, and I guess I can't help but be curious. I know some of the men who were at that party, and I'd sure hate to think one of them is a killer."

"You don't have to worry about a killer being on the loose," Vance said. "The state cop, Warren, arrested and charged someone with the murder just a little while ago."

Wanda Nell had a bad feeling about this. She was pretty sure who Bill Warren had arrested. Still, she had to ask. "Who was it? Can you say?"

Vance shrugged. "Don't see why not. It'll be pretty public soon anyway. It was the victim's brother, Gerald Blakeley."

Ten

Vance didn't give Wanda Nell any time to react to his news. He nodded, said, "Ma'am," and left.

Wanda Nell stared at the closed door for a moment. She had heard what she expected to hear, yet she still felt a bit surprised. Maybe she was just in a contrary mood, or maybe she just didn't like the way Bill Warren had acted last night, but whatever the reason, she didn't want to think of Gerald Blakeley as a murderer.

He had looked so sad and lost last night, not to mention truly puzzled over the glass tube he had been holding. Wanda Nell had been around drunks enough in her life to know when somebody was just putting on. Gerald hadn't been. He had been well and truly inebriated, and therefore Wanda Nell believed him when he said he had found the tube but wasn't sure where.

Everything seemed awfully convenient for Bill Warren all of a sudden, Wanda Nell realized. He obviously had it in for Gerald right away, and Gerald had a motive for getting rid of his brother. Often the most obvious answer was the correct one, Wanda Nell knew, but this time she just didn't believe it. From everything she had heard about Travis Blakeley there was probably a long line of people who wanted him dead.

The question was, had any of them besides Gerald Blakeley been at the bachelor party last night?

Well, it really wasn't up to her, and she knew that. Tuck was Gerald's lawyer, and it would be up to him to cast enough doubt on Gerald's alleged guilt to keep him from going to jail. If the police really believed they had the killer already, they certainly weren't going to be looking at anyone else.

Or were they?

Wanda Nell went to the phone and punched in T.J.'s cell number. She thought about calling Tuck directly, but she figured he was too busy with Gerald to have time to talk. T.J. answered after a couple rings.

"Hey, honey, it's me," she said. "Are you where you can talk?"

"Hi, Mama. You caught me at home," T.J. said. "Well, I've got some news for you."

"They've arrested Gerald," she said.

"Yeah, how did you know?" T.J. was surprised.

"A policeman was just here talking to Lisa, Jack's cousin, about her stalker, and he told me."

"Oh. Well, it happened about half an hour ago," T.J. said. "Tuck had just gotten down to the jail and had about five minutes with Gerald before it went down. Tuck was pretty pissed about the whole thing, because he doesn't think they really have enough evidence to charge Gerald. But obviously the judge thought different."

"Does Tuck think Gerald did it?"

"We talked about it over breakfast this morning," T.J. said, "and he's inclined to think Gerald is innocent. Tuck wants to know where the poison came from, and he thinks that's going to be a key point in the case."

"Do they know yet what kind of poison it was?"

"They won't know for sure until they do the autopsy," T.J. said, "but Tuck thinks, based on what happened and a couple of things he picked up from talking to the EMTs who handled the case, that it might have been cyanide."

"Cyanide?" Wanda Nell asked. "Where on earth would Gerald get hold of cyanide?"

"That's what Tuck wants to know, and he thinks the cops are going to have a tough time proving Gerald had access to it. We're going to be investigating that ourselves, because Tuck doesn't want to leave anything to chance."

"That's why he's so good at being a lawyer," Wanda Nell said.

"He sure is," Tuck said, and Wanda Nell had to smile at the pride in his voice. She hadn't known what to think about her son's relationship with Tuck at first, but as time had passed, she had become more used to it. It wasn't hard to see how they felt about each other, and having Tuck in his life had made a huge difference to T.J. in many ways. Though she worried about how others might treat them, Wanda Nell was happy for them. In the past there had been many nights when she was afraid T.J. would end up spending the rest of his life in jail, but her son had turned out to be a good man after all.

"What do *you* think? About Gerald, I mean," Wanda Nell asked.

"He swore up and down to Tuck that he didn't do it," T.J. replied.

"Do you believe him?"

T.J. didn't answer for a moment. "Yeah, I do. I knew Gerald pretty well back when we were in high school, and even though I haven't been around him that much the last few years, I don't think he's changed, really. Back then he was one of those guys who was always hanging back, never really getting involved in anything. You know what I mean?"

"I think so," Wanda Nell said. "A follower, not a leader."

"Yeah," T.J. replied. "It was always somebody else who had the ideas, and Gerald just kinda trailed along behind like a puppy dog."

"Did he get in trouble?"

"Like me, you mean?" T.J. laughed. "Naw, he always stayed out of trouble. He never got in fights or anything like that, and he sure didn't do drugs."

"It's hard to imagine a guy like that killing somebody," Wanda Nell said.

"It was a pretty sneaky way to do it," T.J. said, "and if Gerald was going to do it, I think he'd do it like that somehow. I mean, he'd never just bash somebody over the head. He's too chicken to do that."

"But if you think he might poison someone, then couldn't he have done it?"

"Not really," T.J. said. "I just don't think he had the nerve."

"Even to protect that girl?"

There was a pause before T.J. spoke again. "You know, there's something kinda funny about that. Back in high school, Gerald was real stuck on Tiffany, and of course she wouldn't give him the time of day. Tuck said when he asked Gerald about her, Gerald said she was just a friend. He's not in love with her anymore."

"Maybe he was putting on so nobody would think he had a motive, like killing his brother to protect her."

"Tuck didn't think so. He said Gerald just shook his

head when he asked him about that. He said he got over Tiffany a long time ago. Gerald didn't want her to marry Travis and tried to talk to her about it. But for some reason, Tiffany wouldn't even go into it with him. And he kept on saying he didn't kill his brother." T.J. paused a moment. "Look, Mama, I hate to cut this short, but Tuck needs me to do some stuff for him. I've got to get on down to the office."

"Okay, honey," Wanda Nell said. "Give Tuck my love, and y'all both be careful."

"We will, Mama," T.J. said, his voice firm. "Now stop worrying about us."

Wanda Nell hung up the phone, shaking her head. T.J. telling her not to worry was like telling the pope not to be Catholic. Worrying about her children was something a mother never stopped doing, no matter how old they were.

That reminded her she wanted to check in on Juliet. She walked down the hall and stepped into Juliet's room. Her youngest child was sound asleep, tangled in the covers, one arm loosely wrapped around a worn teddy bear.

Juliet was a bit warm and sweaty when Wanda Nell checked her forehead, but not enough for her to be alarmed. The best thing for her now was sleep. When she woke up, Wanda Nell would take her temperature.

She headed back to the kitchen to get started on lunch. When she glanced out the window toward Mayrene's trailer, she saw her friend and Lisa getting into Mayrene's car. She checked the clock, and it was ten-thirty-five. Jack would be here around eleven, so she had better get a move on. She would get the potatoes ready for boiling before she started on the chicken.

By the time Jack arrived, Wanda Nell had everything well in hand. She went to let Jack in, and he pulled her into his arms the moment the door shut behind him.

The next few minutes passed in enjoyable fashion, and Wanda Nell had just stepped back when she heard Juliet calling her.

"Go on in the kitchen and get yourself something to drink," she told Jack. "Let me see what Juliet wants."

Jack nodded, and she went down the hall. "Honey, are you okay?" She walked into Juliet's room and sat down on the bed beside her daughter. She checked her forehead again—still warm and sweaty.

"I'm real thirsty, Mama, and my throat is scratchy," Juliet said. "I was going to get up and get some water, but I felt a little dizzy."

"Probably that sinus medicine's making you feel that way," Wanda Nell said. She picked up a cup from Juliet's bedside table. "I'll be right back." She went into the bathroom between her bedroom and Juliet's and filled the cup with cold water.

"Drink this, sweetie," she said as she sat down on the bed again. "Can you sit up?"

Juliet nodded, pushing herself nearly upright with her right arm. She took the cup in her left hand, raised it to her mouth, and drained it. "Thank you, Mama. That makes me feel better."

"Would you like some more?"

"No, that's enough for now," Juliet said, lying down again.

"I'm going to take your temperature," Wanda Nell said. She went back to the bathroom for the thermometer.

Juliet opened her mouth obediently for the thermometer and clamped her lips shut to hold it under her tongue. Wanda Nell sat on the bed and watched a minute tick by on Juliet's bedside clock. She pulled the thermometer out of her daughter's mouth and tilted it, trying to read it.

"Looks like just a very slight fever, honey," she told her daughter. "Not even up to a hundred."

Juliet smiled wanly.

"Do you feel like eating anything?" Wanda Nell asked. "Jack's here, and I'm getting lunch ready."

"I'm a little hungry," Juliet said, "but not much."

"I'll bring you some mashed potatoes with plenty of butter. How's that?"

Juliet nodded.

"Okay, honey," Wanda Nell said. "The potatoes won't be ready for a little while, but I'm going to get you a pitcher of water, so when you get thirsty it'll be right here."

Jack was sitting at the kitchen table, drinking some tea. "Is Juliet okay?" he asked, his face expressing his concern. He set his glass down and got up from the table.

"I think she's got a sinus infection," Wanda Nell said. "She's running a little fever, but it's not too bad yet. I'm probably going to take her to the doctor in the morning. Usually it takes some antibiotics for her to get better."

"Anything I can do?"

"Keep an eye on the stove for me while I take Juliet some water," Wanda Nell said. She retrieved a small plastic pitcher with a lid from the cabinet. She rinsed it out, filled it with water, and carried it back to Juliet's room. The girl had fallen asleep. Wanda Nell set the pitcher down on her bedside table and tiptoed out.

Jack was poking at the potatoes with a fork when she walked back into the kitchen. He turned his head at the sound of Wanda Nell's footsteps. "They're about done."

Wanda Nell nodded. "I'll start the chicken frying, and you can mash the potatoes if you don't mind."

"Sure," Jack said. "What about rolls?"

"I forgot about them," Wanda Nell said, frowning.

"Don't worry about it," Jack said. "It won't hurt us to do without them for once." He grinned.

Wanda Nell patted her hip ruefully. "You're not kidding. I don't need any more padding than I've already got."

"You look just fine to me," Jack said, an amorous glint in his eyes. "In fact, you look better than fine."

With a pang, Wanda Nell thought for a moment how nice it would be to forget about everything else except this wonderful man. She wanted him so badly she almost couldn't stand it. But now wasn't the time, nor was this the place.

Though her pulse was racing, she spoke calmly. "You look better than fine to me, too, mister, but I've got some chicken to fry." She gave him a quick kiss on the cheek before turning her attention to her work.

Jack just smiled, and they worked in companionable silence for a while. When the potatoes were mashed, Wanda Nell asked him to take over watching the chicken while she took a small bowl of potatoes to Juliet.

Juliet was awake, propped up in bed with a book. She accepted the potatoes gratefully.

"Are you sure you don't want something else, honey?" Wanda Nell watched her daughter eat.

"No, mama, this is fine," Juliet said. "I don't think I'll want anything else for a while."

Wanda Nell bent to kiss her forehead. "Just holler if you need me."

Jack was taking the chicken out of the frying pan, placing it on paper towels, when Wanda Nell returned. He set the table for the two of them while she checked on the green beans. They were canned, and all she had done was add some fatback to them while they heated up. They were ready, and she turned the heat off under them. She retrieved some leftover salad from the fridge and set it on the table, found a large spoon from the silverware drawer and stuck it in the bowl.

"Sure you don't want some bread, honey?" she asked. "I've got some loaf bread, and I could toast it real quick if you like."

"No, I'm fine," Jack said. "Let's just sit down and enjoy this. That chicken is making my mouth water."

They filled their plates and sat down at the table. They ate in silence for a while.

"Have you talked to Lisa today?" Wanda Nell asked. She put her fork down and stared at her empty plate. Had she really eaten it all already?

"Just briefly this morning," Jack said. "She called me and said she was doing fine. She told me how nice Mayrene was and how much she appreciated what Mayrene was doing." He pushed his plate aside and picked up his tea glass.

Wanda Nell debated whether to tell him about Mayrene's reaction to his cousin, but for the moment she decided not to. Maybe by the time Lisa finished her shift at the hospital that evening she would have calmed down a bit and wouldn't get on Mayrene's nerves so bad.

"Mayrene took her to work. Are you going to pick her up?"

Jack nodded. "Yeah. I won't be gone that long. You don't mind, do you?"

"Of course not," Wanda Nell said. "I might go with you, if Miranda's back by then. I don't want to leave Juliet by herself."

"Okay," Jack said.

"By the way," Wanda Nell said, "I've been meaning to tell you, a policeman came by to talk to Lisa this morning. Mayrene is dating a cop now, a guy named Dixon Vance, and she asked him to come over."

"How did it go?" Jack asked.

"He was very gentle with her," Wanda Nell said. "He told her they would look into it, and for her to call the police department if she spotted this guy in town."

"That's good," Jack said. "I'm glad she's finally talked to the police here."

"I just hope he'll be so busy being a cop in Meridian he won't have time to drive all the way over here and bother her. Of course, that wouldn't stop him from calling," Wanda Nell said.

"First thing Monday, Lisa's going to call the phone company and have them disconnect her phone. She's going to get a new cell phone, too, and use that. He'll have a harder time getting hold of her new number."

"That's a good idea," Wanda Nell replied.

"She also needs to talk to Tuck and see what they can do, legally, to put a stop to this."

"He'll know what to do," Wanda Nell said. "But he's going to be pretty busy for a while. They've arrested Gerald Blakeley for the murder, and Tuck's his lawyer."

"That's pretty fast," Jack said. "They must think they have a good case."

Wanda Nell told him the gist of her conversation with T.J. "And I'm not too convinced he did it either. I just think they're going a little too fast."

"Maybe," Jack said. "But you say Gerald Blakeley isn't still in love with the bride. What's her name again?"

"Tiffany Farwell," Wanda Nell said. "I don't know her, but I have a vague idea I've seen her picture in the paper."

"Probably," Jack said. "I don't think I know her, though."

"I know," Wanda Nell said, getting up from the table. "Somewhere around here I know I've still got T.J.'s high school yearbooks, and there's bound to be pictures of her in those. Now where are they?"

She thought for a moment. She couldn't remember the last time she had seen them, but she thought they might be in a box in the hall closet. "You just sit and relax, and I'm going to look for them. Back in a minute."

Wanda Nell rooted around in the bottom of the closet and found the large box she was looking for. She pulled it out of the closet and set it down in the hall. It was certainly heavy enough to contain yearbooks, she thought.

Pulling off the lid and setting it aside, she bent over and rummaged through the contents. There were a lot of loose papers at the top. She really ought to go through them at some point and see if there was anything important among them.

Under the layers of paper she could feel the hard binding of a yearbook. She pulled out the first one and glanced at the year. It was from when T.J. was a senior. That would do. She replaced the lid on the box and shoved it back into the closet.

Leafing through the yearbook as she walked back to the kitchen, she found the section with class portraits. The seniors came first, and she put a finger in to hold her place.

"Here it is," she told Jack. She sat down next to him at the table and opened the book. "Here's the senior class the year T.J. graduated. She was in his class, he said."

She quickly found the girl's picture. "She really is pretty," Wanda Nell said.

"Yeah," Jack replied. "But she has a pretty vacant look on her face, don't you think?"

"Somebody said she wasn't supposed to be all that bright," Wanda Nell said. "Let's look for other pictures."

She flipped the pages back to the features section, and they found numerous pictures of the girl.

"Well built, too," Jack commented when they found the picture of her as Miss Tullahoma County High School. The expensive-looking gown she wore left little to the imagination. Now that she saw the picture, Wanda Nell vaguely remembered that there had been a bit of furor at the high school because of that dress.

"Put your eyes back in your head," Wanda Nell said. She poked Jack in the ribs.

"Don't worry, honey," Jack said. "She may have some nice curves, but look at her face. Don't you see?"

Wanda Nell did see. Tiffany Farwell was drop-dead gorgeous, but when you really looked in her face, there wasn't anybody home. She had such a vacant look in her eyes, Wanda Nell felt sorry for her.

"I've seen her before," Jack said, continuing to study the picture. "It was only a couple of weeks ago, too. I had no idea who she was at the time, though."

"Where'd you see her?" Wanda Nell asked.

"Lisa was having some car trouble," Jack said. "She managed to make it to the hospital, but she called and asked if I would come by after school and take a look at it for her. I was out in the staff section of the parking lot of the hospital, poking around under the hood of her car, when this bright red BMW convertible came zooming by. I wondered who was driving it, so I stopped what I was doing and watched."

"And?" Wanda Nell said when he paused.

"The driver parked the car and got out. It was her," Jack said, pointing down at the picture.

"Is that all?" Wanda Nell said, feeling disappointed.

"No," Jack said, "that's not all. She sat down on the

hood of the car. She was obviously waiting for someone, and it was only about five minutes before someone came out to greet her."

"Did you recognize that person?" Wanda Nell wanted to poke him again. He was dragging this out deliberately, because he knew how impatient she was.

Jack grinned. "I sure did, because he's my doctor. Tony Crowell."

"Okay," Wanda Nell said, "he may be her doctor, too. He's mine, and I take the girls to him, too."

Jack grinned, lasciviously this time. "He may be her doctor, but I doubt he greets all his patients the way he greeted her."

"What do you mean?" Wanda Nell asked, though she was beginning to see where this was leading.

"They weren't that far from where I was," Jack said, "and I had a pretty clear view of them. He had his hands all over her, and she wasn't trying to stop him."

"But she was supposed to be getting married to someone else," Wanda Nell said slowly.

"Not from the way she was acting that afternoon, she wasn't," Jack said.

Wanda Nell stared down at Tiffany Farwell's picture. If she was having an affair with the doctor, that meant Tony might have had a motive to kill Travis Blakeley. And who better than a doctor who would be right there when his victim collapsed?

Eleven

Wanda Nell voiced her thoughts to Jack. "What do you think?"

"It's possible, I guess," Jack said, frowning. "But do you really think Dr. Crowell would kill somebody?"

"I sure wouldn't want to think so," Wanda Nell said. "Ever since his daddy retired a few years ago, I've been going to him. He's always seemed like a real nice, caring man. Just like his daddy always was."

"But if he's really in love with Tiffany Farwell . . ." Jack said. He shrugged. "Is he married?"

"No, I'm pretty sure he's not," Wanda Nell said. She thumped the table with her hand. "This is really stupid. Why would he have to murder Travis Blakeley if he's in love with Tiffany? Tiffany didn't have to marry Travis. She could have told him she was in love with someone else, and that would be the end of it."

"Maybe," Jack said. "But what if she was afraid of Blakeley?"

"That's true," Wanda Nell said. "He might have threat-

ened her, I guess. But that just sounds crazy. He could
have found some other girl to marry if she dumped
him."

"Isn't she worth a lot of money, though?" Jack said.
"Her father was supposed to be pretty rich, and she was his
only child, right?"

"Yeah, that's true," Wanda Nell said. "According to
what I heard, she is pretty well off."

"Maybe Blakeley didn't want to let go of a woman with
that kind of money."

"From what Mayrene told me, he collected a lot of life
insurance when his first two wives died." She shivered.
"Lord, this is creepy. What kind of monster was he?"

"If he killed his wives—or had them killed—for the
money," Jack said, his face darkening, "then he deserved
what he got. Men like that shouldn't be allowed to prey on
women, or anyone, for that matter."

"No, they shouldn't," Wanda Nell said. "Look, I think
we need to tell Tuck about this. He needs to know anything
that could help him defend Gerald."

"Sure," Jack said. "I'll tell him about it." He paused for
a moment, regarding her with an odd expression. "Why
are you so intent on helping in this case? I know you saw
it happen, but otherwise, does it really involve you directly?"

"No, not really, I guess," Wanda Nell said. "I don't really know Gerald, and he could be guilty, I reckon. But it
did happen right in front of me." She paused. She had to be
completely honest with Jack. "Mostly I guess I'm just really peeved with Bill Warren. The way he's acting really
makes me mad, and maybe I just want to see him get a
black eye. Instead of him giving one to someone else."

"Remind me not to get on your bad side," Jack said, half humorously.

Wanda Nell grinned. "Yeah, you better remember that, buddy."

"I will." Jack laughed. He got up and retrieved the phone. "What's the number?"

Wanda Nell gave him Tuck's cell phone number, and he punched it in as she spoke.

"Hey, Tuck, this is Jack. How's it going?" Jack listened for a moment. "Good. Look, the reason I'm calling is, I think I have some information that might be useful in your present case."

Jack quickly explained what he had seen, and when. "Yeah, I'm sure who it was," he said. "Right. Talk to you later." He hung up the phone.

He folded his arms and stared down at Wanda Nell. "Now, what do you say we forget about murders and so on, and just concentrate on relaxing?"

Wanda Nell laughed. "Sounds good to me."

For the rest of the day, they did just that. Wanda Nell looked in on Juliet regularly, checking her temperature, making sure she drank enough water, and dosing her with the sinus medication. She decided she would take her to the doctor the next morning, just in case, even though she didn't seem to be getting any worse.

Teddy Bolton brought Miranda and Lavon home around seven, and Lavon was so worn out, Miranda put him to bed right away. Teddy stayed and visited with Wanda Nell and Jack for about half an hour before excusing himself, saying he had to be up early the next day for work. Miranda followed him out to his car, and while she was gone, Jack turned to Wanda Nell.

"Do you think he's really serious about Miranda?"

"He sure seems to be," Wanda Nell said. "He's told me he wants to get married, but he wants to save up some money first."

"How do you feel about them getting married?" Jack asked.

"I was a little nervous about him at first," Wanda Nell said, "but the more I've gotten to know him, I really like him. I think he's good for Miranda."

"I like him, too," Jack said. "He's very mature for his age, and I think he's got his head screwed on right." He paused. "If he and Miranda get married, that would be a big burden off your shoulders."

"Yes, it sure would," Wanda Nell said, eyeing him curiously. He was up to something, and she was beginning to suspect what it was. "I think I could count on Teddy to look after her and Lavon."

"Yeah," Jack said. He glanced at the door, evidently watching for Miranda. "So if that happens, do you think you might be willing to think about marriage yourself?"

Despite the fact that she kept telling herself she wasn't ready for marriage yet, she had actually been thinking about it. Not having to ride herd on Miranda all the time would certainly make her life easier, and as time wore on, she was getting more and more impatient to sort out her own life. She loved Jack and wanted to be with him. She had been reluctant at first, because her first marriage had left a lot to be desired. Jack was very different from Bobby Ray, though, and she knew that. Maybe she should just stop hemming and hawing and admit that being married to Jack would be a good thing.

Wanda Nell clasped one of Jack's hands in hers. He

watched her face intently. "Yes, I would," she said. *There, that wasn't so hard after all.*

Jack smiled, and the love and desire in his face made Wanda Nell feel like she was melting inside. He leaned forward and kissed her.

The sound of giggling brought them back to reality with a thud. Miranda stood over them, arms akimbo. "Get a room, you two," she said, smiling. "I can't leave you alone even for a minute."

"Miranda!" Wanda Nell could feel herself blushing. "What a thing to say." Beside her, Jack was laughing.

"I'll have you know, young lady," Jack said, trying to sound stern, and failing, "your mother and I are now officially engaged."

"What?" Wanda Nell stared at him.

"Well, I suppose it's not completely official," Jack said. He stood up, reached into the pocket of his jeans, and brought out a small box. "Maybe this will make it official." He held out the box to Wanda Nell.

Hands trembling, Wanda Nell accepted the box and opened it. Nestled inside was a beautiful diamond engagement ring. From the cut, she figured it was an old ring.

"It was my grandmother's," Jack said. "She gave it to my father, and he gave it to me after my mother died."

Wanda Nell couldn't speak. She just sat and stared at the ring.

Jack got down on one knee, pushing the coffee table aside as he did so. He clasped one of Wanda Nell's hands and said, "Wanda Nell, will you marry me?"

The lump in her throat felt so big Wanda Nell was afraid she wouldn't be able to respond. She swallowed hard. "Yes, Jack, I will."

Had she really said those words aloud? Her mind was so fuzzy, she wasn't certain what was real and what was only in her mind.

Evidently she *had* spoken the words, because Jack removed the jewelry box from her shaking hand, took the ring out of it, and placed it on her left hand. Wanda Nell stared down at it for a moment. It was so beautiful. Bobby Ray had never given her an engagement ring.

Miranda was hopping up and down, squealing with excitement. Juliet appeared in the room, rubbing her face tiredly. "What's going on? Is everything okay?"

"Jack just asked Mama to marry him," Miranda said, "and she said yes."

"Oh, Mama, that's wonderful," Juliet said with a huge smile as she came forward to stand beside Miranda.

Jack stood, pulling Wanda Nell up with him. He gave her a quick kiss. With an arm around Wanda Nell, he faced the girls. "I'm glad you're pleased, girls," he said. "I love your mother very much, and I'm going to do my best to make her happy."

Wanda Nell still hadn't spoken. She saw the delighted expressions on her daughters' faces and realized they were truly happy for her. "I love Jack, too, and I'm going to do my best to make *him* happy."

"We've got to call T.J. and Tuck," Miranda said. "They have to hear about this, too." She disappeared into the kitchen.

"And Mayrene," Juliet called after her. She gave her mother and Jack hugs in turn. "I'm so glad. Mama, you deserve to be happy."

"Thank you, honey," Wanda Nell said. Everything still felt slightly unreal to her. She realized Jack must have planned this, but she hadn't suspected a thing.

"We ought to do something to celebrate," Juliet said. "We don't have any champagne, but I'll see what we do have." She went into the kitchen.

Miranda emerged a few minutes later as Jack and Wanda Nell were seating themselves on the couch again.

"T.J. and Tuck are coming over," Miranda announced. "*And* they're bringing a bottle of champagne." She giggled. "I've never had champagne before."

"They shouldn't do that," Wanda Nell protested. "We don't need champagne."

"Yes, we do," Jack said firmly. "This is something to celebrate, and the rest of us are going to overrule you. Right, Miranda?"

"We sure are," Miranda said, giggling.

A knock sounded at the door, but before anyone could answer it, it burst open. Mayrene came in, leaving the door open behind her.

"Okay, let me see it," she said, advancing on Wanda Nell.

Wanda Nell held out her hand, the ring flashing in the light from the lamps. Mayrene clasped her hand and examined the ring.

"That's gorgeous," Mayrene said with a touch of envy in her voice. "Oh, girl, I'm so happy for you." She leaned down and gave Wanda Nell a hug. "You, too, you rascal," she said to Jack. "Come here and give me a hug."

Laughing, Jack complied, and Mayrene threw her arms around him. She squeezed hard. "And you listen to me, buster, you better treat her right, or you'll rue the day you were ever born." She gave him a big kiss on the cheek and let him go.

Rubbing his left arm, Jack said, "You don't have to worry about that."

Mayrene had to hug Miranda and Juliet after that. The three of them were so excited, they were chattering nonstop. Wanda Nell and Jack sat on the couch, watching them and smiling. Wanda Nell still couldn't quite take it all in. She supposed it would sink in eventually.

T.J. and Tuck arrived a few minutes later, and Tuck wasted no time in opening the champagne they had brought. Wanda Nell didn't have any champagne glasses, so Miranda brought whatever she could put her hands on from the kitchen. When they all had champagne, except for Juliet who had water because of her medication, Tuck raised his glass.

"To Wanda Nell and Jack," he said. The others echoed him. "Wanda Nell, you've done so much for each and every one of us. You give us so much every day, I bless the day you came into my life." He paused a moment to clear his throat. "You and your family have brought me something— and someone—very special." He looked at T.J., and T.J. gazed back at him.

Wanda Nell couldn't help it, she started crying. She couldn't remember when she had last felt so happy. All the people she loved best—except for her grandson—were here with her, and she would treasure this moment always.

"And here's to Jack," T.J. said, his voice hoarse with emotion. "It takes a very special man for someone like Mama, and I'm glad he had the sense to recognize just how wonderful she is." He raised his glass, and the others did the same.

"Thank you, T.J.," Jack said. He had to clear his throat a couple times before he could go on. "You've all welcomed me into the family, and I love you all for that. Wanda Nell is the most amazing woman I've ever known, and I think I fell in love with her the first time I ever saw her. I'm the luckiest man in the world." He hugged Wanda Nell to him, and she rested her head on his shoulder.

"Okay, enough of all this sappy stuff," Mayrene said in a gruff voice. "Otherwise we'll have to have a contest to see who can cry the most."

That brought laughter, and the mood lightened. Wanda Nell was grateful to Mayrene. She could always count on her best friend to interject a light note to the proceedings when necessary.

Tuck went around with the champagne bottle again, and it quickly emptied. Wanda Nell had kept her eye on Juliet during the celebration, and she could see that her younger daughter was very tired.

"Come on, honey," she said, slipping an arm around Juliet's drooping shoulders. "I think you need to go back to bed."

"Yes, Mama," Juliet said. "I am tired, but I'm so happy."

"Me, too," Wanda Nell said. She walked Juliet down the hall to her bedroom. "You get in bed, and I'll check on you in a little while. Do you need anything?"

"No, Mama," Juliet said. "I've got plenty of water, and I don't feel like eating anything."

"Okay, just get some rest," Wanda Nell said. "I'm going to take you to see Dr. Crowell in the morning."

Juliet nodded, her eyes already closing. Wanda Nell turned off the light and tiptoed out of the room. She pulled the door nearly closed, hoping that would muffle some of the sounds of the celebration in the living room.

When Wanda Nell walked back into the room, Jack was standing with Mayrene and T.J. She caught his eye and smiled. He smiled back, and Wanda Nell went to his side. He put an arm around her, and she leaned against him. He sure felt good.

She could feel the ring on her finger. It was a little heavy, but she found that reassuring. That meant it was all real. She really had said yes. She was going to get married. She didn't know just when, but there would be time to sort that out later. They would have to see whether Miranda was going to marry Teddy before they could finalize their own plans. There would be a lot of things to think about.

The door of the trailer burst open then, startling them all. Lisa Pemberton stumbled into the room, sobbing loudly and waving her arms around. She was speaking, but her words were unintelligible.

Jack was the first to reach her. "Lisa, what's the matter?"

She clung to him for a moment, struggling to catch her breath.

When she did speak, the words came out in a rush. "He's found me again. He knows where I am."

Twelve

Jack led Lisa over to the couch and sat down with her. Wanda Nell sat down on the other side. She took Lisa's hands in hers and started rubbing them. The others, except for Mayrene, stood back out of the way, watching in silence. Mayrene disappeared out the door.

"It's okay," Jack said. "You're safe here with us." He kept repeating the words, and gradually Lisa's breathing settled down to normal.

By then Mayrene had returned, and she had a bottle of whiskey with her. She found an empty glass, sloshed some of the whiskey into it, and gave it to Jack. "Give her that," Mayrene said. "It'll help settle her nerves."

Lisa accepted the glass from Jack. She stared at it a moment before lifting it to her lips and bolting down the contents. She coughed a couple times, but after a moment she nodded.

"Thank you, Mayrene," she said, as the color came back into her face. "I needed that."

Wanda Nell took the glass from her and set it down on the coffee table. "Can you tell us about it now, honey? I don't want to upset you, but we need to know what happened so we can decide what to do."

Lisa nodded. "I guess so." She drew a deep breath. "I got a ride here after work with one of my coworkers who lives out this way." She turned to Jack. "I thought you were coming to pick me up, but when you didn't show up, I asked Sheila if she would mind, and she said she'd be glad to give me a ride."

Jack's face reddened. "Lisa, I'm so sorry. I completely forgot. I, um, I guess I had other things on my mind. Can you forgive me? I promise it won't happen again."

"It's okay," Lisa said, shrugging. "It really doesn't matter."

Wanda Nell, sitting beside her, could tell that Lisa was lying from the way her hands clenched and unclenched in her lap. It did really matter to Lisa, and she was very annoyed with her cousin. Wanda Nell felt guilty, too, because she knew why Jack had forgotten about the younger woman.

"I'm sorry, too, Lisa," Wanda Nell said. "We promised we'd help you, and we let you down."

"I'm okay now," Lisa said, her words slightly clipped. Wanda Nell still didn't believe her.

"What happened?" Jack asked.

"Well, Sheila dropped me off, and Mayrene let me in. She'd fixed us a really nice dinner, and I was so hungry. When I finished eating I went back to my room, and I was looking for a book to read. I heard the phone ring once, but I guess Mayrene must have answered it. I heard her go out of the trailer, but I didn't think anything about it."

"Oh, Lisa," Mayrene said, "I'm sorry, too. I guess I was so excited I didn't stop to tell you what was going on."

"What *is* going on?" Lisa asked, appearing perplexed. "Are y'all having some kind of party?"

"We'll get to that in a minute," Wanda Nell said. "You go on and tell us what happened."

"Okay," Lisa said, shrugging. "Well, a few minutes ago, the phone rang again, but I hadn't heard Mayrene come back. So I got up and answered it." She paused to take a deep breath. "It was him. He told me it was no use me trying to hide from him. He would always find me no matter where I went."

She started crying again, but quietly this time. Mayrene slipped out of the trailer. Wanda Nell noticed her leave and was puzzled. What was she doing now?

Tuck came over to the couch and sat on a corner of the coffee table. "Lisa, I'd like to help you with this, if you want me to. There are things we can do to stop this guy harassing you. You shouldn't have to go through this."

"Thank you." Lisa's voice was little more than a whisper. "I guess I do need help, but I really hate to bother anybody."

"It's not a bother," Tuck said, his voice firm, but kind. "Can you come to see me at my office tomorrow?"

"I guess so," Lisa said. "I'm off tomorrow."

"Good." Tuck pulled out his wallet and extracted a business card from it. "Here's my card, with my numbers. Just call the office in the morning, and let my secretary know when you can come in."

Lisa accepted the card. She stared down at it for a moment. "Okay," she said.

"This is the right thing to do," Wanda Nell said. "Tuck will help you so this guy will have to leave you alone."

Lisa didn't say anything. She leaned against Jack, her eyes closed.

Mayrene had come back, Wanda Nell noticed. "Lisa, honey," Mayrene said, "why don't you come on with me, and let's get you settled down. I think maybe you need some peace and quiet, okay?"

"I think that's a good idea," Jack said. "Come on, I'll go with you."

Lisa allowed Jack to lead her back to Mayrene's trailer. Mayrene trailed behind them, pausing at the door to say she would be back in a little while.

T.J. spoke for the first time since Lisa had made her dramatic entrance. "Well, that's one way to kill a party. I'm sorry, Mama. This should be a night for celebrating."

"Thank you, honey," Wanda Nell said. "But it's not Lisa's fault. I feel so sorry for her. I can't imagine what it's like, having some creep stalking her like that." She looked at Tuck. "You *can* help her, can't you?"

Tuck shrugged. "I'll see what I can do. We can maybe get a restraining order on the guy, but I'll have to find out more details from Lisa. Depends on what he's done in the past, and whether she has evidence of it. Hopefully records of the phone calls, if nothing else. If we can get a restraining order, then we'll have some ammunition if he violates it."

"It's not a good situation, is it?" Wanda Nell said, frowning. "It's almost like he has to attack her or something before you can really do anything about it."

"Unfortunately, yes," Tuck said.

"In a case like this, intent isn't enough," T.J. said. "You have to do something, not just think about it."

"Get you," Miranda said, poking her brother in the side. "Now you're starting to talk like a lawyer, too." She giggled.

"I may be a lawyer one of these days," T.J. said, "and when I am, you better watch out, Randa. I might have to sue you for all those times you were such a pain in the behind when we were kids." He poked her back. "All that pain and suffering you put me through—you know, it probably stunted my growth or something."

Miranda, staring up at her brother who towered over her, stuck out her tongue.

Wanda Nell and Tuck laughed at them, and Wanda Nell was glad for the lightened mood.

"I guess we'd probably better get going," Tuck said. "We've got a long day tomorrow, and you and Jack would probably like a little time to yourselves now."

"Good night, Mama," T.J. said, giving her a hug and a kiss on the cheek. "And congratulations again. We're both thrilled to death for you."

Tuck hugged her, too. "Set a date yet?"

Wanda Nell laughed. "No, we hadn't got that far yet. I'll have to get back to you on that." She followed them to the door. "Y'all be careful."

Jack and Mayrene came out of Mayrene's trailer in time to say good-bye to them. Once Tuck and T.J. had driven off, Jack and Mayrene joined Wanda Nell in the living room. Miranda went to check on Lavon.

"How is she?" Wanda Nell said, patting the couch beside her. Jack sat down next to her.

"She's calmed down," Jack said, shrugging. "She has some sleeping pills her doctor gave her, and she took one of those. She'll be out like a light soon, I hope."

"I turned off the ringer on the phone in her room," Mayrene said, "so if anybody else calls, she won't hear it." She leaned back in her chair.

"Good," Wanda Nell said. "That poor girl. I feel so sorry for her."

"I know," Jack said, "and I feel so bad. I can't believe I forgot to go pick her up."

"She could have called you," Mayrene said. "Don't go beating yourself up about it, Jack. You didn't do it on purpose, and she made it here just fine."

"I know," Jack said, "but I still feel bad. She's going through so much, and I shouldn't have forgotten about her." He shook his head. "Even though she was scared she still wanted to wish us the best. She's very happy for us." He looked at Wanda Nell.

"That's very sweet of her," Wanda Nell said. "And we're all going to do what we can to help her. We won't forget her again." She snapped her fingers. "The police. We should have called the police."

"Don't worry, honey," Mayrene said. "I took care of that. I called Dixon and told him about it. He wants her to come by the police station tomorrow and talk to him about it." She grinned widely. "Plus we have a way to track that jackass down. He left his number on my caller ID."

"That's good," Wanda Nell said. "The faster they can do something about him, the better we'll all feel."

"Amen to that," Mayrene said. She got up from her chair. "Well, I'd better get back over there. I don't like leaving her alone too long, even if she is sound asleep. I don't imagine that creep will call back tonight, but you never know." She grinned. "Besides, you two probably want to be alone for a little while."

Jack got up from the couch and went over to give her a hug and kiss on the cheek. "Thanks for everything you're doing, Mayrene. You're one in a million, you know that?"

"Make it a billion, honey, and I'll agree with you." Laughing, Mayrene waved good-bye and let herself out. The door closed behind her.

Jack resumed his place on the couch beside Wanda Nell. He put his arm around her and drew her close to him.

"This feels nice," Wanda Nell said, her hand on his chest.

"It sure does," Jack said, his mouth against her forehead.

They sat in silence for a few minutes. Finally, Wanda Nell roused herself. "You'd better get on home, honey. It's getting late, and tomorrow's a school day." A teacher's day started pretty early.

"Yeah, I guess you're right," Jack said. "But I'm looking forward to the day when I don't have to go very far to go to bed." He grinned at her. "That day can't come too soon for me."

"Me either, honey," Wanda Nell told him. "But we'll have to talk about setting a date later, okay?"

"I know," Jack said. "I know there are some things to work out before we get married." He nodded his head in the direction of Miranda's room.

"Yeah," Wanda Nell said. "Exactly." She was glad he understood.

They shared one last, long kiss before Jack said good night. Wanda Nell stood in the doorway, watching until he had driven off. She shut the door and locked it.

Before getting ready for bed, she checked on Juliet again. The girl was sound asleep, and Wanda Nell was relieved to find her forehead cool and dry. She would see how Juliet felt in the morning, but she was still going to take her to the doctor, just to be safe.

Wanda Nell went to the other end of the trailer to say good night to Miranda and Lavon. Her grandson was sound asleep in his crib, and Miranda was talking on the phone. Wanda Nell didn't have to ask who it was on the other end. She mouthed "good night" to Miranda and went back the other way to her bedroom.

After changing into her nightgown, washing her face, and brushing her teeth, Wanda Nell sat on the side of the bed for a few minutes, staring at the ring on her finger. It fit just right, and it was so beautiful. She had never owned a piece of jewelry this nice in her whole life. She touched it a couple times to make sure it was real. Her brother Rusty had their mother's engagement ring, but so far he hadn't found anybody he wanted to give it to. She would have to call Rusty and tell him the news.

This was a big step she was taking. Getting married again. Was she really ready to do that? She had known Jack for about a year now, and in that time she had come to love him. He was a good, caring man. Strong, but not rigid. Dependable, thoughtful, patient. She really appreciated his patience. He had made it clear, pretty early on, that he was in love with her, but she had held back. Her marriage to Bobby Ray had made her wary, and it took her a while to let her guard down and let Jack into her heart.

Now that she had, though, she was very happy. She was tired of being alone. Marrying Jack was the right thing to do. She realized she couldn't imagine life without him, and that told her all she needed to know.

She removed the ring, kissed it, and placed it on the nightstand beside her bed. She set her alarm and turned out the light, and after her eyes adjusted to the darkness, she fancied she could see the ring glow occasionally. Smiling, thinking of the future, she fell asleep.

The alarm roused her at six-thirty the next morning, and after she switched it off, she picked up her ring and slid it onto her finger. She couldn't help smiling as she looked at it.

After a quick trip to the bathroom, she checked on Juliet.

Her daughter was awake, and her fever was back. Wanda Nell took her temperature, and it had climbed to a little over a hundred. She gave Juliet some water and a small dose of the sinus medicine.

"We are definitely going to see the doctor this morning," Wanda Nell said. "I'm going to call as soon as they're open and see if we can get you in there today."

"Yes, ma'am," Juliet said. "I sure don't feel very good. My throat's real scratchy."

"Keep drinking water," Wanda Nell told her. "You need me to help you to the bathroom?"

"No, I'm okay," Juliet said, smiling a little. "I'm not totally helpless, Mama."

"I know that, baby," Wanda Nell said, smoothing the hair back from Juliet's face. "Do you think you could eat something?"

"Maybe a little toast."

"Okay, you stay in bed, and I'll bring you some in a few minutes," Wanda Nell told her.

In the kitchen she popped some bread into the toaster. Next she put the coffee on. There was no sign of Miranda and Lavon yet, but Wanda Nell figured it wouldn't be long before Lavon was up, and he would be hungry. She got his oatmeal started so that it would be ready when he did get up.

The toast popped up, and Wanda Nell buttered it lavishly so it would be easier for Juliet to swallow. She cut the two slices into triangles, put them on a plate, and poured a small glass of orange juice.

She took the toast and juice to Juliet, sitting up in bed. Juliet accepted the plate and glass, saying, "Thank you."

"If you want some more, I'll come back and check on

you in a few minutes," Wanda Nell said. "I can't call the doctor's office until eight o'clock. If you feel like it, though, you ought to have a shower."

"I think that might make me feel better," Juliet said. "I'm feeling kind of icky right now."

Wanda Nell patted her daughter's head. "Call me if you need me," she said.

The coffee was ready when she returned to the kitchen, and she poured herself a cup, adding some cream and sugar. She sat down at the table and sipped at her coffee. Memories of the night before danced through her head, and she replayed the proposal over and over, smiling.

The phone rang, startling her. She set down her coffee cup and got up to answer the phone.

"Hello," she said.

"Honey, are you up?" Mayrene spoke in a low voice.

"Yeah," Wanda Nell said. "You want to come over for some coffee?"

"Be right there," Mayrene said.

The phone clicked in Wanda Nell's ear. Frowning, she hung up the receiver and went to open the door for her friend. There had been an odd tone in Mayrene's voice, and that worried Wanda Nell.

She opened the door, and Mayrene strode in. Wanda Nell shut the door and followed Mayrene into the kitchen.

Mayrene plopped down in a chair and stared up at Wanda Nell.

"What's wrong?" Wanda Nell said. "Did Lisa get another phone call?" She poured Mayrene a cup of coffee and set it down in front of her before resuming her seat at the table.

Mayrene shook her head. "No, she didn't. But something weird happened."

"What?" Now Wanda Nell was really getting alarmed.

"I checked my caller ID this morning," Mayrene said. "I was going to write down that phone number. But it's not there anymore. Somebody erased it."

Thirteen

"But that's crazy," Wanda Nell said. "How could it just disappear like that?"

"You tell me," Mayrene said. She folded her arms across her chest and stared hard at Wanda Nell.

"Your electricity didn't go out during the night, did it?" Wanda Nell knew she was clutching at straws, but she didn't want to have to believe the obvious.

"Nope, it didn't," Mayrene said. "I did check that, but it didn't happen." She added some cream and three spoons of sugar to her coffee.

"And you didn't accidentally do it yourself?"

Mayrene just snorted in response. She stirred her coffee.

"No, I guess not," Wanda Nell said. "Why would she erase the number? Is she so afraid of this man that she thinks if the police talk to him, he'll try to kill her?"

"Come on, Wanda Nell," Mayrene said after a sip of coffee. "I didn't see any turnip trucks driving by here this morning, so I know you ain't been falling off of one."

Wanda Nell sighed heavily. Her heart constricted in her

chest. "The only other reason I can think of is that this whole thing is made up. But why would Lisa be faking something like this? It just don't make sense."

"Not to you and me it don't," Mayrene said, "but look at her situation. She's young, she's alone with no family to speak of, except a cousin. And he's just asked you to marry him to boot. She's desperate for attention."

"She didn't even know Jack had asked me to marry him last night when she came over and told us about the phone call," Wanda Nell said. "And Jack said when he did tell her she was real happy for us."

"I think she knew, all right," Mayrene said. "And I think maybe that's why she staged that big scene last night. She wanted to break up the party. She didn't like it that you were getting all the attention and not her."

"You can't know that," Wanda Nell said. She wanted to be fair to Lisa. "Besides, Jack may have told her some time before this all happened that he was going to ask me to marry him last night."

"I bet if you ask Jack, he'll tell you that Lisa didn't know nothing about him going to pop the question last night," Mayrene said.

"I might just do that," Wanda Nell said. "But why are you so convinced that Lisa knew?"

"Because I think she was listening in on the phone when Miranda called me to give me the news." Mayrene paused for a moment. "I thought at the time, when I first answered the call, that I heard a click like somebody else picking up. But then I forgot all about it because I was so excited by the news."

"Are you sure about hearing that click?"

"Yeah," Mayrene said. "I think it was Lisa. I think she did it deliberately, because I caught her doing it one other time."

"This is awful," Wanda Nell said. "I hate like anything to think she's made this whole story up just to get attention."

"Well, think about it for a minute," Mayrene said. "I've been sitting over there this morning, going over and over it while I was waiting to be sure you were up. The only evidence anybody has is what she has told people, right?"

"As far as I know," Wanda Nell said. "I'd have to ask Jack, though, if *he's* seen or heard anything to the contrary."

"I bet you he hasn't either," Mayrene said. "But of course he's going to believe her, he's her cousin."

"He's going to be devastated if this turns out to be true," Wanda Nell said.

"What do you mean, 'if'?" Mayrene asked in a tone of outrage. "I'll bet every last cent I own that this whole thing is a scam. That's why she hadn't been in a hurry to talk to the police about it. It probably started in Meridian, and I bet the people there got wise to her. That's why she decided to move. That, and to be closer to Jack."

"I guess you're probably right," Wanda Nell said, "but first we have to prove it, beyond a shadow of a doubt. And then we need to see about getting that poor girl some help. She can't go on like this."

"No, she can't. There's no telling what she might do, to herself or to somebody else, if we don't put a stop to this." Mayrene regarded her friend with an odd expression.

Wanda Nell stared back at her, and it took her only a few seconds to realize what Mayrene was thinking. "You really don't think she would try to hurt me, do you?" She shuddered. "Surely not."

"I don't know," Mayrene said, "and I don't really want to find out. But look at it this way: Jack's been spending as much time as possible with you, hasn't he? And that means he ain't been spending much time with her. And now he goes and asks you to marry him. That might send her over the edge if she's getting really desperate."

Wanda Nell wanted to think that Mayrene was just getting a little too carried away herself, but now she was more than a little spooked by the situation.

"What are we going to do?" she asked.

"First thing is, I'm going to have a nice quiet chat with Officer Dixon Vance," Mayrene said. "I'll lay it all out for him and see what he thinks. Heck, this probably won't be the first time he's seen a problem like this."

"Maybe not," Wanda Nell said. "You know what? This makes me kind of angry, though. Somebody making all this up to get attention, so it's no wonder the cops don't want to believe women sometimes when they swear they're being stalked. It's just not right."

"No, it sure ain't," Mayrene said before draining her cup. She stood up. "I'm going to take Lisa by her house so she can get her car in a little while. She wants to run some errands, plus she was talking about going to see Tuck." She shook her head. "Maybe she's deluded herself into believing it's true. If she really goes and talks to a lawyer about it, I'd say she's getting seriously loopy."

"Maybe so," Wanda Nell replied. "But before I say anything about this to Jack, I want to be more sure that she really is faking it. Can you imagine how he'd feel if I told him right now, and her story turned out to be true? He'd think I was the crazy one then."

"You're right, honey," Mayrene said, "and I promise I won't say anything to him either." She headed for the door.

"Do you think I should talk to Tuck before she goes to see him?"

Mayrene paused, considering. "No, I don't think you

should. Wait and let him talk to her first, then you can tell him. That way he can look at it and be fair."

"Good point," Wanda Nell said. "Talk to you later."

Mayrene waved good-bye, and moments later Wanda Nell heard her front door open and close.

She glanced at the clock then and decided she should probably call the high school and let them know Juliet wouldn't be in school today. She looked up the number, punched it in, and waited for the receptionist to answer.

A few minutes later, that duty discharged, Wanda Nell decided to start trying to call Dr. Crowell's office. It wasn't quite eight yet, but sometimes somebody in the office was there early and would pick up the phone.

She was lucky this morning, and on a Monday, to boot. Usually she could hardly get an answer from the doctor's office on a Monday. Today it was the doctor's nurse, Martha Farrington, who took her call.

"Good morning, Martha," she said. "This is Wanda Nell Culpepper. My daughter Juliet's running a fever and has a scratchy throat. I'd like to bring her in to see the doctor this morning if he can work her in."

"Hang on a moment and let me check," said the nurse. Wanda Nell could hear her tapping at the keyboard. People used computers for everything these days. Wanda Nell remembered how the sound you heard used to be the rustling of pages as someone flipped through an appointment book. She kind of missed that. It seemed more personal somehow.

"Wanda Nell?" Martha spoke, bringing Wanda Nell back to the present. "I think we can work her in at nine-thirty. How's that sound?"

"That's just fine, Martha," Wanda Nell said. "Thank you so much. We'll be there."

She hung up the phone, and as she did, she caught sight

of the stove. *Oh, good Lord*, she thought, *I forgot all about the baby's oatmeal*. There it was, just bubbling away in the pot. Wanda Nell checked it, relieved to see that it hadn't scorched on the bottom. She took the pot off the stove and set it on a trivet on the counter.

She decided it was time to get Miranda up. Even though Miranda didn't have to work at Budget Mart today, she still had some things to do around the house. Wanda Nell hated having to remind her, but Miranda was still slack sometimes when it came to housework.

Miranda was on the phone when Wanda Nell tapped on her door. One of the first things Miranda had done, once she was working at Budget Mart again, was to have her own phone line put in. Wanda Nell didn't begrudge her that, though Miranda still had a tendency to act like the phone was an actual part of her ear and not just a helpful device for occasional use.

"Hang on, honey," Miranda said. "It's Mama." She pulled the phone away from her and rested it against her chest. "Yes, Mama, what is it?"

"Time for breakfast," Wanda Nell said, walking over to Lavon who held his arms out for his grandmother. She picked him up and set him down on the floor. "Have you checked his diaper?"

"Yes, Mama," Miranda said. "I was just about to bring him into the kitchen, but Teddy called me. Take him on into the kitchen, if you don't mind, and I'll be there in a minute. Teddy's at work, so he can't talk long anyways."

Suppressing a sigh, Wanda Nell took her grandson by the hand and led him to the kitchen. He talked nonstop the whole way, and Wanda Nell interjected the occasional word. Lavon was more than capable of carrying on a conversation by himself, however. Wanda Nell marveled at his imagination. He was always talking about things he and his bunny had done.

By the time Wanda Nell had Lavon in his high chair and eating his oatmeal, Miranda wandered into the kitchen. "Do you want some breakfast?" Wanda Nell asked her.

Miranda shook her head. "No thanks, I'm not that hungry." She rubbed her stomach.

"What's the matter, honey? Are you sick?"

"No, I'm fine," Miranda said. "I'm just not hungry."

Wanda Nell didn't believe her. Miranda had a drawn look to her, a sure sign to her mother that she wasn't feeling good. Wanda Nell decided not to push her this morning. Miranda could be pretty stubborn when she wanted to. That was one thing she had inherited from her mother.

"Then you take over here with Lavon," Wanda Nell said, "and see if you can get more of the oatmeal *in* him instead of on him."

"Sure," Miranda said.

"I've got to get ready so I can take Juliet in to see the doctor this morning," Wanda Nell said. She put a couple more slices of bread in the toaster for her own breakfast.

"Is she still feeling bad?" Miranda asked. "What is it?"

"Sinus infection, I think," Wanda Nell said. "You and Lavon will be all right here by yourselves while we're gone, won't you?"

"Yes, ma'am," Miranda replied. "We'll be just fine."

When the bread popped up in the toaster, she removed the slices and buttered them. She stood at the counter, munching on toast while she watched Miranda supervise Lavon's breakfast. Miranda had been a lot better about looking after her son once Teddy entered the picture, but Wanda Nell shuddered to think what Miranda would do if she had more than one child to take care of.

She carried the second piece of toast with her, munching as she walked, on her way to check on Juliet. She found her daughter dressed and sitting at the computer.

"I took a shower," Juliet said, turning to Wanda Nell as she entered the room. "When's the appointment?"

"Nine-thirty," Wanda Nell replied. "If you're ready, then I'll have a shower myself. We ought to leave around nine. It won't hurt to get there a little early."

Juliet nodded and turned back to her computer.

By the time Wanda Nell was dressed and ready to go it was about five minutes before nine. She stuck her head in Juliet's room and said, "Come on, honey, time to go."

Juliet shut down her computer and followed her mother down the hall.

"We're leaving, Miranda," Wanda Nell called out. She picked up her purse from the kitchen counter. "Don't forget to clean up in here, okay?" Miranda had gone off and left Lavon's bowl, spoon, and high chair messy. "And get started on the laundry, too. It's your turn."

"I will, Mama," Miranda responded from down the hall.

In the car, Juliet leaned her head against the window and closed her eyes. "I hate being sick," she said. "I'm sorry, Mama."

"Honey, don't be silly," Wanda Nell said as she backed her car out and headed out of the trailer park. "You can't help being sick, so don't even say things like that. The doctor will give you some antibiotics or something, and you'll be feeling a lot better soon." She reached over and patted Juliet's leg.

Juliet, of her three children, had always been the "good" one. She had never given Wanda Nell a minute's trouble, unlike her older sister and her big brother. Wanda Nell had had more than enough heartache and headaches over T.J.

and Miranda. She was thankful that Juliet was such a sweet girl.

The drive to the doctor's office, in a building near the hospital, took about fifteen minutes. Wanda Nell parked the car, and she and Juliet entered the building. Dr. Crowell's office was on the first floor. There were several people in the waiting room when she and Juliet entered.

"You go sit down, honey," Wanda Nell said in a low voice. "I'll go let them know we're here."

She walked up to the desk and waited until she could catch the receptionist's attention. Martha, a trim, white-haired woman, had worked for the older Dr. Crowell for as long as Wanda Nell could remember. When his son took over the practice a few years ago, she had stayed on. Wanda Nell had no idea how old she was, but she didn't look much older than she had when Wanda Nell was a teenager.

"Good morning, Wanda Nell," Martha said when she put down the phone. "Just sign in on that sheet there, if you don't mind."

"Morning, Martha," Wanda Nell said. She signed Juliet in as requested.

"Would you mind seeing Dr. Crowell Sr. this morning?" Martha asked. "We're pretty busy, and he came in to help out. There's some kind of bug going around, and we got a whole bunch of people calling in today."

"That's fine," Wanda Nell said. "It'll be good to see him."

"Y'all just have a seat," Martha said, beaming, "and someone will call you back real soon."

Wanda Nell flipped through one of the magazines, while Juliet leaned against her. They had to wait about ten minutes before someone called out Juliet's name.

"Come on, honey," Wanda Nell said.

She led Juliet through the door, smiling at the nurse as

she did so. This girl must be pretty new, Wanda Nell figured, because she hadn't seen her before.

"In here," the nurse said, indicating a small room. She followed them in and asked Juliet to sit on the examination table. "Now what seems to be the problem?"

"Sinus infection, I think," Wanda Nell said. "She's been running a low-grade fever off and on, and she's got a scratchy throat."

The nurse jotted something on Juliet's chart. Next she took her temperature and checked her blood pressure. "She does have a little temperature this morning," the nurse said. "Now, Miss Juliet, if you don't mind, we need to weigh you." She held out a hand.

Juliet got down from the table and followed her into the hall. Wanda Nell waited, and they were back in less than a minute. Juliet climbed back on the table while the nurse noted Juliet's weight on her chart.

"The doctor will be with you in a moment," the nurse said. She left the room, shutting the door behind her.

"You can lie down if you want to, sweetie," Wanda Nell said. "It may be a few minutes before the doctor comes."

"I'm okay," Juliet said.

The door opened then, and the elder Dr. Crowell entered. He was a distinguished-looking man in his early seventies. Tall, portly, and white-haired, he reminded Wanda Nell of Colonel Sanders, but without the facial hair. He also loved to talk, and Wanda Nell, struck by a sudden thought, decided she might try to get him talking about the bachelor party once he was finished examining Juliet.

"My goodness, Wanda Nell Culpepper, how are you doing? I'm sorry I didn't get to talk to you the other night, but with everything going on, it was impossible." The doctor beamed at her. "And what's the matter with Miss Juliet this morning?" He read the notes the nurse had made.

"I'm fine, doctor," Wanda Nell said. "And I think Juliet may have another sinus infection."

"Let's check this out," the doctor said. He proceeded to examine Juliet's throat, eyes, and ears. He took her temperature again, as well. He also checked her breathing.

"I think you're right," he finally said. "Miss Juliet, I'm going to give you a shot to give you a jump start on some antibiotics, and then I'm going to give you some pills to take for a few days. If this hasn't cleared up by the end of the week, I want your mother to bring you back."

Juliet nodded, though she looked a bit apprehensive at the mention of a shot. She never had liked needles, and Wanda Nell didn't blame her. She wasn't fond of getting shots herself.

"I'll be back in just a minute," the doctor said.

He was as good as his word, and he administered the shot quickly, without giving Juliet too much time to dread it and tense up. After he disposed of the needle, he reached into the pocket of his white coat and pulled out a couple small bottles.

"Here you go," he said, handing them to Wanda Nell. "These are samples, and they should be enough to do the trick. I doubt you'll need any more than that, but if you do, just call up here and tell them I said to give them to you."

Wanda Nell was touched by the doctor's thoughtfulness. He was well aware that she didn't have any kind of health insurance, and in the past, whenever she had been to see him, he had always done what he could to help her like this.

"Thank you, doctor," she said, accepting the pills. "I really appreciate this."

"Don't even mention it," he said. He showed no inclination to leave, so Wanda Nell decided to get him to talking, especially since he had already referred to the night of the murder.

"That was pretty awful Saturday night," Wanda Nell said. "I thought I'd have nightmares after the way that poor man collapsed like that."

"Yes, wasn't that something?" Dr. Crowell said, frowning. "Such a shock to see a young man collapse right in front of you."

"I heard he was poisoned," Wanda Nell said. Juliet was staring at her, eyes round with horror, and Wanda Nell realized she had neglected to tell Juliet about it. She would just have to do that later. She smiled to reassure her daughter. "Do you think that's true?"

"Very likely," the doctor said. "Men that age don't collapse like that unless something is very wrong. It could be something to do with his heart, I suppose. But from the way the police were acting, I think it must be like you say."

"It's terrible to even think about," Wanda Nell said. "And he was real happy one minute, and the next, well . . ." She trailed off, shaking her head.

"Looking forward to his wedding," the doctor said, "and now instead he'll be going to a funeral."

"I wonder who could have done such a thing?" Wanda Nell said. "Him being a policeman and all. Though I did hear some bad things about him, I have to say."

Dr. Crowell looked away from her. "Those were probably just rumors. I doubt there was anything to them."

Wanda Nell didn't think he believed that, judging by the way he had avoided looking at her when he spoke.

She tried another tack. "I have to say, I was kind of surprised to see you and your son there," Wanda Nell said. "Were you friends of the groom?"

"Not really," Dr. Crowell replied. "More like friends of the bride, I guess you'd say. The bride's father and I were good friends, and I've known Tiffany since she was born. In fact, I'm her godfather."

Fourteen

Wanda Nell was so surprised at what Dr. Crowell had said that she couldn't think how to respond. Her first thought was that the doctor's relationship to the bride gave him a motive for murder—if he believed the stories about Travis Blakeley, that is. If he did, he certainly wouldn't want his goddaughter to marry such a man.

But would he really murder someone just to stop the wedding? It simply didn't square with what Wanda Nell knew of the old man. To her he had always been a figure of kindness, caring, and general goodwill. She couldn't see him as a killer.

If it meant his son's happiness, though, would that change things? If the younger Dr. Crowell really was involved with Tiffany Farwell and wanted to marry her, might his father be willing to act for his son's sake? Wanda Nell knew the old man doted on his son.

If Tiffany didn't want to marry Travis Blakeley, though, surely she could have broken off the engagement? This was the same bit of reasoning that had brought Wanda Nell up short before when she was thinking about motives.

There had to be some reason that Tiffany wasn't willing to end the engagement, then. Wanda Nell was willing to bet that it was because Tiffany was afraid of Travis Blakeley.

"Wanda Nell, are you all right?"

Dr. Crowell's voice broke into her thoughts, and she came back to reality. She smiled and said, "Sorry, Doc, I was just thinking about something." She looked at Juliet, slumped over on the exam table, and had a pang of guilt. "Come on, sweetie, we'd better get you back home and into bed."

Juliet stirred and got down from the table. Dr. Crowell held out a hand for her to grasp to steady herself, and Juliet smiled shyly at him. "Thank you, Doctor Crowell."

"My pleasure, my dear," he said, beaming. "Now you be a good girl and do what your mother tells you. You'll be feeling much better in no time."

"Thank you again, Doc, for everything," Wanda Nell said. She led Juliet out of the room and toward the front of the office. She stopped at the cashier's desk where she wrote a check for the bill. She was relieved to see that the charge for an office visit hadn't gone up since the last time she had been here.

Wanda Nell was getting ready to start the car when her cell phone started ringing. She dug through her purse until she located it. Her home phone number flashed on the small screen. She answered the call, afraid that something had happened to Miranda or Lavon.

"Hello."

"Hey, Mama, it's me," Miranda said, sounding perfectly normal. Wanda Nell relaxed slightly.

"Hi, sweetie," Wanda Nell said. "What's going on?"

"This man called here a couple minutes ago looking for

you," Miranda said. "I wouldn't give him your cell phone number, though. I told him I'd call you and give you the message."

"Who was it?"

"He said he was Master Sergeant Warren with the state police," Miranda said. "He wants to see you in his office down at the courthouse as soon as you can get there."

Wanda Nell grimaced. The last thing she wanted to do was talk to Bill Warren, but she didn't have much choice. He would come looking for her if she didn't turn up at his office soon.

"Did you write down his number?" she asked.

"Yes, ma'am," Miranda said. "You want me to give it to you?"

"No, I want you to call him back and tell him I'll try to get to his office in thirty minutes or so. We're just leaving the doctor's office, and I want to bring Juliet home and get her settled before I go see him."

"Okay, Mama," Miranda said. "I'll call him for you."

"Thanks, sweetie. We'll see you in a few minutes." Wanda Nell ended the call and dropped her cell phone in her purse. She cranked the car and started backing out of the parking space.

"Mama, what's all this about?" Juliet asked.

"I'm sorry, honey," Wanda Nell said. "I know I surprised you back there in the doctor's office." She pulled out of the parking lot onto the street.

As she drove home Wanda Nell gave Juliet as many details as she thought necessary to explain the situation. Juliet didn't say much, though she did express concern for the bride.

"She may be better off in the long run," Wanda Nell

said, "because the guy she was going to marry was supposed to be a pretty bad person. But we don't really know
for sure yet."

"It's all really sad," Juliet said. "I'm sorry you had to
see it happen, Mama."

"Me too," Wanda Nell said.

Wanda Nell pulled her car into its space by the trailer.
She and Juliet got out and went inside. "You get yourself in
bed," she told her daughter. "I'm going to talk to Miranda
for a minute, and then I'll come say bye before I go."

Juliet went to her room, and Wanda Nell went in search
of Miranda. As she expected, she found Miranda in her
room, on the phone, and Lavon playing in his crib.

Wanda Nell knocked on the open door to get Miranda's
attention. Miranda broke off her conversation, telling the
person on the other end that she would call back in a few
minutes.

At the sight of his grandmother, Lavon stood up and
started talking to her, telling her another of his stories.
Wanda Nell went to him and gave him a hug and a kiss and
listened for a moment to his excited babbling.

"What did the doctor say?" Miranda asked.

"Sinus infection," Wanda Nell said. "He gave her a shot
and some pills to take. I'm going to put the bottles in the
cabinet over the sink so these busy little hands can't get to
them, okay?" She rubbed Lavon's head, and he laughed up
at her.

"Good idea," Miranda said, smiling over at her son. "I
have to watch him every minute."

Wanda Nell pulled one of the bottles from her purse and
examined the label. "Juliet doesn't need to take one until
tonight, after she's eaten something. You'll have to be sure
she takes it. After that she takes one every eight hours."

"Okay, I won't forget," Miranda said.

Wanda Nell stepped over to her and gave her a quick peck on the cheek. "Thank you, sweetie. I'm going to check on Juliet and put away this medicine. I don't know how long this talk with the state cop will take, but call me if you need me."

Miranda nodded. Before Wanda Nell was out the door Miranda was on the phone again, chatting with one of her friends. Wanda Nell shook her head. She wondered what Miranda would do without a phone.

Juliet was curled up in bed, reading. Wanda Nell made sure she had fresh water on her bedside table. "Get Miranda to fix you something to eat later if you get hungry. Maybe some scrambled eggs or some soup, okay? Don't forget to eat something."

"I won't," Juliet said. "I'm going to read a little, and then I'll probably take a nap." She yawned. "I feel really tired."

Wanda Nell bent to kiss her forehead. It was a little cooler and not as clammy. "Tell Miranda to call me if you need anything."

"I will," Juliet said. She smiled. "Now go on, Mama. I'll be fine."

"See you later, then," Wanda Nell said. She hated leaving home, even for a little while, with Juliet not feeling good, but she couldn't ignore a summons from the state police.

She put the medicine the doctor had given her in the cabinet over the kitchen sink, and she found a can of Diet Coke in the fridge. She needed a little boost right now.

There were no signs of life in Mayrene's trailer as Wanda Nell got into her car. Mayrene was at work, she knew, and she had no idea where Lisa was. Wanda Nell hoped that she had gone to talk to the police or to Tuck. She might not have, though, if what Mayrene and she suspected was true.

Wanda Nell thought about that while on her way back into town. As she drove down Main Street she glanced at Mrs. Culpepper's house. That gave her an idea. After she finished with Bill Warren, she would drop in for a visit. If anyone knew anything about Tiffany Farwell's family, it would be Mrs. Culpepper. Wanda Nell figured the solution to the murder had something to do with Tiffany and her family, and the more she knew, the better it would be for Tuck and his client Gerald Blakeley.

Wanda Nell found a parking space on the square across from the county courthouse. As she locked her car she glanced up at the building to her right. Tuck's law offices were in that building. She wished she had time to go up there and say hello.

Instead she crossed the street to the courthouse. In the lobby she consulted the building directory and found the number of Bill Warren's office. It was on the third floor, and she decided to take the elevator up.

First, though, she had to pass through the security check-point. She handed the officer her purse, and he examined its contents while she walked through the screening mecha-nism. On the other side, the officer gave her back her purse and said, "Have a nice day, ma'am."

Smiling her thanks, she headed to the elevator. When the door opened on the third floor, she followed the signs and wandered down the corridor toward the state police district office. Bill Warren's name was emblazoned in gold letter-ing on the door along with the insignia of the state police.

She had reached for the door when it suddenly opened, startling her. A balding man in coveralls stopped in the doorway, glowering at her. Wanda Nell stepped aside, and he brushed past her. Wanda Nell glared at his retreating back. What a rude man, she thought. Then it struck her that his face had been somewhat familiar. Where had she seen him before? She watched him as he practically stomped his way down the hall.

Shrugging, Wanda Nell dismissed him from her thoughts. She needed to focus on the interview ahead with Bill Warren. She would need all her wits about her around that man.

Pushing the door farther open, she stepped inside. She paused a moment to get her bearings before shutting the door. No one else was waiting. She approached the secretary's desk and gave her name. "He asked me to come in," she said.

Nodding, the secretary said, "Just have a seat, honey, and I'll tell him you're here."

Wanda Nell sat down, feeling suddenly nervous. What was it that Bill Warren wanted from her? Was he going to try to get back at her somehow because she slapped him?

Maybe this was just a routine thing. She sure hoped it was. Maybe all she would have to do was to give him a statement and sign off on it.

About ten minutes passed before the secretary told her, "Master Sergeant Warren will see you now, Miz Culpepper."

Wanda Nell followed the woman to the door that led into an inner office. Bill Warren was stuffing a large manila envelope in the drawer of a file cabinet when she walked in. He turned, frowning, as he slammed the drawer shut. He nodded curtly at his secretary. She shut the inner office door, and Wanda Nell stood, staring at Bill.

"Have a seat, why don't you?" Bill indicated a chair across from his desk.

Wanda Nell relaxed a bit. He was treating her like a stranger, courteous but distant. She took that as a good sign.

She sat down and waited. Bill sat down again and stared across the desk at her.

"I'm sorry to hear your daughter's ill," he said, surprising her.

"It's a sinus infection," Wanda Nell said. "She gets them sometimes. She'll be better real soon." She shut her mouth, realizing she was starting to babble.

"That's good," Bill replied. He leaned back in his chair and tented his fingers. He flexed them while he stared at her.

The silence was irking her. She knew she ought to wait for him to speak first, but she didn't want to sit around playing games with him.

"You wanted to see me about something?" she said.

"Yes," Bill said. He leaned forward, propping his elbows on the desk, his lower arms extended on the desktop. "I want to go over what happened Saturday night with you. See if there's anything we might have missed. Okay?"

"Sure," Wanda Nell said. This she could handle. "Where do you want me to start?"

"When the first guests arrived," he replied. "Just go on from there, and tell me every little detail you can remember."

Wanda Nell nodded. She didn't speak for a moment, marshaling her thoughts. She had a pretty good visual memory, and she concentrated on trying to call up the sights and sounds of that evening.

Once she was ready, she began talking. Bill occasionally jotted something down on a pad on his desk, but he didn't interrupt her. It took her about fifteen minutes, and as she talked she was aware of something niggling in the back of her mind. Something she couldn't quite recall—but whether it was important she had no idea. It would come to her later, probably, and if it was important she would tell Bill then.

"That's all pretty clear," Bill said. "You've obviously had experience doing this."

"A little," Wanda Nell said. "More than I'd like to think about, actually."

Bill had no comment for that. Instead, he glanced down at his pad and read.

"So you don't recall seeing anybody near the victim's glass just before he collapsed?"

"No, I don't," Wanda Nell said. "They were all moving around so much, any one of them could have dropped something in his drink and I probably wouldn't have noticed." That elusive memory flickered in her mind and then was gone again.

"Too bad," Bill said. "Nobody seems to have seen anything." He picked up a piece of paper from his desk and held it across to Wanda Nell. "Why don't you take a look at this for me? See if you can tell me anything."

Wanda Nell took the piece of paper and turned it around. It was a list of names, fifteen or twenty. She recognized a few names on the list.

She looked up at Bill. "I know a few of the men on this list. Is it a list of who was at the bachelor party?"

"Yes," Bill said. "Tell me who on that list you know."

Wanda Nell glanced down at the paper. "I know both Dr. Crowell and his son. In fact, I just saw the older Dr. Crowell this morning with my daughter."

She scanned the names again. "Dixon Vance, the policeman. He's dating a friend of mine, but I don't really know him all that well."

"Was there anybody at the party whose name isn't on the list?" When Wanda Nell looked at him, Bill had an enigmatic expression on his face.

She went through the names on the list again. Most of

them were men she didn't know, but the number of names seemed about right.

"I don't think so," she said finally, and Bill leaned back and his chair, regarding her in silence for a long moment.

When he spoke again, Bill had an edge to his voice that made Wanda Nell wary. "What about Gerald Blakeley?"

"He was in my son T.J.'s class in school. I knew him to speak to, I guess, but before Saturday night I don't think I'd seen him in several years."

"Your son," Bill said. "I found out something interesting about him."

Wanda Nell didn't like the tone of his words. "And what would that be?"

"That he's that fairy lawyer's boyfriend," Bill said. He was sneering openly now. "God, Wanda Nell, how can you stand letting your son be involved with that guy?"

"Just who the hell do you think you are?" Wanda Nell asked. Her temper hit white hot, but she was determined to keep herself under control. "My son is a good man, and so is Tuck. Yes, they're both gay, and yes, they're a couple. What the hell business is it of yours?"

"It's against the law in this state," Bill said, "what they do to each other. I ought to arrest them both and put them in jail. Keep them away from decent people."

Wanda Nell was trembling, and she felt like throwing up. She couldn't believe what Bill had just said to her. He looked dead serious when he said it, and Wanda Nell was afraid of what he might do.

"Are you doing this to get back at me because I slapped you the other night?"

Bill laughed, surprising her. "I forgot all about that. But now that you mention it . . ." He leaned forward across his desk again.

Wanda Nell tensed. He was up to something, but what?

"Are you sure you didn't see anyone put anything in the victim's glass?" he asked, once again surprising her. "Say, for example, you didn't see Gerald Blakeley do it? It sure would make things a lot easier if we had an eyewitness in this case." He watched her, his head cocked to one side, his face devoid of expression.

Fifteen

Wanda Nell couldn't believe what she had just heard. Bill Warren was trying to blackmail her into saying she had seen Gerald Blakeley put the poison into his brother's glass. If she would do that, then he wouldn't go after her son and his partner.

"You are about the lowest thing I have come across in all my life," Wanda Nell said. "I can't believe you sitting there, threatening me like that." She felt like the top of her head was going to come off, she was so angry.

"I don't recall threatening you," Bill said. He shrugged and leaned back in his chair. "I just asked you whether or not you saw Gerald Blakeley put something into the victim's glass."

"And if I go along with you and say I *did* see him do it, you'll leave my son and Tuck alone, is that it?" Wanda Nell had to struggle to keep her tone even, her words intelligible.

Again, Bill shrugged. "I don't recall saying that either. You certainly do have a vivid imagination, Wanda Nell. I can't help it if you misconstrue what I'm saying to you."

"Like hell you can't," Wanda Nell said, getting to her

feet. She leaned forward over his desk and pointed a finger right in his face. "You listen to me, Bill Warren, you're not going to threaten me or anybody in my family, do you hear me? If you do anything to harm my son or Tuck, I will come after you so fast you won't know what hit you."

"So now you're threatening *me*?" Bill said. To Wanda Nell's satisfaction, he appeared to be losing his cool. "I'm an officer of the law, and you'd better watch what you say. You just might find yourself in jail."

"You try that, buster, and I'll raise such a stink you'll be lucky to *have* a job, any kind of job. You think you can treat me like this because you think I'm a nobody, and you think you can get away with it. You'd be surprised at who I know in this town and just how they'd react if I told them what you're trying to do."

Bill laughed. "I'm real scared, Wanda Nell."

She stared him straight in the eye until he stopped laughing. "You'd better listen to me, Bill. You start something, and I'll finish it. You will *not* threaten me and my family and get away with it. And I *will* not lie for you. I didn't see anybody put anything in that man's drink, and I'm not going to say I did, no matter what you threaten to do to me." She paused, watching him closely. Despite his earlier statements, he seemed to be wilting under the force of her words. "I don't know what it is you're up to, but I'll be damned if you treat me like this."

She turned and headed for the door, not wanting to see his face another minute. She half expected him to speak to her, but he didn't say a word. She grabbed the door handle, twisted it, and pulled the door open. She thought about slamming it back against the wall, but she didn't. The sooner she got out of this place, the better.

The secretary didn't say a word, and Wanda Nell gave

her only a cursory glance as she stalked past. Out in the hall, she made her way rapidly to the elevator. By the time she reached it, her chest was heaving, and she was trying not to break down.

She was so angry right now she was afraid she might have a stroke any minute. She couldn't believe what he was threatening her with. He had to be stark raving mad to try something like that.

The elevator doors opened, and Wanda Nell stepped inside, only half aware of what she was doing. The only other occupant, an elderly man, asked her, "What floor, miss?" He looked like he wanted to say something else to her, but evidently he changed his mind.

"One," Wanda Nell said, trying hard to get herself under control.

The button for the first floor was already lit. The old man nodded and stepped back into the other corner of the elevator. During the brief trip down two floors he kept an eye on her. The moment the doors opened, he hopped out, not waiting for Wanda Nell to exit first.

That made Wanda Nell calm down a bit. Here she was, scaring old men in elevators. Her face must look a sight. She stepped out of the elevator and walked to the exit.

On the steps outside, the sun shining in her face, Wanda Nell paused for a few deep, steadying breaths. She was still very angry, but at least she had gained some control over herself.

Shading her eyes against the sun, Wanda Nell strode down the steps and across the street on the north side of the courthouse. The sheriff's department had its headquarters here, along with the county jail. With any luck, Elmer Lee would be in his office. She was going to give him an earful if he was.

She pushed open the door and stepped inside, giving her eyes a moment to adjust to the change in light. She walked up to the desk. The officer on duty behind it looked familiar, but she couldn't remember his name. He certainly remembered her, though, she could tell by the look on his face as he rose from behind his desk.

"Morning, Miz Culpepper," he said. "What can I do for you?" He continued to eye her warily.

"Is the sheriff in?" she said. "I really need to talk to him. It's real important."

"Let me check," the deputy said. He turned his back to her and picked up the phone. He spoke in a low voice, and Wanda Nell couldn't catch what he said.

After a moment he put down the phone and turned back to her. "The sheriff can see you."

He opened the door for her and led her back to Elmer Lee's office, despite her protests that she knew the way. He left her with a quick nod at the open office door.

"Come in, Wanda Nell," Elmer Lee said. He stood up and motioned for her to take a seat in a chair across from his desk. "What can I do for you?"

Wanda Nell sat down and waited until Elmer Lee had taken his seat. "I was just over at Bill Warren's office." She hesitated.

"Did he have some more questions for you?" Elmer Lee asked.

"Sort of," Wanda Nell said. "Look, I guess there's no other way to tell you this but to come out and say it." She paused for a breath. "He threatened me. He wants me to say that I saw Gerald Blakeley put something in his brother's glass."

Elmer Lee stared at her like she was a creature from

another planet. "I've heard some good ones from you, Wanda Nell, but this takes the cake. Why on God's green earth would Bill Warren threaten you? And how? How did he threaten you?" He shook his head. "It just don't make sense."

"Well, if you'll stop talking long enough for me to get a word in edgewise," Wanda Nell said, trying not to snap at him and not succeeding too well, "I'll tell you. Now just sit there and be quiet a minute."

He gave her a hard look, but he did as she asked. He kept his mouth shut while she told him what had happened to her in the state cop's office. To her satisfaction, she could see the erosion of his disbelief as she talked.

When she finished, Elmer Lee sat there a moment in silence. When he spoke, his tone was flat. "And you're sure you didn't misinterpret anything he said?"

"Come on, Elmer Lee, I'm not stupid, and neither are you," Wanda Nell said, "though sometimes I do wonder. First he tells me he could arrest Tuck and T.J. and put them in jail. Then he asks me, flat out, was I sure I didn't see Gerald Blakeley put something in that glass. How would you interpret that?" She sat back in her chair, her arms crossed over her chest, and glared at him.

Elmer Lee scratched his head. "You got me, Wanda Nell. I can't see any way around it."

"So what are you going to do about it?" Wanda Nell asked.

"I'm gonna have to think about that," Elmer Lee said. "I can't just go over there and accuse him, because the only proof we have is what you've told me. He would just say you were lying for some reason."

Wanda Nell sighed. "That's what I was afraid you were

going to say." She uncrossed her arms and rested them on the arms of her chair.

"Sorry, but that's the way it is." Elmer Lee's gaze softened for a moment. "Look, I know you don't lie about things like this, but I'm going to have to handle this real careful like. You understand?"

"Yeah, I do," Wanda Nell said. "But it makes me so angry." She leaned forward. "Can he really do that? Arrest Tuck and T.J., I mean."

Elmer Lee focused on something on the top of his desk. "He'd have to catch them in the act, so to speak. It's still a crime here in Mississippi."

"How could he do that unless he just waltzed right into their house one night?"

"There was a case like that in Houston a few years ago," Elmer Lee said, raising his eyes to look at her. "Went all the way to the United States Supreme Court, I think." He shrugged. "If he wanted to do it, he'd find a way, believe you me."

"We've got to stop him," Wanda Nell said. "He just can't ruin people's lives like that."

"No, he can't," Elmer Lee said, "and I promise you, I'll do my best to see that he doesn't do anything to harm your son, Wanda Nell."

"Thank you," Wanda Nell said. "I appreciate that."

Elmer Lee stared off into space. "You know, what I don't get is why he's so bound and determined to pin this on Gerald Blakeley. What does he get out of it, other than wrapping up the case pretty quickly?"

"Beats me," Wanda Nell said, "but there must be some reason. Especially if Gerald *didn't* do it. What do you think? Is Gerald the killer?"

"I don't know," Elmer Lee said. "He could have done it. Hell, anybody in the room that night could have done it. The only fingerprints we found on that glass tube were Gerald's, and that don't make it look too good for him."

"But how would he have got hold of cyanide?" Wanda Nell asked.

Elmer Lee's eyes narrowed. "Who said anything about cyanide? There hasn't been any official report from the medical examiner's office yet."

"It was just a guess somebody made," Wanda Nell said, realizing she should have kept her mouth shut.

"You're meddling again, Wanda Nell," Elmer Lee said. "You need to back off and leave this one alone. You can trust me, even if you can't trust Bill Warren. Can you do that for me, just this once?"

Wanda Nell leaned forward, putting both her hands, palms down, on Elmer Lee's desk. "I'm sorry. I know I can trust you on this, but you've got to understand. This is my family I'm talking about. I can't just sit back and let that bastard walk all over us."

Elmer Lee didn't say anything. His eyes focused on the ring on her left hand. The diamonds shone in the light.

"That's a mighty fancy ring you got there," he said.

Wanda Nell leaned back in her chair. She looked down at the ring. "It's an engagement ring. Jack asked me to marry him, and I said yes."

When he spoke, his tone was grudging. "I guess congratulations are in order. When are you getting married?"

"We haven't set a date yet," Wanda Nell said, ignoring the oddness of his reaction. "I'll let you know when we do, though." T.J. had told her, more than once, that Elmer Lee had feelings for her, but Wanda Nell wasn't really sure. She had come to have respect for Elmer Lee, even though he drove her nuts sometimes. She could never feel about him, though, the way she felt about Jack.

Elmer Lee seemed to have forgotten—for the moment, at least—his insistence that she keep herself out of the investigation. He wouldn't forget for long, she knew.

"Do you think I should tell T.J. and Tuck about this?" she asked.

Elmer Lee nodded. "Yeah, I think you should. They need to know what Warren's up to so they can watch out for him."

"They told me they'd talked to you about some of the nasty things somebody's been doing to them."

"Yeah, they have," Elmer Lee said. "I'm not sure who's doing it, but I've put the word out, here in this department at least, that it had better not be any of my men."

"If you do find out who's behind it, I hope you can put a stop to it," Wanda Nell said.

"I will. You can count on that," Elmer Lee said. "You better get going. I've got some things to look into." He stood up.

"Thank you," Wanda Nell said. She held out a hand for him to shake. He was obviously surprised by the gesture, but he accepted her hand and shook it briefly.

She left his office and walked back down the hall. The officer who had let her in opened the door for her, and she walked across the lobby and out into the bright sunshine again.

She stood for a moment, dreading what she was about to do. She wished she could keep all this from T.J. and Tuck, but she knew Elmer Lee was right. They had to know so they could protect themselves.

She made her way across the street to the building

where Tuck had his office. She glanced at her watch and was surprised to see that it was nearly eleven-thirty. *Better get a move on*, she told herself. She still wanted to drop by and talk to Mrs. Culpepper, and she needed to get home to check on Juliet before she had to go to work at the restaurant.

A couple minutes later, Wanda Nell opened the door to Tuck's office and stepped inside. There was no one in the outer office except Tuck's new secretary who looked up when Wanda Nell came in.

"Hey there, Miz Culpepper," the young woman said with a broad smile. "How are you?"

"I'm fine, Ginger," she said, smiling back. Ginger Newsome was a briskly efficient, perpetually sunny woman, and Tuck and T.J. thought a lot of her. Whenever Wanda Nell talked to her, Ginger was friendly but professional. "How are you?"

"Great, just great," Ginger said. It was the same response she gave whenever Wanda Nell asked. "Do you need to see T.J.?"

"Actually I need to see both him and Tuck, if they're here," Wanda Nell said.

"They are," Ginger said. "Let me just tell them you're here. I think they were about to go out for lunch." She picked up her phone and punched in a few numbers. "Miz Culpepper is here to see you and T.J., Mr. Tucker." She listened for a moment before replacing the phone on its cradle.

"Go right on in," she said.

"Thank you," Wanda Nell replied.

T.J. met her at the door to the inner office. He gave her a quick peck on the cheek.

"What's going on, Mama?" he asked as he escorted her into Tuck's office.

"Hey, Wanda Nell," Tuck said, getting up from behind his desk and coming to give her a quick hug. "What are you doing here? I was going to call you, as a matter of fact."

"I've got something to tell you about," Wanda Nell said, sitting down in the chair T.J. pulled out for her. "You both better be sitting down."

Tuck resumed his seat behind his desk while T.J. pulled another chair up beside Wanda Nell's.

"What's wrong?" Tuck asked. "What can we do to help?"

"I was in Bill Warren's office a little while ago," she said. Tuck and T.J. exchanged a swift glance, and Wanda Nell saw it. "He called the house, saying he wanted to talk to me. So I went to see him after I took Juliet to the doctor."

"How is she?" T.J. asked. "Is it a sinus infection like you thought?"

"Yes," Wanda Nell said. "We saw old Dr. Crowell, and he gave her a shot and some pills to take. And don't let me forget, there's something I need to tell you about Dr. Crowell."

"Okay," Tuck said. "So what about this talk with Bill Warren?"

Wanda Nell told them, not holding back anything. By the time she finished, Tuck's face had gone white. Wanda Nell knew him well enough to know he was furious. His eyes blazed as he stared at her. Beside her, she could feel the same anger emanating from her son.

Before either one of them could speak, she went on. "I went right over to Elmer Lee's office and told him everything. He believes me, and he said he's going to look into it."

"Good," Tuck said. "What the hell is that jackass up to? There's got to be something behind it."

"Besides the fact that he's a raging homophobe?" Wanda Nell asked. "That's the right word, isn't it?"

"It is, Mama," T.J. said. Once again, he and Tuck looked at each other.

"Okay, what's going on?" she asked. "Is it something to do with Bill Warren?"

Tuck nodded. "Yes, it is. I'm afraid we know exactly why he's acting this way. And it probably explains some of the things that have happened to us lately."

"So what is it?" Wanda Nell asked, feeling her stomach knotting up.

"We've spotted him a couple of times in a bar in Memphis."

Wanda Nell stared at her son. "So what if he was in a bar? What does that matter?"

T.J. smiled grimly. "It was a gay bar, Mama."

Sixteen

Wanda Nell stared at her son in disbelief. "Are you telling me Bill Warren is *gay*?" She shook her head. "That just don't make sense to me. If he's gay, why is he harassing you two?"

"Because he's so deep in the closet he's behind the wallpaper," Tuck said, half jokingly. "Seriously, though, Wanda Nell, it's not unusual. Men like Warren who can't accept being gay can be worse homophobes than just about anybody."

"Are you sure?" Wanda Nell asked. "Maybe he was undercover or something."

"He was out of his jurisdiction, for one thing," Tuck said.

"And for another, if he was undercover, he sure was enthusiastic about it," T.J. said, grinning. "I don't want to embarrass you, Mama, but if you'd seen him doing what I saw him doing on the back patio at that bar, you wouldn't doubt it for a second."

Wanda Nell blushed as she tried to rein in her imagination. She didn't want to even think about it. She also didn't want to know what T.J. was doing out on that patio. Evidently a lot went on there.

She had to clear her throat before she could speak. "Does, um, does he know you saw him there?"

"We're not sure," Tuck said. "It's a very popular place, and it's usually packed."

"I'm pretty sure he didn't see me when he was out on the patio that time," T.J. said. "But he could have seen one of us inside the bar at some point."

"Was it just the one time?" Wanda Nell asked.

"No, about three times, I guess, since the first of the year," T.J. said.

"He took over the district office here in Tullahoma in January. The first time I ran into him here in town was at a Rotary Club breakfast the first week of January, and T.J. was with me," Tuck said. "It was back in late February when T.J. spotted him on the patio."

"Maybe he saw you two there but doesn't think you saw him," Wanda Nell said.

"Could be," Tuck replied. "But at the moment, I don't think I'm going to ask him about it."

"No, but I think maybe you ought to talk to Elmer Lee about it," Wanda Nell said.

"Why?" T.J. asked. "What's Elmer Lee going to do?"

"It would at least be some insurance," Wanda Nell said. "So if Bill tries to do anything against you, that way Elmer Lee already knows what's going on, and maybe he can put a stop to it before it goes very far." She paused, frowning. "But how can you prove he was there? And more than one time?"

"Actually, that's not a very big problem," Tuck said, smiling. "Right, T.J.?"

T.J. laughed. "Yeah. You remember that camera phone Tuck gave me for Christmas?"

Wanda Nell nodded. "You mean you took pictures of him at that place? And he doesn't know that you did?"

"Yes, I did," T.J. replied. "And no, I don't think he knows about them."

"Then you better give them to Elmer Lee," Wanda Nell said.

"You're right," Tuck said. "I don't like having to do it, but if attempts to arrest us, we'll need some ammunition."

"I just thought of something," Wanda Nell said, turning to T.J. "What made you take the pictures of him in the first place? That's not something you normally do when you go to that bar, is it?"

"No, of course not," T.J. said, sounding indignant. "Look, by the time we saw him in the bar, we'd already run into him two or three times in town. It was pretty clear somebody had told him about us, because he made some derogatory remarks." He shrugged. "So when I spotted him out on the patio doing what he was doing, I didn't even think twice. I took the pictures, and I made sure he didn't see what I was doing."

"Wasn't there a flash, or something?" Wanda Nell asked. "I'm assuming it's kind of dark on that patio."

"Yes, it is," T.J. said, "but if you weren't paying close attention you would probably think it was just somebody lighting a cigarette."

Wanda Nell shook her head. It was all pretty sordid, but when someone threatened her family, she figured they had to use whatever weapons were at hand to protect themselves.

"Well, you just promise me you'll talk to Elmer Lee today and show him those pictures, too."

"We will, Wanda Nell," Tuck said. "I think you're right. We can't afford to take any chances."

"Why didn't y'all tell me about any of this before now?" Wanda Nell asked with a frown.

"We didn't want you to worry, Mama," T.J. said.

Wanda Nell looked at him, and he shrugged. "I know, I know," he said.

"I'd rather know what's really going on," Wanda Nell said, "instead of imagining Lord knows what."

"Point taken, Wanda Nell," Tuck said. "We won't purposely keep things like this from you anymore, but you have to remember that we can take care of ourselves. We appreciate your support, but you don't need to lose any sleep over us." He smiled to take any sting out of his words.

Wanda Nell sighed. "I know that, but you know how mothers are. We just can't help worrying. We don't ever want anything bad to happen to our kids." She smiled back.

"Getting back to the main subject here," T.J. said with a frown. "What I don't get is why Warren is so determined to pin this on Gerald."

"You still think Gerald didn't do it?" Wanda Nell asked. "I hope he didn't, because he seems like a nice boy. Plus, right now, if Bill Warren told me the sun was up in the sky, I'd argue with him it wasn't. He makes me feel real contrary."

T.J. and Tuck both laughed at that. "No, I don't think he's guilty," T.J. said, "and neither does Tuck. We just don't have a clue right now who else might have done it."

"Didn't you say you had something to tell us about your visit to old Doc Crowell this morning?" Tuck said.

"Yeah, I sure did," Wanda Nell replied. "You remember what Jack told you he saw?"

"Yes, and what do you think it means?" Tuck asked.

"They were making out in the parking lot," Wanda Nell said tartly. "You want me to draw you a picture?"

Tuck grinned, and T.J. laughed. "No, I get it," Tuck said.

"What about this morning, Mama?" T.J. asked.

"Guess who Tiffany Farwell's godfather is?" Wanda Nell asked. "Old Dr. Crowell, that's who."

"Interesting," Tuck said. "So the old man is her godfather, and the son has a decidedly unprofessional interest in her." He shook his head. "But if Tiffany is in love with the son, why didn't she just break off the engagement? Why would somebody have to kill Travis Blakeley to stop the marriage?"

"That's what I want to know, too," Wanda Nell said. "Maybe she was too afraid of Travis and what he might do."

"That's certainly possible," Tuck responded. "But if she was that afraid of him, wouldn't she also be afraid of getting caught running around on him?"

T.J. laughed. "You don't know Tiffany, believe me. That girl has about as much brains as a clod of dirt. Thinking is *not* her strong suit. Knowing her, she figured she could get away with it, because that's what she wanted to think."

"If she's that dumb," Tuck said, "why are these men so hot to trot for her?"

"You haven't seen her, have you?" T.J. laughed again. "She's the most beautiful girl I've ever seen, let me tell you. And when guys catch sight of her, well, you can just imagine what part of their anatomy they're thinking with."

"I see," Tuck said. "That certainly explains a few things." He leaned forward, his elbows on the desk. "But it still doesn't explain why she just didn't end the engagement."

"Maybe somebody should ask her," Wanda Nell said. "You know her, T.J. Can't you talk to her?"

"Actually, I tried calling her," T.J. said, "but she won't return my calls. I thought for Gerald's sake she might be willing to talk. But maybe I'm wrong about that."

Tuck stood up. "I don't know about you two, but I sure

could use something to eat right about now. How about it, Wanda Nell, can we take you to lunch?"

T.J. stood also and held out a hand to his mother. Wanda Nell let him pull her to her feet. "Thank you, Tuck, but I've got a couple of things I need to do. And I really need to get home to check on Juliet. Y'all go on without me, but don't forget about seeing Elmer Lee this afternoon."

"We will," Tuck said. "I'll have Ginger call and make an appointment before we go to lunch."

"Oh, before I forget," Wanda Nell said, thinking about Lisa Pemberton. "Did Lisa call your office or come by?"

"No," Tuck said. "I thought she would, but she hasn't yet." He shrugged. "There's still the afternoon."

"Yeah, I guess so, but it seems kind of odd to me. Nobody can make her do it, though." Wanda Nell shook her head. "Y'all be careful. If I find out anything, I'll let you know." She headed for the door.

"You be careful, too," T.J. said, shaking a finger at her.

Wanda Nell just grinned. She opened the door and left. She paused only to say good-bye to Ginger, and then she made a beeline for her car.

She wanted to stop by to see Mrs. Culpepper and Belle. They might be having their lunch right now, and Mrs. Culpepper would be peeved at her for interrupting. "Too bad," Wanda Nell muttered. She didn't want to put off talking to her former mother-in-law, and it certainly wouldn't be the first time the old battle-ax had been annoyed with her.

Five minutes after leaving Tuck's office, she pulled her car into the driveway of Mrs. Culpepper's antebellum home, one of the oldest in Tullahoma. It was a beautiful place, full of antiques, but it had never felt much like a home to Wanda Nell. Mrs. Culpepper wasn't exactly the happy homemaker type, and her late husband, old Judge Culpepper, had been a hard-drinking, woman-chasing tyrant. It was no wonder Bobby Ray, their only child, had insisted they not live there after they were married. He couldn't wait to get out of that house.

Wanda Nell proceeded up the walk to the front porch, what Mrs. Culpepper always referred to grandly as her "veranda." She climbed the steps and crossed the porch to the door. She rang the doorbell and waited. After a moment, through the smoky glass she could see a dim figure moving toward her.

The door swung open, and plump Belle Meriwether, Mrs. Culpepper's cousin and now live-in companion, beamed at Wanda Nell.

"What a nice surprise," Belle said. "Honey, come on in here. It sure is good to see you." She gave Wanda Nell a quick hug before shutting the door behind her.

"It's nice to see you, too, Belle," Wanda Nell said. "I hope I'm not interrupting your lunch or anything."

"Oh no, we had that about an hour ago," Belle said, still smiling. "You know Cousin Lucretia doesn't sleep that much most nights, so she's always awake early. I have to fix her breakfast around five-thirty, and then she's real peckish again by eleven o'clock."

Wanda Nell was about to ask whether Mrs. Culpepper was resting after her meal, but a querulous voice emanating from the front parlor answered the question for her. "Belle! Who is it? If they're selling something, send them away. I'm not feeding any more of those people so you stop asking them in for coffee."

"She's having one of her cranky days," Belle said, shaking her head slightly. "Of course, she was always more than usual cranky. I believe her mama once told me Lucretia was the most colicky child anyone had ever seen. And I guess it just goes to show what can happen when a colicky baby grows up."

As usual, Wanda Nell didn't know quite how to respond when Belle darted off on a tangent. Pretty much any conversation with Belle consisted mostly of tangents, but she never seemed offended if no one responded. She was more than capable of carrying on a conversation by herself. *Just like Lavon*, Wanda Nell thought, trying not to smile.

Belle turned and led Wanda Nell into the front parlor. "It's Wanda Nell, Lucretia. She dropped by to visit with us. Isn't that nice of her?"

Mrs. Culpepper sat in her favorite chair, her eyes bright and her posture erect. Since Belle had come to live with her, Mrs. Culpepper had fewer and fewer encounters with Jack Daniel's and Jim Beam. She was a lot more alert these days, but Wanda Nell wasn't totally convinced that was a good thing. The more sober she was, the sharper her tongue, in Wanda Nell's experience.

"I reckon you've come because you want something," Mrs. Culpepper said. "That's about the only time *you* come to see me."

"Now, Lucretia, don't talk like that to Wanda Nell. You know how busy she is, having to work those two jobs and look after everybody." Belle motioned for Wanda Nell to take a seat on the sofa near Mrs. Culpepper, while she sat a few inches away from her.

"She ought to get one job that pays better," Mrs. Culpepper said.

Wanda Nell had heard this so many times it no longer bothered her the way it used to. "It's nice to see you, too, Miz Culpepper," she said, smiling sweetly. She knew it irritated the old battle-ax when she didn't rise to the bait.

She set her purse down on the couch between her and Belle and placed her hands demurely in her lap.

"Where did you get that ring?" Mrs. Culpepper said, staring at Wanda Nell's left hand. "Don't tell me you went out and spent your hard-earned money on that. It must be worth at least five thousand dollars."

Wanda Nell stared down at the ring in surprise. She hadn't really given much thought to how much the ring might be worth, because it really didn't matter to her. What was important was the man who had given it to her and how much she loved him. Wanda Nell didn't doubt Mrs. Culpepper was right about the value of the ring, because the old woman always knew the monetary value of anything.

"That sure looks like an engagement ring to me," Belle said, leaning forward to get a better look. "How exciting! When are you getting married, Wanda Nell? What can I do to help?"

"Is that an engagement ring?" Mrs. Culpepper demanded in a harsh voice before Wanda Nell had the chance to respond to Belle. "What are you doing getting married again at your age?"

"Yes, it is an engagement ring," Wanda Nell said, determined not to let the old biddy get to her. She turned to Belle. "We haven't set a date yet. Jack just asked me last night."

"You're going to marry that schoolteacher fellow?" Mrs. Culpepper said. "Well, at least he seems like a sensible man, and he's nice looking. But if you have to get married again, Wanda Nell, you ought to get yourself a man who makes more money than a teacher does."

"Lucretia Culpepper, what a terrible thing to say!" Belle was highly indignant, to say the least. "Wanda Nell isn't some mercenary creature out for what she can get, and you ought to know that by now. She's a good girl, and

she deserves a nice man like Jack. Why, the very idea!" She
sat, arms crossed over her chest, and glared at her cousin.

"Oh hush, Belle," Mrs. Culpepper said, her voice as tart
as a fresh lemon. "The good Lord knows he didn't give you
the sense he gave a goose. I know that teacher is a nice
man, I'm just saying it would be nice if he made more
money so Wanda Nell didn't have to work so hard. That's
all." She sniffed loudly, glaring right back at her cousin.

Wanda Nell's irritation rapidly turned into amusement.
The way the two women bickered was harmless fun, and
she knew Mrs. Culpepper relished her verbal battles with
her cousin. They were a satisfactory replacement for her
tippling, or so Wanda Nell believed.

"Jack is a wonderful man," Wanda Nell said, trying to
keep a straight face as the two older women continued to
stare at each other. "I feel very lucky, and I hope both of
you will wish us the best."

"Of course we will," Belle said. "*Won't* we, Lucretia?"
She gave her cousin a pointed look.

"Yes, yes," Mrs. Culpepper said. "But I suppose you'll
be expecting an expensive wedding gift from me. Won't
you?"

"If you want to give us a wedding present," Wanda Nell
said, "I can't stop you. The main thing is that I want you
both to come to the wedding. Whenever and wherever we
decide it will be."

Mrs. Culpepper sniffed again.

Before either of the older women could say anything,
Wanda Nell decided she had better get to the point of the
visit.

"Actually, Miz Culpepper, I did want to ask you something," Wanda Nell said. "Just for information, though,
since you know so much about people in Tullahoma."

Mrs. Culpepper eyed her suspiciously. "Does this have anything to do with that man dying at that diner place where you work? I heard about it at church yesterday morning."

"It does," Wanda Nell said. "You probably know that Gerald Blakeley has been arrested. Tuck is representing him, and none of us really think he did it. So we're trying to figure out who else might have done it."

"What is it you want to know?" Mrs. Culpepper asked, her eyes now alight with curiosity.

"I need to know more about the bride," Wanda Nell said. "Tiffany Farwell. Do you know her or her mother?"

"I do," Mrs. Culpepper said. "They used to go to our church. I think they stopped after the girl's father died. He was real big on putting on a show by being at church every Sunday. He gave a lot of money to the church, too. But I doubt it bought him a room in heaven. Nobody makes as much money as he did and does it legitimately."

"I see," Wanda Nell said, though she wasn't quite sure that information would be of any use. It might simply be Mrs. Culpepper's spite talking. "What about Tiffany's mother?"

Mrs. Culpepper thought for a moment. "I believe her daddy was a policeman. I know Thaddeus thought a lot of him at one time." Thaddeus was her late husband, the judge. "Now, what was his name?" She thought for a moment longer. "Oh yes, now I remember. His name was Vance. Robert Vance, and he had a son and a couple of daughters. I think the son is a policeman now, too."

Wanda Nell's heart sank. She had to be talking about Dixon Vance, Mayrene's new boyfriend. If he was Tiffany's uncle, then he, too, might have a motive for killing Travis Blakeley.

Seventeen

"Cat got your tongue, Wanda Nell?" Mrs. Culpepper's waspish tones broke through Wanda Nell's reverie.

"Oh yes, ma'am," Wanda Nell said. "That's the kind of thing I want to know." She wondered if Mayrene knew her boyfriend was related to Tiffany Farwell. Surely if she did know, she would have said something. "Anything else about the family you can think of?"

Mrs. Culpepper cocked her head to one side, like a thoughtful parrot. "I do seem to recall that Mrs. Farwell remarried a couple of years ago." She frowned. "But for the life of me I cannot remember who she married. Since she stopped attending my church, I've lost track of her."

"Are you sure you don't know anything about the Blakeleys?" Wanda Nell asked. "The man who died, well, there were stories about him. You know he was married twice before, and both his wives died in accidents. Some people say he was responsible."

"Merciful heavens," Belle said with a gasp. "That's horrible. What kind of man would do something like that? I just do not know what this world is coming to. I guess he

did it for money, didn't he? Money is the root of all evil."
She sighed heavily.

"Fool woman," Mrs. Culpepper said. "It's not money
that's evil, it's the idiots who are too greedy for it."

"Isn't that what I said?" Belle asked, appearing puzzled.
"I said money was the *root* of all evil, not evil itself. I do
declare, Lucretia, I think sometimes you don't really listen
to what I say." She winked at Wanda Nell who had to work
hard to keep from laughing.

"Of course I don't listen to you, Belle. If I did, I'd go
stark raving mad and run screaming down the street," Mrs.
Culpepper said. "I listen to about every fifth word you say,
and since you talk so much, I still get an earful."

Wanda Nell would have sworn she saw Mrs. Culpepper's lips crease briefly in a smile, but it was gone as soon
as she noticed it. "Now, to answer your last question, I do
recall hearing about those tragic deaths. But I didn't know
any of the people involved."

At this point, Wanda Nell figured she had as much useful
information as she was likely to get from Mrs. Culpepper.

"Thank you, Mrs. Culpepper," she said. "I'll let Tuck
know what you told me, and if you should think of anything else, I'm sure you'll let one of us know."

She was ready to be on her way, but before she could
start saying her good-byes, Mrs. Culpepper began quizzing
her about Juliet, Miranda, and Lavon. Wanda Nell answered
her questions patiently. This was a big change, because
before Bobby Ray's death, Mrs. Culpepper had expressed little interest in her granddaughters and great-
grandson.

Belle had to chime in as well, and it was another twenty
minutes before Wanda Nell could safely leave without appearing rude. Belle saw her to the door and made her swear

she would call and tell them the minute she and Jack set a wedding date. Wanda Nell gave her a quick kiss and a hug before she practically ran out the door to her car.

Before she pulled out of the driveway, she retrieved her cell phone from her purse. She'd better call Tuck right now and tell him what she had learned from Mrs. Culpepper. Otherwise she might forget about it until later.

She punched the speed dial number for Tuck's cell phone. She was disappointed when it went to voice mail. She left a message about the connection between Dixon Vance and Tiffany Farwell. Ending the call, she dropped her phone in her purse.

She headed home. She wanted to see how Juliet was doing, plus she realized she was really hungry. That skimpy breakfast of toast hadn't stuck to her ribs very long. If everything was calm at home, she might even have time for a quick nap before she had to get ready for the evening shift at the Kountry Kitchen.

Juliet was asleep, and Miranda was feeding Lavon his lunch when she got home. Lavon held out his arms for his grandmother, and Wanda Nell picked him up for a moment, trying her best to keep his sticky fingers out of her hair. Then she set him back down, and he began playing with his food again.

"I checked her temperature, Mama," Miranda said proudly. "It was only a teensy bit over normal, so I think she's doing a lot better. She was up for a while, and we watched some TV, but then she said she felt like taking a nap again."

Wanda Nell patted her older daughter's shoulder. "Thank you for taking such good care of her, honey. And Lavon, too. Have you had time to have lunch yourself?"

"Oh, I'm not real hungry right now," Miranda said. "I

might eat me a sandwich or something when I put Lavon down for his afternoon nap."

"Okay then," Wanda Nell said. "I'm so hungry right now I could eat a bear." She headed for the fridge.

"Gamma eat teddy?"

Wanda Nell turned to see Lavon's lower lip trembling. She went back to him and rubbed his head. "No, honey, Grandma is not going to eat your teddy bear. All I meant was that I'm really hungry. Okay?"

Reassured, Lavon smiled. Wanda Nell and Miranda exchanged smiles. She really had to be careful what she said around him these days. He picked up the oddest things sometimes.

Wanda Nell went back to the fridge and peered inside. There was still some of the chicken salad she had made on Friday, or she could have a ham sandwich. She decided on the chicken salad. She made a sandwich with it and washed it down with Diet Coke. Still feeling hungry, she made herself another sandwich and finished off the chicken salad.

While she was eating, Lavon finished his lunch. Miranda carried him off to the bathroom to clean him up. They came back in a few minutes, and Lavon wandered around the kitchen with his teddy bear, talking a mile a minute, while Miranda sat at the table and talked to her mother.

"I saw your grandmother and Belle just before I came home," Wanda Nell told her. "And of course the first thing your grandmother did was spot my ring."

"What did she say? Was she mad?"

"No, she wasn't," Wanda Nell said. "I know she misses your daddy, but she knows we have to get on with our lives. She made some fuss about a wedding present, but you know how she is."

Miranda laughed. "I sure do. She's like that old chihuahua

Mayrene used to have. She growls a lot, but if you pay her some attention, she's okay."

"She's been easier to get along with since Belle came to live with her," Wanda Nell said. "I hate to say it, but I guess she was pretty lonely for a long time. She and Belle entertain each other. You should have heard them today." She laughed as got up to put her plate in the sink and throw away her empty Coke can.

"They're kinda like watching a rerun of *Golden Girls*," Miranda said. "Belle is like Rose, and Grandma is Dorothy. She was the real cranky one, wasn't she?"

"Yeah," Wanda Nell said. "She was." She had to laugh again. Miranda had hit the nail on the head. "I think I'm going to try to nap a little. I've got a long night ahead of me. Make sure I'm up by four-thirty."

"Okay, Mama," Miranda said. "We'll be real quiet so you can sleep. And if Juliet needs anything, I'll look after her."

"Thank you, honey," Wanda Nell said. She was touched. Miranda really was making an effort to be more thoughtful and to be more of a help around the house.

"Mama," Miranda said, and Wanda Nell turned back to face her. "You think you might be able to quit one of your jobs when you and Jack get married?"

"I don't know," Wanda Nell said. "I hadn't thought about it, to tell the truth. I guess it's something Jack and I'll have to discuss."

"I hope you can," Miranda said. "You work so hard all the time, and as old as you are, I know you must get real tired." Her face was so earnest Wanda Nell didn't have the heart to tell her she didn't appreciate being considered too old to work hard.

"Thank you, honey," she said. "We'll see what happens."

She headed for her room before Miranda could say anything else.

She peeked in Juliet's room first to satisfy herself her
younger daughter was okay. Juliet was sound asleep, and
Wanda Nell went to her own room feeling relieved. She
hated it when one of her children was sick.

As she undressed, she thought back to what Miranda
had said. Miranda, at eighteen, thought anyone over twenty-
five was on the downhill slide into senility. Wanda Nell
would be forty-two her next birthday, and that wasn't old,
not by a long shot. Jack was a year younger than she was,
and that wasn't so bad. She hoped they'd have a lot of
years together before either one of them felt old.

She lay down on the bed and pulled the sheet over her.
She closed her eyes and willed herself to relax. Miranda's
question came back to her, though, keeping her awake.
Would she give up one of her jobs after they got married?
And if she did, which one would she give up?

That part was easy. She would give up the job at Budget
Mart. The work wasn't that hard, but she wouldn't miss
having to work from ten at night till six in the morning.
She made better money at the Kountry Kitchen because
she always got really good tips from her customers.

Giving up the job at Budget Mart also would mean she
could be at home with her husband during the night. She
grinned at that thought. If she kept up her current work
schedule after they were married, she would hardly ever
sleep in the same bed as Jack. He would be up and getting
ready for school when she came home, and when she was
leaving for the Kountry Kitchen he would just be getting
home from school.

She would have to give up one of her jobs if she wanted
her marriage to work. Maybe she could work two shifts at

the Kountry Kitchen instead. She would have to talk to Melvin about that. It would mean a long day for her, but at least she would be at home when Jack was at home. She was sure Jack would think it was a good idea.

Having come to that conclusion, she felt a little better. Now, however, she started thinking about Jack and his cousin, Lisa. What were they going to do about her? If it turned out she really had made up the whole story about being stalked, she was going to need some serious help. What effect would that have on Jack, though? She couldn't ask him to ignore his cousin's troubles in order to pay attention to her. She wouldn't respect him much if he did that, anyway. Family ties were important, and you did what you could to help your family. That was the way she had been raised, and she couldn't expect Jack to do anything else.

It'll all work out somehow, she told herself. *Now stop thinking about it and try to get some sleep.* She thought about other, less challenging things, and soon she drifted off.

When Miranda woke her up, Wanda Nell was just coming out of a dream in which she and Jack were getting married on the football field at the high school. Her parents were there, and they were smiling at her to show their approval. She realized she was crying a little as she came out of the dream.

"Mama, are you okay?" Miranda asked, alarmed.

"Oh, I'm fine, honey," Wanda Nell assured her. "I was just dreaming, and Mama and Daddy were in the dream. They were really happy, and I guess I was crying happy tears, too."

"Well, that's okay, I guess," Miranda said, though she didn't look convinced. "It's a little after four-thirty."

Wanda Nell nodded. "I'm up now. You go on and do whatever you were doing. I'm going to take a quick shower."

She sat on the bed for a few minutes after Miranda left her, thinking about her dream. The part about having the wedding on the football field was weird, and she had no idea what that was supposed to mean. She couldn't stop thinking about seeing her parents in the dream and how happy they were for her. She hadn't dreamed about them in a long time.

In a book she had read a few years ago, the author claimed that when people who had died appeared in dreams, they were trying to get a message to the dreamer. Wanda Nell wanted to believe that was true, especially in this case. She knew how much her parents would have loved Jack, and she wished they could be here to know how happy she was.

Wiping away a few stray tears, she got out of bed and took a quick shower.

Juliet was in the kitchen, eating some cereal, when Wanda Nell had finished getting ready for work.

"How are you feeling, sweetie?" she asked her daughter.

"Better, Mama," Juliet said, "but my throat is still a little itchy."

"I think there's some of that sore throat spray in the bathroom. Use some of that if it gets to bothering you too much," Wanda Nell said. "And don't forget to take your medicine this evening before you go to bed."

"I won't," Juliet said. "Don't worry about me. Miranda's taking good care of me." She grinned, and Wanda Nell smiled back. It was usually Juliet who looked after Miranda, and this reversal of roles was almost unheard of.

"Where is Miranda?" Wanda Nell asked.

"In her room, on the phone," Juliet said, raising one eyebrow as if to say, "Where else?"

"Okay, well, I'd better get going. Call me if you need me, and remember I have a shift at Budget Mart tonight after I get off at the restaurant."

Juliet nodded. "Be careful."

Wanda Nell kissed her good-bye. As she let herself out of the trailer she glanced across at Mayrene's. It was a little too early for Mayrene to be home from the beauty salon where she worked, and there was no sign of Lisa or her car. Wanda Nell frowned. If she had time tonight, she would give Mayrene a call and see if she had heard anything from Dixon Vance. Maybe he'd had time to do a little digging into Lisa's case.

As she pulled out of the trailer park driveway, Wanda Nell thought about Dixon Vance. He had to be Tiffany Farwell's uncle from what Mrs. Culpepper had told her. Tuck would surely verify that, and she would double-check with him before she said anything to Mayrene, just in case.

When she reached the Kountry Kitchen, she said hello to Melvin, busily bussing tables, and waved at a few of the regulars. She passed Ruby Garner behind the counter and patted her on the shoulder. Stopping to chat with the kitchen workers, Lurene the cook and Elray the dishwasher, she found out that the police had made a real mess in the back room. Melvin had paid Elray extra to help clean up this afternoon and get it ready for the evening.

"It's a good thing they finished, though," Wanda Nell said after commiserating with Elray. "It sure would be awful if we had to turn people away because we couldn't use the back room."

Her purse safely stowed away in its usual place in the

back, she went back out front. She was wearing her ring, and she thought about telling Melvin and Ruby right away about her engagement. Then she decided, just for fun, to see how long it took them to notice. She figured Melvin would probably see it first.

She was making a fresh pot of coffee when she heard the door open. Turning to see who the newcomer was, she almost dropped the coffee pot.

What on earth was Tiffany Farwell doing here?

Eighteen

Tiffany Farwell paused inside the door of the restaurant, staring about uncertainly. Wanda Nell set the coffeepot down and made her way to where Tiffany stood.

Now that she saw the young woman in the flesh, Wanda Nell could understand why men acted like rutting stags around her. T.J. had said she was the most beautiful girl he'd ever seen, and Wanda Nell had to agree with him. Tiffany had a figure that called to mind some of the movie bombshells of days gone by, and her face was breath-stoppingly lovely. The dress she wore complemented her coloring but did little to conceal the voluptuous curves beneath it. The men in the restaurant had all stopped talking, eating, or drinking. Their eyes were practically out on stalks, Wanda Nell noted with amusement. Tiffany appeared not to notice what was going on. She was probably well used to it.

"Good evening," Wanda Nell said. "Would you like a table? Or can I help you with something else?"

"I'm not sure," Tiffany said. "Is this where it happened?" Her voice was low and vibrant. She stared at Wanda

Nell, and, looking into those blue eyes, Wanda Nell had the distinct feeling there was plenty of empty space in Tiffany's head.

Even though she knew what Tiffany meant by her question, Wanda Nell nevertheless had to ask. "Where did *what* happen?"

Tiffany blinked. "Didn't I just ask you?"

"You did," Wanda Nell said, suppressing a sigh. "Are you talking about the man who died here on Saturday night?"

Nodding, Tiffany said, "Yes. Can you show me where it happened?"

The younger woman's request made Wanda Nell uneasy. It was more than a bit morbid, Wanda Nell thought.

"I guess so," Wanda Nell said. "Come with me." She led the way toward the restaurant's back room. As she walked, she was very conscious that every male eye in the place was following Tiffany's progress behind her.

Wanda Nell stepped aside, and Tiffany walked past her into the back room. This early in the evening, the room was still vacant. Wanda Nell could talk to the girl without anyone overhearing.

"Here?" she asked. She glanced around, cowering a little, almost as if she were afraid.

"Yes," Wanda Nell said. "The party was in this room."

"Did you see him die?" Tiffany asked, turning to stare at her. Her whole body was trembling.

"Yes, I did," Wanda Nell said. This was getting more and more creepy by the moment. What was the point of all this?

Her legs a bit shaky under her, Tiffany wandered over to a table, pulled out a chair, and sat down. Wanda Nell followed her and sat down across from her. "Are you okay, honey?"

Tiffany blinked, breathing deeply. "They told me he's

dead, and that it happened here." She shivered. "But I'm afraid they're just telling me that. What if he really didn't die?" Her eyes implored Wanda Nell, and Wanda Nell was astonished to read the fear there.

Impulsively, she held out a hand to the younger woman. Tiffany stared at it for a moment before she grasped it. Wanda Nell almost gasped aloud. Tiffany's hand was ice cold.

"He really did die," Wanda Nell said gently. She hated having to recall that scene, but it was obvious this poor girl needed reassurance. "I was here when it happened, and people I know and trust told me he died."

Tiffany relaxed. "Good." Her hand went limp in Wanda Nell's grasp, and Wanda Nell released it.

"Weren't you supposed to marry him?" Wanda Nell asked as gently as she could.

The girl nodded, her lower lip trembling. "I thought he was so handsome, at first. And the way he looked in his uniform. He was so, you know, manly. He was always telling me how beautiful I was, and all kinds of things." She closed her eyes. "But I didn't really love him."

"Why were you going to marry him, then?" Wanda Nell said.

"He asked me first," Tiffany said, opening her eyes and frowning at Wanda Nell. "It was on our second date, and it was real romantic. He said it was love at first sight, just like in the movies."

"I see," Wanda Nell said, though she really didn't.

"I had my wedding dress already picked out, and Mama and I had planned everything," Tiffany said. "Ever since I was seventeen."

"You said he asked you *first*," Wanda Nell said. "So does that mean someone else asked you to marry him?"

Tiffany nodded. "But by then it was too late. I'd already said yes to Travis." She sighed. "But Tony is so much nicer than Travis."

Wanda Nell knew she must be talking about Tony Crowell.

"If you liked Tony better, why didn't you just tell Travis you didn't want to marry him?"

Tiffany stared at her, her face paling beneath the makeup. "I did. But Travis said I had to marry him."

"You didn't have to marry him if you didn't want to," Wanda Nell said. "Surely he didn't want to marry you if you were in love with somebody else."

"Travis didn't care," Tiffany said, staring down at her hands. "He said we were getting married, and I'd sure enough be sorry if I tried to dump him."

"What did he mean by that?" Wanda Nell asked. She was not surprised Travis Blakeley had threatened the poor girl. It certainly explained a lot.

"He told me not to tell anybody," Tiffany said. She looked like she was going to faint.

"But he's dead, honey," Wanda Nell said firmly. "He can't do anything to you now."

"That's right," Tiffany said, hope dawning in her eyes. "He's really gone, and now he can't hurt my mama."

"Did he say that he would hurt your mama if you didn't marry him?"

"Yes," Tiffany said. "He said it would be a shame if Mama wasn't around to see her grandchildren." Just saying the words made Tiffany go pale again.

"Did you tell anybody about this?" Wanda Nell asked.

Tiffany didn't respond. She stared at Wanda Nell.

"I know you said Travis told you not to tell anyone,"

Wanda Nell said. "But maybe you did tell somebody. You did, didn't you?"

Tiffany licked her lips, and for a moment Wanda Nell thought she wasn't going to answer. Tiffany's head dropped, and the words came out in a whisper. "I told my mama."

And Mama probably told several people, Wanda Nell thought. That was the reason Travis Blakeley had to die. His threat to Tiffany had been all too real. With his history and the rumors that surrounded him, anyone would be terrified by such a threat.

This meant that Dixon Vance and both Dr. Crowells could legitimately be considered suspects now.

"Do you remember when you told your mama about it?" Wanda Nell asked.

Tiffany nodded. "It was on Friday."

That meant there was plenty of time for someone to plan to murder Travis Blakeley at his bachelor party and rescue Tiffany from a very bad mistake in judgment.

"Travis must have wanted to marry you really bad if he threatened you like that," Wanda Nell said.

"Yeah, he did," Tiffany said. "He always talked about how beautiful I am." Her face clouded. "But he talked a lot about all the things he was going to buy when we got married. He said he wouldn't have to work anymore."

"I see," Wanda Nell said. She felt so sorry for the poor girl.

"You know what? I think he didn't really care about me," Tiffany said. "I think he just wanted to marry me because of all the money my daddy left me." The way she spoke it sounded like it was the first time the idea had occurred to her.

Wanda Nell wanted to comfort her, but there wasn't

much she could say. "Some men are like that," she said. "I know it's awful, but it just happens that way sometimes. You're very lucky you don't have to marry him now."

"I sure am," Tiffany said, sounding happier. "Now I can marry Tony. He asked me again last night."

"That's nice," Wanda Nell said. As far as she could tell, Tiffany hadn't made the connection yet between Travis Blakeley's sudden death and her own good fortune. How would she react if she knew someone had murdered Travis to save her from marrying him?

Another thought struck her. She might as well ask, because Tiffany seemed a little too dim to understand the import of the question. "Tiffany, honey, did Travis know about you and Tony? That you really wanted to marry him instead?"

"Yeah," Tiffany replied. She screwed her face up like a little child who knows she's done something bad but doesn't really know why. "I guess I kind of told him the other day."

"When you told him that, did he say he would hurt Tony, too?"

Tiffany nodded.

"Did you tell anybody about that? Like Tony, maybe?"

Tiffany ducked her head. "I guess I might've." Her voice was barely audible. "Like maybe my mama and Tony."

"It's okay, honey," Wanda Nell said in soothing tones. "You couldn't keep something like that to yourself." She paused. The next bit was going to be difficult, she knew. "The thing is, Tiffany, now you need to tell the sheriff what you just told me. Can you do that?"

"Why? Why do I have to talk to the sheriff?" Tiffany's mouth set in mulish lines. "Now that he's really dead, I don't have to talk to a policeman ever again."

"It's information the sheriff needs to know so they can figure out who murdered Travis," Wanda Nell said.

Tiffany had to think about that for a moment, and Wanda Nell could see that it took some effort. Finally, Tiffany spoke. "I guess so, but my mama's not going to be happy about that." As she said the words, her eyes widened, and she clapped a hand over her mouth.

"What's the matter, honey?"

Tiffany just shook her head, her hand still over her mouth.

Wanda Nell made a shrewd guess. "Your mama told you not to talk to anybody about any of this, didn't she?"

If anything, Tiffany's eyes widened even more. Her hand dropped from her mouth. "How did you know that?"

"I'm a mama, too," Wanda Nell said. "I understand why your mama told you that. She just wants to protect you. But it's not that simple, honey. This affects other people, and somebody innocent could get hurt. You wouldn't want that, now would you? You're a nice girl, aren't you?"

Tiffany nodded. "Yes, ma'am. But who might get hurt?"

"Gerald Blakeley. They've put him in jail because they think he murdered his brother."

"I didn't know that," Tiffany said, frowning. "Gerald's really nice. He was always so sweet to me. He asked me to marry him a long time ago, back in high school." She shook her head. "But I couldn't marry him. He's only a boy."

"He's a *nice* boy," Wanda Nell said, "and he needs your help, honey. That's why you need to talk to the police and tell them just what you told me. Okay?"

"I guess so." Tiffany frowned again. Wanda Nell wasn't sure the girl could work out just *why* what she had to say could help Gerald.

They both heard a ringing sound, and it was coming

from Tiffany's purse. She opened it and pulled out her cell phone. "Hello." She listened a moment. "I'm at that restaurant, Mama, and I've been talking to a real nice lady."

Wanda Nell was close enough to hear the sharp tones, but not the words, emanating from Tiffany's phone. Evidently Mama wasn't too happy about Tiffany being there and talking to someone.

"Okay, Mama," Tiffany said. "I'll be right home." She shut the phone and dropped it back in her purse. "Mama wants me to come home right now." She stood up. "It's been real nice talking to you, ma'am."

Wanda Nell stood, too. "It's been nice talking to you, too, Tiffany. Now, I know your mama wants you to come right home, but you think about what I told you. About how you need to talk to the sheriff and tell him what we talked about. It's real important, okay?"

Tiffany nodded, and Wanda Nell had to be content with that. She was afraid that once Tiffany was back under her mother's protective wing, she would never go to the sheriff's department. Mama might very likely do her best to keep Tiffany from talking to anyone, because no matter how dim Tiffany was, Wanda Nell had an idea her mother was a lot sharper.

Ruby Garner stepped into the back room. "Hey, Wanda Nell, that policeman's here again, and he wants to talk to you."

"Okay," Wanda Nell said. Her stomach knotted up. Ruby must mean Bill Warren. He was the last person on earth she wanted to see right now.

She followed Tiffany into the front room, and Tiffany continued on to the door, oblivious as before, while the male customers got an eyeful.

Bill Warren stood by the cash register. Wanda Nell

watched him for a moment as he watched Tiffany. The look
he gave the beautiful girl was nothing like the looks she was
getting from the other men. That was when Wanda Nell had
no further doubts about what Tuck and T.J. had told her.
Bill obviously knew who the girl was, but he might as well
have been looking at a cow or a dog walking by.

Tiffany went out the door, and Bill Warren turned away.
He caught sight of Wanda Nell and walked forward to meet
her.

"I need to talk to you," he said.

"I'm at work, in case you hadn't noticed," Wanda Nell
said. "Besides, I don't have anything else to say to you."

"I'm investigating a murder," Bill said, "and if I have to
talk to you, I don't care where it is. You get your tail back
here on the double." He walked past her, heading for the
back of the restaurant. He didn't look back.

Wanda Nell felt her blood pressure shoot up, and the
top of her head throbbed. He had some nerve, talking to
her like that. If she could have put her hands on a baseball
bat or a sturdy piece of lumber, she would have knocked
his head off. She didn't care who was watching.

She stomped after him, determined to give him a piece
of her mind.

Bill stood waiting for her in the center of the back room.

"You've got a hell of a nerve, talking to me like that,"
Wanda Nell said. "I don't care who you think you are, don't
ever speak to me like that again. You hear me?" She got
right up in his face, and she was pleased to see him flinch.

"Chill, Wanda Nell," Bill said. His face had reddened.
"You're going to have a stroke one of these days, you keep
on acting like that."

Wanda Nell didn't reply. She simply stood there, glaring at him hard enough to strip the paint off the walls.

"I just needed to talk to you," Bill said, not looking at her. "It occurs to me you really got bent out of shape when we were talking earlier, and you got the wrong end of the stick. You didn't really think I wanted you to lie about seeing Gerald Blakeley put something in the victim's drink, did you?"

What was he up to now? He was sounding almost apologetic, and that was a far cry from the way he had been earlier in the day.

Wanda Nell didn't say anything. She wanted to think about this for a moment.

The only answer she could come up with was maybe he had got wind of the fact that she had gone to see Elmer Lee. If that was true, then it meant that Bill was probably afraid of Elmer Lee and what he might do. She got a certain grim satisfaction out of that. She wanted to see him squirm.

Taking a deep breath to steady herself, Wanda Nell said, "I don't think I got the wrong end of the stick at all, Bill. I'd have to be about as dense as a fence post not to understand what you were getting at. So don't come in here and try to pretend it didn't happen."

Bill's nostrils flared, and his face reddened again. "I swear, Wanda Nell, you screw with me, and you're going to be real sorry."

"Funny," Wanda Nell said, smiling, "I was just about to say the same thing to you." The smile disappeared, and she said, "Now get the hell out of here, and leave me alone."

Bill didn't move. He tried to stare her down, but finally he turned away. "I'm going, but I want to know one thing."

"What?"

"What was Tiffany Farwell doing here? Did you call her and ask her to come here?"

Wanda Nell laughed. "Why would I call somebody I

don't even know and ask them to come here? For your information, she showed up all on her own. She wanted to
see where her fiancé died, the Lord only knows why." She
wasn't about to tell him about the conversation she had had
with the girl. "I showed her, and that was that."

Bill's eyes narrowed in suspicion. She could tell he
didn't really believe her, but she didn't care.

Wanda Nell turned and walked away. She half expected
him to call her back, but he didn't. She headed straight for
the women's bathroom. She locked herself in and turned to
stare at her face in the mirror. She was surprised her eyes
hadn't bugged out completely because Bill had made her
so mad. Her head was throbbing, and she wet a paper towel
with cold water. She wrung it out and pressed it against her
forehead. Closing her eyes, she leaned against the wall and
concentrated on relaxing.

She wet the paper towel and wrung it out a couple more
times. When her head finally stopped feeling like it was going to jump off her shoulders, she threw away the paper
towel and left the bathroom.

Bill Warren was gone, and for that she was thankful.
She couldn't take much more of him, or she really would
have a stroke. She got busy helping Ruby clean off some of
the tables, and soon she was feeling much better.

Melvin had been absent while Wanda Nell had been
talking to Tiffany and Bill. He reappeared, coming through
the kitchen door, while Wanda Nell was pouring one of
their regulars, Junior Farley, a cup of coffee.

"Where've you been?" Wanda Nell asked Melvin.

"Doing some paperwork back in the office," Melvin responded with a scowl. "It seemed pretty quiet out here, and
I was a little behind on some of it. Y'all didn't need me, did
you?"

"No, not really," Wanda Nell said. She would have to do something nice for Ruby, who had taken up the slack while Wanda Nell had been in the back room. Ruby never uttered a word of complaint, however, and when Wanda Nell had tried to thank her, Ruby would have none of it.

Melvin looked around. "Where's Mayrene?"

Wanda Nell was surprised. "Mayrene? You mean she was here?"

"Yeah," Melvin said. "I came out a few minutes ago to get me some coffee, and Mayrene was waiting here by the counter. She was looking for you, but you were back there talking to that cop. I thought she said she was going to wait for you."

"I sure didn't see her," Wanda Nell said. "She must've decided not to wait for some reason." She frowned. "I sure hope everything's okay."

"She didn't seem upset or anything," Melvin said. "I would've stayed and talked to her, but I really had to get some of that work done before we get busy tonight."

Wanda Nell was debating whether she should try calling her friend when Mayrene came waltzing through the front door.

"Where did you go?" Wanda Nell said. "Melvin just told me you were here a few minutes ago, and then you were gone. I was getting worried."

Mayrene shrugged. "Yeah, I was here, but I could see you talking to a man. I figured you might be a few minutes, so I went and got my car filled up next door. And now I'm back."

"Thank goodness nothing's wrong," Wanda Nell said, feeling mighty relieved. "It's been such a day, I just knew something had to be wrong."

"Now, honey," Mayrene said, "don't get so worked up

about things." She sat down at the counter. "How's about some iced tea?"

"Coming right up," Wanda Nell said. She fetched a glass of tea, a napkin, and teaspoon, and set them down in front of her friend.

"That sure was a good-looking man you were talking to," Mayrene said, "though you didn't look real happy about it. He seemed real familiar to me, too, and I've been trying to figure out where I seen him before." She frowned. "There was something different about him, maybe."

Wanda Nell didn't say anything. It was obvious Mayrene didn't know who Bill Warren was, and she was curious to hear what her friend would tell her.

Mayrene tapped her teaspoon on the side of her glass. "Now I know where I seen him before. It was in Tunica a couple months ago." She grinned. "You remember I went up there one weekend to the casinos with a couple of the girls from the beauty shop?"

Wanda Nell nodded.

"Well, that's where I seen him," Mayrene said, "except that he looked a little different. He had a moustache and some glasses, but I know it was him."

"So he was in one of the casinos?"

"Yeah," Mayrene said. "And he wasn't really happy either. From what I could see, he'd been losing a lot of money, and he looked about ready to kill somebody."

Nineteen

Wanda Nell stared at Mayrene for a moment, trying to figure out whether what she had just heard could have any bearing on the murder of Travis Blakeley. At the moment she couldn't see any connection between the two, but if Mayrene was really sure about seeing Bill losing money at a casino, she sure would tell Elmer Lee about it.

"Are you sure it's the same man?" Wanda Nell said, glancing toward the back room of the restaurant. "If you were right about here when you saw him"—Mayrene nodded—"you were kinda far away to get a real close look."

Mayrene laughed. "Honey, when it comes to a good-looking man, you know I can see pretty darn good."

Wanda Nell shook her head. "Seriously, Mayrene, are you sure? This could be important."

"Who was it you was talking to?" Mayrene asked, sobering.

"Bill Warren. He's the state policeman who's investigating the murder," Wanda Nell said. She leaned forward and lowered her voice. "I've got some stuff to tell you about him, but I can't do it here."

Mayrene nodded. "Okay. But you know I'm going to be about dying of curiosity until you do."

"Can't help that," Wanda Nell said, grinning. "But, tell me, are you really sure he's the same guy you saw in Tunica?"

"Yeah, I'm sure," Mayrene said, beginning to sound impatient. "I could see him pretty clearly from here. I recognized his hair first."

Wanda Nell rolled her eyes. This wasn't the first time Mayrene had told her she could recognize hair without seeing the face it was attached to. "How? What's so special about his hair?"

"For one thing, I don't see that shade of blond in men his age that often," Mayrene said with some asperity. "Either he's putting some kind of rinse on it, or it runs in the family. The other thing is he has a funny little cowlick at the front of his hairline, right where he parts his hair. Didn't you notice it?"

Shrugging, Wanda Nell said, "Now that you mention it, I remember it. But I knew him back when we were in high school. I guess knowing him all those years ago, I didn't even think about the cowlick."

"Anyhow, that's how I'm sure he's the same guy I saw at the casino," Mayrene said. "Just for that, you can pay for my tea."

Wanda Nell resisted the urge to stick out her tongue at her friend. "Okay, that's fair, I guess. Back to Bill and the casino. You said he was real mad and had lost a lot of money?"

"Yeah," Mayrene said. "I happened to be passing his table, and he was arguing with somebody. That made me kinda curious, and I kept an eye out for him the rest of the night. He kept on losing and kept on losing, but he just came back for more. I don't know how much money he lost, but it looked like pretty serious bucks the way he was acting."

"Sounds like he could have a real bad gambling problem," Wanda Nell said.

"Maybe," Mayrene replied. "But what the heck does that have to do with the murder?"

"I don't know," Wanda Nell said, "but I bet it does somehow. We've just got to figure out how." She sighed. "I'll call Tuck and tell him, see if he knows anything. Maybe he's heard something. And he can also let Elmer Lee know about it." She remembered something.

"I seem to recall you went to Tunica two weekends in a row," Wanda Nell said.

Mayrene nodded.

"Can you be sure which weekend it was, just in case it's important?" Mayrene wasn't always good with dates, and Wanda Nell wanted to be sure of her facts.

Mayrene thought for a minute, frowning. Then her face cleared. "Yeah, I know. It was the first weekend. I remember because my friend Teresa was with me that weekend, and she couldn't go the second one. You don't know Teresa, do you?"

"No, I don't think so," Wanda Nell said.

"Well, Teresa—Teresa Taylor, she's a great girl, I know you'd like her. Anyway, the reason I remember is because while we were there and I saw your guy, guess who Teresa saw?" Mayrene was practically crowing, so Wanda Nell knew whatever it was, it must be good.

"Who?"

"Her boss," Mayrene said. "He had his hands all over this woman who was with him, and according to Teresa, she wasn't his wife," Mayrene said.

"Did he see Teresa?"

"No," Mayrene said. "We made sure we stayed out of his way. Teresa's got a real good job in the office at the factory this guy owns, and she don't want to lose it. She makes good money, and she's got good benefits, too."

"Good for her," Wanda Nell said, feeling envious.

"Anyway, that's why I'm so sure of which weekend it was. And Teresa saw this guy, too, so she could be a witness, probably."

"I don't know if it's important," Wanda Nell said, "but it's good to know about your friend, just in case."

Mayrene slapped a palm down lightly on the counter. "I almost forgot why I stopped by here in the first place," she said, frowning at Wanda Nell.

"Why did you?" Wanda Nell said.

"I talked to Dixon late this afternoon," Mayrene said. "He called me to tell me what he found out from talking to the police over in Meridian."

"Okay, tell me," Wanda Nell said. "I'm all ears."

"According to the guy Dixon talked to, they don't have any records of Lisa ever talking to them about a stalker," Mayrene said.

"That's not good," Wanda Nell said.

"No, it sure ain't," Mayrene replied. "But it gets worse. You remember the other night, Lisa mentioned a name? Lester Biggs."

Wanda Nell nodded.

"Well, no such person works for the Meridian PD and never has," Mayrene said. "Sounds to me like she just made up a name."

"This is bad," Wanda Nell said. "How am I going to break this to Jack? He's going to be real upset."

"I know, honey," Mayrene said. "But just to be sure about this, Lisa really did tell y'all she called the cops in Meridian about her stalker?"

"She sure did," Wanda Nell said. "She told us she called them a couple of times before she found out he was a cop himself. That was about when she decided to move to Tullahoma."

"What makes a woman lie about something like that?" Mayrene said. "I just don't get it."

"I've been thinking about that," Wanda Nell said. "What I figure is that she's real lonely. You've seen how shy she is around people a lot of the time. And she doesn't have any family to speak of, except Jack. Her parents died several years ago, and she don't have any brothers or sisters. Heck, I don't think she and Jack even have any other cousins, at least not close ones."

"So she kinda depends on Jack for male attention," Mayrene said.

"Exactly," Wanda Nell said. "And maybe if I wasn't in the picture, she might have been okay once she moved here. But now, well, she can't have Jack to herself."

"That's pretty sad," Mayrene said.

"It is," Wanda Nell replied. "And I bet it's going to get worse. Jack will take it hard."

"You got to tell him."

"I know. That don't make it any easier though."

"You want me to be with you when you do it?" Mayrene asked.

"Thanks, honey," Wanda Nell said. "But this is something I better do just him and me. You know how men are. If somebody else is there, no telling how he'll take it."

"Ain't that the truth," Mayrene said, shaking her head.

She drained her glass and set it down. Rising from her stool, she said, "I better be getting on home. I gave Lisa a key, but I don't know if she'll be there or not."

"I asked Tuck this morning if she had called him or come by, and she hadn't. I doubt she made it by this afternoon either, or even called him," Wanda Nell said.

"I bet you she won't," Mayrene said, "unless she's getting so far into this game she really has lost touch with reality." She opened her purse and started rummaging around.

"No, it's on me, remember?" Wanda Nell said with a smile.

"That's right, it sure is." Mayrene laughed. "Give me a call when you can, or if you need me for anything. I'll keep an eye out on the girls, too."

"Thanks," Wanda Nell said.

Once Mayrene was gone, Wanda Nell focused on actually doing her job. Ever since she had come in tonight she had been standing around talking to people and not getting anything done. Customers were beginning to trickle in for dinner, and soon she and Ruby were constantly on the move.

Wanda Nell halfway expected Jack to turn up that evening, because he so often did. When eight o'clock came and he still hadn't appeared, she stopped looking for him. He might have had a lot of papers to grade tonight, and when that was the case, he usually ate at home. That was the bad thing about being an English teacher, he had told her several times. English teachers always had more papers to deal with than teachers in other subjects.

For a moment Wanda Nell enjoyed thinking about her and Jack together, him grading papers and her reading a book. Just being able to be together, even if they were doing different things, would be wonderful.

Around nine business began slowing down, and Wanda

Nell had a few minutes to take a break. She called Tuck on his cell phone, and he answered on the second ring.

"Tuck, it's me," she said.

"What's up?" he asked.

"I don't have very long, but I've got some things to tell you," she said. As succinctly as possible, she recounted the conversations she had had with Tiffany Farwell, Bill Warren, and Mayrene.

Tuck didn't interrupt her. When she was done, he said, "Now at least we have clearer motives for someone beside Gerald to kill Travis. Not to mention some other lines of inquiry that occur to me."

"Good," Wanda Nell said. "Before I forget, did Lisa ever call you, or come by?"

"No, neither one," Tuck said. "Frankly I find that a bit strange."

Wanda Nell didn't want to get into any explanations for Lisa's behavior, not until she had talked to Jack first. "Look, I've got to get back to work. I'll talk to you tomorrow."

"Thanks for your help, Wanda Nell," Tuck said before ringing off.

The last customer was gone by nine-forty-five, and by then Wanda Nell and Ruby had finished their side work. Melvin let them leave early, but Wanda Nell stayed long enough to make herself a sandwich to eat on the way to Budget Mart. She needed an energy boost for her overnight shift, and she wouldn't be able to take a break for a snack until around two a.m.

As she restocked shelves that night, Wanda Nell found her mind flitting back and forth between the murder and the problem of Lisa. She went over and over different ways of breaking the news to Jack, but none of them seemed quite right. Then she would start thinking about the murder, wondering how they would ever figure out who was really guilty. Maybe it was Gerald Blakeley, after all, and they were just spinning their wheels trying to prove someone else had done it.

Wanda Nell had to ask herself whether she would have made such an effort on Gerald's behalf if Bill Warren hadn't been involved in the case. Bill had turned out to be such a colossal jerk, and he had made her so mad, she was bound to act contrary in response. She hated to think Bill was right, that Gerald really was the murderer.

By the time her shift ended at six a.m., Wanda Nell was worn out mentally and physically. All she could think about was getting home and climbing into bed. After checking on Juliet first, of course. She hadn't forgotten about her daughter during all that back-and-forth musing on murder and fraud.

Everything was quiet at home when she let herself into the trailer. She dropped her purse on the counter in the kitchen before heading back to Juliet's room.

Juliet was sound asleep, and Wanda Nell gently placed a hand against her forehead. To her relief, it was cool and dry. As she pulled her hand away, one of Juliet's eyes opened, quickly followed by the other one. Yawning, Juliet pushed herself up into a sitting position.

"Good morning, Mama," she said. "Did you just get home?"

"Yes," Wanda Nell said. "I'm sorry, honey, I didn't mean to wake you up. You go back to sleep."

Juliet shook her head. "No, I've had enough sleep, I think. I feel a lot better. My throat isn't hurting much at all this morning." She reached for the pitcher of water on her bedside table. Wanda Nell took it from her and poured water into her glass for her.

"Thank you," Juliet said. She drained the glass and set it back on the table. "Can I go back to school today, Mama? I really do feel a lot better."

Wanda Nell frowned. Juliet was such an eager student, this wouldn't be the first time she had overestimated how well she was because she wanted to be at school.

"I'm not sure, honey," Wanda Nell said. "I think you need to stay home another day, just to be safe. You need to keep taking those pills the doctor gave you, too."

Juliet's face fell. "Okay, Mama, if that's what you think."

"I know you're probably getting really bored here at home," Wanda Nell said. "But I want to make sure you're really over this before you get back. I promise you, though, if you feel good tomorrow, you can go to school then. Okay?"

"Okay," Juliet said with a smile. "I'm going to have some breakfast, I think. Are you hungry?" She pushed the covers aside and got out of her bed, stretching.

"A little bit," Wanda Nell said, "but mostly I'm tired, so I think I'll wait till later to have something to eat."

Juliet nodded. She followed her mother out the door, but she paused to use the bathroom before going to the kitchen.

Wanda Nell changed into a nightgown and was about to climb into bed when the phone rang. She answered it, sitting down on the bed as she did so. "Hello."

"Morning, love," Jack said. "Did I catch you before you got in bed?"

"You just barely did," she said. "Good morning, honey. How are you?"

"I'm fine," he said. "I bet you're pretty tired."

"Yeah," she said, trying to suppress a yawn but failing. "Sorry."

"That's okay."

"And I bet you were at home grading papers last night, weren't you?" Wanda Nell asked.

"For a while, anyway," Jack said. "But then Lisa called me and wanted to come over and talk to me. By the time she left it was pretty late, and I was too tired to finish grading. I guess I'll just have to do it during my free period this afternoon."

"Was Lisa okay?" Wanda Nell didn't want to think about Lisa just now, but she couldn't ignore the subject.

"About the same," Jack said with a heavy sigh. "It was the same stuff, all over again. I did my best to keep her calm, but she just kept talking about how she was going to have to move to Alaska to get away from this guy."

"Oh dear," Wanda Nell said. She was going to have to tell him what was really going on, and soon. But this wasn't the right time to do it. "I'm sorry, honey. I know that wore you out."

"Yeah," Jack said, "but I feel so sorry for her. And I feel helpless, too. There doesn't seem to be much I can do for her."

"Well, I've got some ideas about that," Wanda Nell said. "We'll talk about it later, okay? And in the meantime, don't let it get you down."

"I'll try." Jack laughed, and Wanda Nell hated to hear the sound of defeat in his laughter. "You better get to bed and get some rest. I'll come by the Kountry Kitchen tonight."

"Good," Wanda Nell said. "I want to see you."

"And I want to see you," he replied. "Love you."

"Love you, too." They said good-bye, and Wanda Nell hung up the phone. She sat for a moment, staring at her ring. She still couldn't quite believe she was engaged now. But the ring was beautiful proof that she was. She smiled.

Once more she was about to get into bed, but she remembered something. She had better go remind Juliet to take her medicine this morning, and she really ought to check in on Lavon and Miranda. Lavon might be awake and need changing, plus Miranda had a shift at Budget Mart this morning.

Sighing, she left her bedroom. In the kitchen, Juliet was eating cereal. "Don't forget to take a dose of your medicine, honey," she told her daughter.

"Already did," Juliet said.

"Good," Wanda Nell said. "I'm going to make sure Miranda is up. She's got to work today, and she needs to get Lavon ready to drop off at day care."

"I think I heard her stirring around a few minutes ago," Juliet said.

Wanda Nell nodded. She walked down the hallway toward Miranda's bedroom. Sounds of retching coming from the bathroom halted her. Pushing open the bathroom door, she found Miranda down on her knees, clutching her stomach, and holding her head over the toilet.

All at once, Wanda Nell realized what was going on.

"Oh Lord, Miranda," she said, her heart sinking. "You're pregnant, aren't you?"

Twenty

Wanda Nell felt like she wanted to start throwing up, too. What would they do with another baby to take care of?

Miranda stared at her mother. When Wanda Nell stepped forward, Miranda drew back as if she expected her mother to strike her.

Instead, Wanda Nell reached for a washcloth, soaked it under the cold water tap, wrung it out, and knelt down to wipe Miranda's face. Miranda held still while her mother cleaned around her mouth and bathed her forehead.

"Are you pregnant?" Wanda Nell got up to rinse out the washcloth.

"I think so," Miranda said, her voice faint. Wanda Nell had to strain to hear her above the running water.

"Why did you lie to me the other day, then?" Wanda Nell asked. "You told me you had an upset stomach." She wrung out the washcloth again and handed it to her daughter.

Miranda got up from her knees and perched on the edge of the bathtub. She wiped her face again before answering.

"I was afraid to tell you," Miranda said. She looked down at her feet. The washcloth dangled from her hands.

Once the initial shock wore off, Wanda Nell found she was actually pretty calm. They would simply have to deal with the situation and move forward.

"There's no point in trying to hide things like this, honey," Wanda Nell said. "I was going to find out eventually."

"I know, Mama," Miranda said. Her eyes welled with tears. "But you were so happy because Jack asked you to marry him and everything, and I didn't want to tell you and make you mad."

"I'm not mad at you," Wanda Nell said, and it was true. She was disappointed, but not angry. Getting angry with Miranda wouldn't help the situation any. She put the lid of the toilet down and sat on it. Her knees touched Miranda's.

Miranda scrunched closer to her mother and laid her head in Wanda Nell's lap, wrapping her arms around her mother's waist. Wanda Nell stroked her hair while Miranda cried.

When the burst of sobbing stopped, Wanda Nell pulled Miranda back up into a sitting position. She took the wadded-up washcloth from her daughter's hand and wiped her face with it.

"We need to talk, Miranda," Wanda Nell said, softly but firmly. "No point in any more crying, okay?"

Miranda nodded.

"First thing," Wanda Nell said. "How sure are you?"

"Pretty sure," Miranda said.

"Okay, second thing. Does Teddy know?"

"No, ma'am."

"Then you need to tell him, and right away," Wanda Nell said, her tone even more firm.

"But, what if he . . ." Miranda's voice trailed off, and the tears flowed again.

"What if he walks away, you mean, and doesn't want to

have anything more to do with you or the baby?" Wanda Nell sighed. "If he does that, then we'll just cope with the situation, honey. We don't have any choice."

"But I love him, Mama," Miranda wailed.

"I know you do, and he loves you, too," Wanda Nell said. "I don't think he's the kind of man who would walk away and leave you and your baby. You have to tell him, because it may take him a little while to get used to the idea, though."

"He told me he wanted us to get married," Miranda said, sniffling every few words, "but he wanted to wait until he had saved up enough money so we could get us our own house, or maybe a trailer."

"How long did he think that was going to take?" Wanda Nell wasn't sure she wanted to hear the answer.

Miranda hung her head, and her reply was barely audible. "Another year or two."

"Well, we'll just have to wait till you tell him, and go from there," Wanda Nell said. She got up and held out a hand to Miranda. Her daughter stood and wrapped her arms around her. Wanda Nell hugged her back. She felt sorry for Miranda because she knew the girl was upset and afraid.

"Do you think you can get ready for work?" Wanda Nell said. "Is your stomach settling down now?" If she didn't get Miranda to go to work, the girl would just sit around moping at home all day.

"I think so," Miranda replied. She glanced at the clock mounted on the wall over the toilet. "But I'm going to be late. I need to clean up, and I haven't got Lavon ready yet either." She gave her mother a hopeful look.

"You get yourself ready, and I'll take care of Lavon," Wanda Nell said, suppressing a sigh. The girl was too transparent, but she knew her mother would help. "You'll make it on time."

Twenty minutes later, feeling like she was going to drop from fatigue, Wanda Nell stood in the doorway, watching as Miranda drove off to work. Lavon was strapped into his car seat in the back, and Wanda Nell could see him bouncing up and down.

Wanda Nell shut and locked the door behind her. She leaned against it for a moment, her eyes closed. She pushed away from the door and walked down the hall to her bedroom.

Juliet had gone back to her room and was using the computer, checking e-mail or whatever else it was she did on the darned thing. Wanda Nell was glad she was occupied with something, because she wasn't ready to tell Juliet the news that she was going to be an aunt again.

After setting her alarm and placing her ring on the nightstand, Wanda Nell climbed into bed and pulled the covers around her. She closed her eyes and willed sleep to come. She didn't want to think about Miranda or the murder or Lisa or anything. She just wanted to sleep.

Sleep wouldn't come, though, and she felt like hitting herself on the head with a hammer to knock herself out. She was desperate for rest, but all she could think about was Miranda being pregnant again.

What were they going to do? She didn't want another person to have to take care of. Maybe that was selfish, but she couldn't help it. She would have to tell Jack right away. All she could think about was how this pregnancy might make her have to postpone her own wedding. Jack might be pretty upset over that, and she couldn't really blame him.

What if Teddy decided he didn't want to be a father? Miranda would be heartbroken if he dumped her, and Lavon would miss him, too. In her heart of hearts, Wanda Nell believed that Teddy wouldn't behave like that. If he did, well, it wouldn't be the first time a man had let her or Miranda down.

Would Teddy want to go ahead and marry Miranda right away? That might be the best thing, but Wanda Nell wasn't sure Miranda was really ready to be a wife. Getting married with a baby on the way could put a big strain on a marriage. Wanda Nell knew that much from her own experience.

But if Miranda and Teddy get married, said a little voice in her head, *then someone else will have to take care of her. You won't have to anymore.*

Wanda Nell felt ashamed at wanting to shift the burden onto someone else. *You can't still be taking care of Miranda when she's forty years old*, said that same voice. *She's eighteen, and it's time she was someone else's responsibility if she's not going to look after herself.*

"Oh hush," Wanda Nell said. She turned over in bed and tried to get comfortable. All this worrying about what might happen would drive her crazy if she let it. She would take one step at a time, and whatever would be, would be.

At times like this Wanda Nell really missed her own mother. Her mama had always been so calm and so strong, no matter what happened. She knew how her mama felt when she broke the news of her own pregnancy nearly twenty-four years ago. Mama had never said a bad word to her, though. She had coped, and that was what Wanda Nell would do. No matter what, she would cope. There were no easy answers, whichever way she looked.

Comforted by thoughts of her mother, Wanda Nell at last was able to drift off to sleep.

She slept soundly until her alarm roused her at four-thirty. Yawning, she sat up and fumbled for the alarm. Once the insistent beeping ended, she sat on the side of the bed for a moment, trying to wake up. She felt better for the sound sleep, but she decided she sure would like to go to bed for another couple of hours.

She stood up and stretched. She felt a little stiff, but a hot shower would soon limber her up.

By five o'clock she had showered, done her makeup and hair, and dressed, not forgetting her engagement ring. She picked it up, still amazed by the fact of it. She slid it on her finger and smiled.

Now that she had rested, she felt less pessimistic about Miranda's situation. For once, she decided, she was going to believe things would work out in a good way. Her engagement ring would be her good luck charm.

Juliet was in the living room watching TV. She turned the volume down when her mother entered the room. "Did you sleep well, Mama?"

"I did," Wanda Nell said. "How are you feeling, sweetie?"

"Just fine," Juliet said. "I'm sure I'll feel like going back to school tomorrow."

"Okay," Wanda Nell said, smiling. "You're probably right, but I still want to be sure before you do go back."

"Yes, ma'am," Juliet said. "I'm going to call Jennalee in a little while to find out about homework and stuff. I promise I won't talk too long."

"That's fine, sweetie. I think I'm going to have a little something to eat," Wanda Nell said. "Miranda ought to be home soon, or at least she had better be. I don't want to be late to work."

While Wanda Nell was making herself a ham sandwich, she heard a car pull up outside. Peering out the window over the sink, she saw her little red Cavalier in its parking space. Miranda got out of the car and opened the back door. She freed Lavon from his car seat and set him on the ground. He immediately headed for the steps up to the door of the trailer. They were shallow enough that he could easily climb up them.

Miranda grabbed her purse from the car, along with Lavon's bag, and she caught up with him before he reached the top step. She waited until he was patting his hand on the door—his way of knocking—before she gently pulled him back. Then she opened the door, and he clambered inside with his mother close behind.

Wanda Nell brought her sandwich and a can of Diet Coke with her into the living room. She greeted Miranda and Lavon, who ran over and grabbed one of her legs and hugged it tight.

Miranda dropped her purse and Lavon's bag on the couch by Juliet. She pulled Lavon loose from his grandmother's leg and picked him up. He laughed and chattered. Wanda Nell leaned over and kissed him, and he laughed some more. He really was a happy baby, and Wanda Nell was very thankful.

"How was everything at work?" Wanda Nell asked.

"Just fine," Miranda said. She avoided her mother's eye.

"I'm going to finish this," Wanda Nell said, brandishing her sandwich. "Then I'd better get on to work. Don't forget about talking to Teddy."

"I won't forget, Mama," Miranda said. She still wouldn't look her mother in the face.

"Good," Wanda Nell said. "Keep an eye on your sister. I think she's pretty much over her sore throat, but make sure she takes her medicine."

"I will. Bye, Mama," Miranda said, following her mother to the door. Wanda Nell heard the lock click behind her.

She had put the car in gear and was about to back out of her parking space when her cell phone started ringing.

Frowning, she put the car back in park and reached for her phone.

She didn't recognize the number. She punched the button and stuck the phone to her ear. "Hello."

"Wanda Nell, is that you?" A woman's voice, sounding a bit harried, spoke in her ear.

"Yes, it is," Wanda Nell said. She thought she recognized the voice. "Is that you, Luann?"

"Yep, it is," her coworker at Budget Mart said. "I'm so glad I caught you. Listen, I need to ask you a favor."

"Sure, go ahead," Wanda Nell said.

"Can you swap shifts with me tonight? I can work for you tonight if you'll work for me tomorrow night. See, the thing is, my mama is having surgery over in Greenwood tomorrow, and I want to be able to stay at the hospital tomorrow night with her. Mr. Higgins said it was okay with him as long as it was okay with you."

"Sure, Luann," Wanda Nell said. "I'll be glad to swap with you. I'm sorry about your mama, though. Is it something serious?" Luann was several years older than she was, and Wanda Nell figured Luann's mother had to be in her seventies.

"It's a hip replacement," Luann said. "The doctor says she'll be just fine, but I want to be there in case she needs anything. You know how it is."

"I sure do," Wanda Nell said, recalling the times she had spent in the hospital with her own mother. "You don't worry about a thing. It's not a problem at all."

"Thanks, Wanda Nell, I'll owe you one," Luann said. "Bye."

Wanda Nell ended the call and dropped the phone back into her purse. Once again she put the car in gear and headed out.

Not having to go to Budget Mart tonight was an unexpected bonus. Maybe if they weren't too busy at the Kountry Kitchen tonight, she could leave there a little early. She knew Mayrene was dying to hear more about Bill Warren, and this would be a good time for them to talk. She also wanted to get Mayrene's advice on talking to Jack about Lisa. Her stomach started knotting up every time she thought about that, but she knew she'd have to face up to it, and soon.

Business was slow at the restaurant when she arrived, but it started picking up around six-thirty. For once, Wanda Nell was hoping Jack wouldn't come by for dinner. She didn't think she could face him without telling him about his cousin, and she wasn't quite ready to do that. He knew her so well by now, he would realize something was bothering her, and she hated not confiding in him.

To her relief, he didn't come. He did call, however, and they spoke briefly. He had a lot of papers to grade, and he was keeping an eye on Lisa. She had decided not to stay at Mayrene's any longer, so Jack was letting her stay with him. Wanda Nell didn't say anything, and thankfully Jack didn't notice her silence on the subject.

T.J. and Tuck turned up around seven, and Wanda Nell was glad to see them. She showed them to a table in the back room, and she decided she had time to sit down for a minute with them.

"I'll get you something to drink in a minute," she said. "First, any news?"

"Not a lot," Tuck said. "We did talk to Elmer Lee, and I also passed along the information you gave me from Mayrene."

"What did he say?" Wanda Nell asked.

"Not much," T.J. replied. "He's interested, but you know

how the sheriff is." He grinned. "He doesn't like anybody knowing what he's really up to."

Wanda Nell sighed. "Yeah, I know. We'll just have to trust him to do what's right."

"I'm sure he will," Tuck said. "He really is a good guy, you know."

"As much as I hate to admit it, you're right." Wanda Nell laughed. "But don't you dare tell him I said that."

"I won't," Tuck promised. "Can you come by the office some time tomorrow morning?"

"Yeah," Wanda Nell said. "What time?"

"How about nine? Is that too early?"

"No, it's fine," Wanda Nell said. "I'll take Miranda to work and drop Lavon off at day care, and then I'll be by your office."

"Good," Tuck said. "I want you to take a look at that list of men who were at the party. I want to be sure we're covering every angle we can."

"Sounds like a good idea to me," Wanda Nell said. She stood up. "Okay, boys, what will it be? Can I interest you in something fried, with lots of gravy?" She grinned.

T.J. made a point of shuddering. "Now, Mama, you know we can't eat that kind of stuff and not be as big as the side of a barn."

"Speak for yourself," Tuck said, poking a finger in T.J.'s side. "Just because you don't like to get up in the morning and work out as much as I do, don't blame your mother."

T.J. rolled his eyes at his mother, as if to say, "See what I have to put up with?"

Wanda Nell sometimes still had odd feelings, thinking of the two of them as a couple. But when she saw the way they looked at each other, she realized it didn't matter.

"Okay, Tuck, you're doing the big talking," she said. "Does that mean you want chicken-fried steak?"

Tuck laughed. "I do, but I know if I order it, T.J. will rub it in for a week. No, I'll have a steak, medium well, with baked potato, green beans, and salad."

"Me too, Mama," T.J. said.

"Next time I'm not even going to ask," Wanda Nell said, shaking her head. "I'll be back in a minute with some tea and water."

After that, Wanda Nell didn't have much time to chat. She and Ruby stayed pretty busy until around eight-thirty, when business really slacked off. By nine, the restaurant was empty except for the staff.

"Go home," Melvin said to her and Ruby. "It's going to be dead until ten, and there's no sense in you hanging around."

"Good," Wanda Nell said. "I can use the break, since I don't have to go to Budget Mart tonight."

"Thank you, Melvin," Ruby said. "I've got a big test in the morning, and I can use the study time." Ruby was taking courses at the community college, and she took her studies very seriously.

"The side work's done," Wanda Nell said, "so everything is set for the morning crew."

Fifteen minutes later, she was pulling her car into its covered space beside her trailer. Mayrene's lights were on, and Wanda Nell was glad to see them. Mayrene might very well have had a date with her cop tonight, but Wanda Nell really wanted to talk to her.

She knocked on Mayrene's door, and Mayrene answered it right away. "Hey, girl, what are you doing home? Is Juliet sick again?"

"No, she's fine, far as I know," Wanda Nell said. "Melvin let us go early, and I swapped nights with one of my coworkers, so I don't have to go in tonight."

"Well, come on in then, and let's talk," Mayrene said.

"I was hoping you'd say that," Wanda Nell said, "but let me just pop my head in at home and make sure everybody's okay."

"Sure, just come on back when you're ready," Mayrene said. "I'll leave the door unlocked."

Wanda Nell crossed over to her trailer and unlocked the door. Juliet, Miranda, and Lavon were watching TV. She explained why she was home early, and after finding out they were fine, she told them she would be over at Mayrene's for a little while.

"Okay, Mama," Miranda said. "I'm going to put Lavon to bed in a few minutes."

"Good," Wanda Nell said. "And if you're still up, maybe we can talk for a few minutes?"

Miranda nodded, though she didn't look too happy at the prospect. From that Wanda Nell figured Miranda hadn't talked to Teddy yet. She would deal with that later.

"You better go to bed soon, too, honey," she told Juliet.

"I will," Juliet said. "I'm fine, Mama."

Wanda Nell left them and went back to Mayrene's. She opened the door and went in. Mayrene was in the kitchen.

"You want something to drink, honey?" she called.

"Maybe just some water," Wanda Nell said, walking into the kitchen.

"Here you go," Mayrene said, handing her a glass. "But I would have brought it to you."

"I know," Wanda Nell said, "but I was coming this way anyway." She grinned. "You want to talk in here?"

"No, let's go back in the living room," Mayrene said. "I

want to sit back and stretch out my legs. I was on my feet every minute today at work."

Wanda Nell headed for Mayrene's couch. There was a newspaper in her favorite spot. She picked it up, holding it while she sat down and got comfortable.

Mayrene plopped down in her recliner and pulled the lever to bring her feet up. "That's better," she sighed. She squirmed for a moment in the chair. "This is worth every penny I paid for it."

Wanda Nell was about to drop the newspaper on the coffee table when Mayrene spoke again.

"I was going to show that to you," she said, indicating the paper.

"Why?" Wanda Nell asked. "Is there something about the murder in here?"

"There is," Mayrene said, "but that's not why. I wanted you to see a picture in it. You remember I told you about my friend Teresa, and how we saw her boss at that casino in Tunica? With some woman besides his wife?"

"Yeah," Wanda Nell said. "Is his picture in here?"

"It sure is, right on the front page," Mayrene said. "And just look at him, standing there with his wife, like he ain't never cheated on her." She shook her head. "I tell you, some men ought to be turned into steers after they get married."

Laughing, Wanda Nell held the paper closer to the lamp on the end table beside her. The light shone down on a couple who smiled in strained fashion into the camera.

With a shock, Wanda Nell realized she recognized the man, though his name wasn't familiar to her.

He had been at the bachelor party. He was the bald-headed man who had been talking to Gerald Blakeley just before Travis collapsed and died.

Twenty-one

Wanda Nell read the caption beneath the picture. "Mr. and Mrs. Barnard Roberts at the opening reception for the Tullahoma Family Center, which they have generously helped fund."

"So he owns a factory?" Wanda Nell said. "What do they make?"

"I don't know," Mayrene admitted. "It's one of those plants out in the industrial park. That's all I know."

"He was at the bachelor party," Wanda Nell said.

"Really?"

"Yeah, I saw him talking to Gerald Blakeley."

"Guess he must be a friend of the family, then," Mayrene said.

"I guess so," Wanda Nell said. She kept staring at Barnard Roberts' face. Another memory surfaced. He was also the man she saw in the hall of the courthouse building coming out of Bill Warren's office. But he hadn't been wearing an expensive suit then. He was dressed in coveralls. That seemed odd. Was it supposed to be some kind of disguise?

What kind of business could he have had with Bill Warren? Maybe Bill has asked him to come in and make a statement about the night of the murder. That was only natural.

But why would a rich businessman show up dressed in coveralls? Unless he was just really eccentric and went around dressed like that, but somehow Wanda Nell doubted that was the reason. He was sure dressed up in the picture in the paper.

The coincidence niggled at her. She would talk it over with Tuck tomorrow when she went to his office.

"Pretty funny," Mayrene said, "him giving money to help fund a family center, and there he was, hands all over some floozy at the casino."

"Sounds like a real nice guy," Wanda Nell said. "Thank the Lord for men like Jack."

"Amen to that, honey," Mayrene said, "and I'm hoping like Mr. Dixon Vance, too."

"For your sake, I hope so, too."

"Enough about all that," Mayrene said. "I want to hear all about this Bill Warren guy."

"It's going to take a while," Wanda Nell said.

"I got the time," Mayrene said. "So shoot."

"It all started at the bachelor party," Wanda Nell said. "Or really, afterwards, when they were starting the investigation." She described Bill Warren's arrival, and from there went on to tell Mayrene all that had happened since. Mayrene occasionally muttered a word like *jerk* or *slimeball*, but otherwise she let Wanda Nell talk.

By the time Wanda Nell finished it was nearly eleven o'clock. She was surprised when she saw the time. She wasn't too tired, but she figured Mayrene must be getting sleepy by now.

"He sure is some kind of jerk," Mayrene said. "I'd like

to hear him say some of that crap to me. You should've slapped him a lot more than you did, honey."

"Believe me, I sure felt like it," Wanda Nell said. "I don't know when I've been so angry. And he was so cold-blooded about it, too. How he can play with somebody's life like that is beyond me."

"He better not try to do anything to T.J. or Tuck," Mayrene said, "or I'll fix his little red wagon for him. Me and Old Reliable."

Mayrene's shotgun had been persuasive on more than one occasion when Wanda Nell needed backup. She didn't doubt for a minute that Mayrene meant what she said. The expression on her friend's face actually made her a little uneasy. If Bill crossed Mayrene's path anytime soon, he would surely regret it.

"What I can't quite work out," Wanda Nell said, "is exactly how he's connected to this business, other than investigating. I just know something else is going on here, but I can't put my finger on it."

"You think Mr. Factory Man there," Mayrene said, pointing at the newspaper on the coffee table, "is involved?"

"I'm not sure," Wanda Nell said. "I mean, he was at the party, and then I saw him again at the courthouse when I went to see Bill. He came out of Bill's office, but maybe he was just there to make a statement. I can't figure out how he's connected, other than that."

"If he is, you'll find out somehow," Mayrene said, "and when you do, I hope that nasty Bill Warren lands deep in the doodoo where he belongs."

"I still can't believe how Bill is acting," Wanda Nell said. "He was such a nice boy in high school."

"Well, if the boys are right about him," Mayrene said,

"he's real mixed up. I can't imagine hating myself that much, twisting myself into that kind of a knot." She shook her head. "Why can't he just accept who he is?"

"I don't know," Wanda Nell said. "What makes me really sad is to think about T.J. and what he must have been going through all those years. And I never knew. Maybe I could have helped him if he'd've talked to me."

"Don't be blaming yourself," Mayrene said, her tone sharp. "You did everything you could for that boy, and you never stopped loving him. He knows that, don't you think for a minute he don't. He just had to work it out for himself, honey, and thank the Lord he did. Otherwise he could've turned into somebody like Bill Warren."

"You know, I actually feel sorry for him," Wanda Nell said, surprising herself. "I really do. I mean, I'd like to take a baseball bat and beat the crap out of him for what he's tried to do. But at the same time, can you imagine how miserable he is?"

"You got a lot more compassion for him than I would in your place," Mayrene said. "I'm not sure he deserves it, frankly."

Wanda Nell shrugged. "I don't imagine he'd be too happy if he knew I felt sorry for him."

"No, he wouldn't," Mayrene said. "It'd just make him act like more of a bastard."

"Maybe it will all be over soon," Wanda Nell said. "I sure hope so. I've got too many other problems to think about."

"Like Lisa, you mean?" Mayrene said.

"Well, there's that," Wanda Nell said, hesitating. She had to confide in someone and share her frustrations. "There's Miranda, too. I found her throwing up in the bathroom twice in the last few days. This morning I finally figured it out."

"She's pregnant," Mayrene said in a flat tone. "I swear, sometimes I'd like to jerk a knot in that girl's tail."

"I know," Wanda Nell said. "Believe me, I've been tempted to do it many a time myself. But there's no point in getting angry about it."

"Are you sure she's pregnant?"

"She's pretty sure," Wanda Nell said. "And the way Miranda's life seems to go, well, I don't doubt it for a minute."

"She hasn't told Teddy yet, has she?"

"I don't think so," Wanda Nell said. "I told her she needed to talk to him right away, but you know how she is. She always tries to put things off."

"Well, she damn sure can't this time," Mayrene said. "How far along is she, do you think?"

"I'm not sure," Wanda Nell said. "Probably not more than a month or six weeks."

"How do you think Teddy's going to take it?"

"Who knows?" Wanda Nell said. "He seems like a very mature, responsible young man. And I know he wants to marry Miranda. They've already talked about it. But he told Miranda he wouldn't be ready to get married for another year or two. He wants to save up enough money for them to get a house or their own trailer."

"Smart boy," Mayrene said. "He's got his head on straight."

"I think so," Wanda Nell replied. "But with something like this, who knows? He may feel like Miranda's trying to force him into getting married right now."

"You think she got pregnant on purpose?"

"I hate to say this about my own daughter," Wanda Nell

said, wincing as she spoke, "but I wouldn't put it past her. She has this crazy way of looking at things sometimes, and I know she's really crazy about Teddy. So . . ." She threw her hands up.

"Yeah, I know," Mayrene said. "I'm sorry, honey. I know this is the last thing you need right now. Have you had a chance to talk to Jack about it?"

"No, not yet," Wanda Nell said. "And I can't imagine what he's going to say. If I have to help Miranda raise this baby, I wouldn't blame him if he asked for his ring back." She stared at her left hand. "I just can't turn my back on my daughter because I want to get married."

"No, I know you. You can't, and you won't," Mayrene said. "That girl doesn't know how lucky she is. A lot of mamas would have put her hiney out by now." She shook her head. "But don't underestimate Jack, Wanda Nell. He's a good man, and I don't think he's going to stop loving you or wanting to marry you because of this."

"I know," Wanda Nell admitted. "Deep down I know that. I guess I'm just feeling selfish. It took me a long time to admit I really loved him and wanted to be married again. And when I finally say yes, look what happens."

"Don't let all this get you down," Mayrene said in bracing tones. "You've got a lot of people on your side, and I know things will turn out okay."

"If you say so," Wanda Nell said with a wan smile. She pushed herself off the couch. "I better go and let you get to bed. Plus I need to talk to Miranda before it gets too late."

Mayrene got up and walked with Wanda Nell to the door. She gave her friend a fierce hug. "Don't worry."

"I'll try," Wanda Nell said. "Good night."

"Night, honey," Mayrene said.

Wanda Nell stood outside for a moment, gazing at the

sky. The night was cool and clear. Beyond the glow of lights from the trailer park, she could make out the stars. She stared at them until her neck started to ache. With a sigh she climbed the steps to her trailer and let herself in.

Everything was quiet inside. She moved softly down the hall to Miranda's room. Pushing the door open, she found both Miranda and Lavon sound asleep.

She didn't have the heart to wake Miranda. She would let her sleep, and they would talk in the morning. She might have to give Miranda an ultimatum, or just invite Teddy over herself so he and Miranda could talk. She didn't like being high-handed like that, but with Miranda, that was the only way sometimes.

At the other end of the trailer, she checked on Juliet. Her youngest child was also sound asleep. She looked so young and so innocent, lying there. Wanda Nell said a quick prayer of thanks for her sweet baby who never gave her a moment's trouble.

In her bedroom she found a note in Juliet's handwriting on her bedside table. "Jack called," she read, "and he wants you to call him no matter how late it is."

Wanda Nell's stomach did a couple of flip-flops. For some reason, this alarmed her. Jack was normally in bed by ten-thirty, and here it was, just past eleven-thirty.

She sat down on the bed and picked up the phone. Her hand trembled as she punched in the number.

The phone rang four times before Jack answered. "Hello," he said, and in those two syllables Wanda Nell heard a note that scared her.

"Honey, it's me," she said, trying to keep her voice steady. "Is everything okay?"

"No, it's not," Jack said. "My god, Wanda Nell, what am I going to do with Lisa?"

"What happened?"

"About three hours ago, I found her passed out on the floor of her room," Jack said. "And there was an empty pill bottle beside her."

"Oh my Lord," Wanda Nell said. "She tried to kill herself?"

"Yeah," Jack said. "I called for an ambulance, and they got here pretty quickly. They took her in, and I followed." He paused, and Wanda Nell could tell he was trying hard to hold it together. "They got her into the emergency room and pumped her stomach. The doctor said she would be okay, but they're going to keep her in the hospital for a few days. After that, I'm not sure what we're going to do."

"Oh honey, I'm so sorry," Wanda Nell said. "Why didn't you call me to come with you?"

"It all happened so fast," Jack said, "and I knew you were still at work. Besides, there wasn't really anything you could do. She was in good hands." He sighed. "I got home about ten-fifteen and called you. Juliet said you were next door talking to Mayrene, but I told her not to bother you."

"Lord, Jack, you should have had her *bother* me," Wanda Nell said. "Now, listen, I'm coming over there. I'll be there in about ten minutes, you hear?"

"It's too late," Jack said. "I'll be okay. You need your rest."

"You think I can go to sleep after hearing this?" Wanda Nell said. "I'm too worried about you. No, I'm coming over there. You just sit tight."

She didn't give him time to argue. She hung up the phone and almost ran down the hall to the kitchen to grab her purse and keys. The girls and Lavon would be fine for a little while without her. Once she was on her way, she pulled out her cell phone and called Mayrene.

"Honey, what's up? Where are you?" Mayrene said, recognizing the number.

Wanda Nell explained, her voice terse.

"Oh good Lord," Mayrene said. "That girl is seriously nuts. Are you going to tell him what we suspect?"

"I may have to," Wanda Nell said. "I could just about wring that girl's neck for what she's doing to him. All I care about is seeing that he's okay."

"Call me if you need me," Mayrene said. "And don't worry about the girls and the baby."

"Thanks, honey," Wanda Nell said. She ended the call and dropped the phone in her purse.

If she had crossed paths with a policeman on that short, wild ride, Wanda Nell had no doubt she would have gotten a lulu of a speeding ticket. But luck was with her. She made it to Jack's house in record time.

He was waiting at the front door when she pulled her car into his driveway. She grabbed her purse, stuffed her keys into them, and barely remembered to lock her car. She ran up the walk to Jack, who met her halfway. He wrapped his arms around her and whispered, "Thank you for coming, love."

Wanda Nell hugged him. "Come on inside," she said. "We don't want to give your neighbors a show." She tried to make a joke of it, and she was gratified to see Jack smile a little.

She led him back into the house, and they went into his living room. He sat down on the couch, and she sat down facing him, only a couple of inches between them.

For a moment they simply sat and looked at each other. Wanda Nell took Jack's hands in hers and held them. He smiled faintly before leaning forward to kiss her. Several minutes passed before he leaned back, his smile radiant this time.

"Thank God for you," he said.

"Honey, I'm so sorry about all this," Wanda Nell said. Her pulse was still racing, and her heart was having trouble slowing down to a normal rate. "This whole situation is so awful."

"Yeah, it is," Jack said. He closed his eyes for a moment. "And I just don't know what set this off. I know she was upset, but I didn't think she was suicidal. We'd actually had a quiet night up to that point."

"What were y'all doing before this all happened?"

"We talked about the wedding for a while," Jack said, giving her a sheepish look. "I know I should have waited to talk to you about all this, but I just couldn't help it. So I was talking to Lisa about things, and everything seemed okay."

"Then what happened?" Wanda Nell said. What Jack had just told her confirmed her worst suspicions about Lisa and her problem.

"Then Lisa said she was tired and was going to get ready for bed," Jack said. He shook his head. "I'm not sure why I went to check on her, but thank the Lord I did. That's when I found her." He shuddered. "I'll never forget the sight of her, lying on the floor like that."

"Oh honey," Wanda Nell said. "I'm so sorry she's put you through this."

"She can't help herself, I guess," Jack said, his tone becoming slightly defensive. "She's so terrified of what this guy might do to her, she's just not herself."

When Wanda Nell didn't say anything for a moment, Jack looked at her oddly. "What is it?" he said. "What is it you're not telling me?"

He really did know her, Wanda Nell thought. He could

tell she was holding something back. She couldn't put it off any longer. She had to tell him.

"It's about Lisa," she said. "There are some things I think you should know."

"Like what?" Jack sat back, his arms crossed over his chest.

Wanda Nell took a deep breath. "I don't think she's really being stalked by anybody. I think she's making all this up because she wants your attention."

She waited for an explosion, but Jack sat there, a stunned expression on his face. Why wouldn't he say anything?

Twenty-two

"Jack, honey, say something. Please." The longer Jack went without responding, the more uneasy Wanda Nell grew.

"Tell me why you think she's making all this up," he finally said. He uncrossed his arms and lowered them.

At least he wasn't telling her *she* was crazy, Wanda Nell thought with relief. She exhaled a shaky breath.

"There's a few things," she said. "First, you remember Dixon Vance? Mayrene's cop friend."

Jack nodded.

"Well, he did some checking with the Meridian police, and told Mayrene what he found out, and she told me," Wanda Nell said. "And I've been waiting for the right moment to tell you."

"Okay," Jack said. "What did he find out?"

"According to him, the Meridian police don't have any record of Lisa making a complaint against somebody stalking her," Wanda Nell said. "And you remember how she gave us a name? Lester Biggs, she said his name was."

"Right," Jack said, nodding.

"The Meridian police say there's no cop by that name

on their force, and there hasn't ever been," Wanda Nell said. She paused, watching for Jack's reaction.

His expression softened, to her relief. "Go on," he said. "What else?"

"The other night, when you asked me to marry you," Wanda Nell said, "you remember Lisa came over and said this guy had called her at Mayrene's?"

Again, Jack nodded.

"Mayrene saw the number on her caller ID that night," Wanda Nell went on, "but she didn't write it down. The next morning, she looked on her caller ID so she could. It was gone. Somebody deleted it."

"That could have been an accident," Jack said.

"Yes, it could have," Wanda Nell admitted. "But just think about this. It wasn't long after you proposed and Miranda called Mayrene to come over, when Lisa burst in and told us she'd gotten a call."

Jack's eyes narrowed. "If you're saying what I think you're saying, Lisa didn't know I proposed to you. How would she have known? I didn't tell her I was planning to propose to you."

"I said that to Mayrene," Wanda Nell said. "She told me she was so excited she didn't think about telling Lisa before she rushed over to see us." She paused. "But she did say she was pretty sure she heard somebody else on the line. She thinks Lisa was listening in when Miranda called her."

"I see," Jack said.

"And the other thing," Wanda Nell said, to press home the point, "you just told me yourself."

"The last thing Lisa and I talked about before I found her," Jack said, "was the wedding. Me marrying you." He closed his eyes, his head shaking back and forth.

"Yes," Wanda Nell said. She felt so sorry for him. This

had to be so hard to hear and to think about, but he had to know the truth. "And let me ask you this."

"What?" Jack said, his eyes opening.

"Have you seen anything that could be proof that this stalker really exists? If you have, then maybe Mayrene and I are wrong."

Jack stared at her, and it was obvious to Wanda Nell that he was searching his memory for anything, some shred of proof that Lisa wasn't lying.

Finally, he shook his head. "No, nothing. All I've got to go on is what Lisa has told me herself. Every time this guy was supposed to have called her, it was while she was by herself somewhere."

Wanda Nell didn't say anything for a moment.

"Lord, how blind could I be?" Jack said, shaking his head. "I just felt so sorry for her, I didn't even think about the possibility she might be making it up."

"I know, honey," Wanda Nell said, reaching out a hand to him. He grasped it as she continued. "She's your cousin, and you love her. None of us wants to think anything bad about her. She's obviously very lonely. She needs help."

"She does," Jack said. "And I should have seen it myself."

"How?"

"Because I should have remembered what Lisa was like when we were kids," Jack said. He massaged her hand as he spoke. "Things were always happening to her, whenever everybody's attention was somewhere else. You know, her parents were in their late forties when she was born, and they hadn't planned on having any children."

"Let me guess," Wanda Nell said. "They didn't really want her."

"No, they didn't," Jack said. "They made sure she had all the material things she could want, and they sent her to good schools and all that, but that was it. Not at all like my parents," Jack said. "In fact, I had a hard time believing my dad and hers were really brothers. They weren't anything alike."

"That's so sad," Wanda Nell said. "That poor girl."

Jack nodded. "She's always been insecure, but I guess I thought maybe she had grown out of some of it. She did really well in nursing school, and I know they really liked her at the hospital in Meridian.

"But underneath it all, she was lonely, really lonely, I guess," Jack said. "And she never talked about doing much outside of work, now that I think about it."

"I was afraid you were going to be angry with me," Wanda Nell said. "With me saying such things about your cousin."

Jack smiled at her. "Honey, I know you well enough by now to know you'd never say something like that unless you had a good reason for doing it. I'll admit I was shocked, but the more you talked, I began to realize you were right."

Wanda Nell smiled back at him. She loved him even more then. "Believe me, I almost wish I had been wrong. But the thought of her being stalked by some maniac may be even worse."

"Yeah," Jack said. "This way she's really only in danger from herself." He rubbed his forehead. "But what am I going to do about her? I'm the only family she has."

"What are *we* going to do about her, you mean," Wanda Nell said gently. "We're going to see that she gets the help she needs. The people at the hospital will know what to do, and I'm sure they can recommend somebody who can help her."

"You're right," Jack said, squeezing her hand. "But you

realize this means we might have to put off our wedding just a little while longer." He shrugged. "Until she's stronger, I don't think it would be a good idea. If she's so attached to me that she would do these things, well . . ." His voice trailed off unhappily.

"I know, honey," Wanda Nell said. She wondered whether she should bring up Miranda's situation now. She decided she would wait, give Jack a little time to deal with the present situation first. "We need time to plan things, anyway."

Jack opened his arms, and Wanda Nell moved into them. He held her close, stroking her hair. She could hear his heart beating.

"Stay with me tonight," he said softly. "Please."

Wanda Nell pulled back so she could look into his face. He was hurting, she knew, and she didn't want to leave him, she realized. She wanted to stay with him, because she needed him right now as much as he needed her.

She nodded, and Jack pulled her close again. They sat that way for a little while longer.

Wanda Nell was the first to break the silence. "I need to make a phone call, honey," she said.

Jack nodded. Wanda Nell reached for her purse and pulled out her cell phone, since it was closer than Jack's phone. She punched in Mayrene's number.

Mayrene answered after a couple of rings. "Hello," she said, and Wanda Nell could hear her yawning. She felt bad about waking her friend, but she knew Mayrene would understand.

She told Mayrene she was spending the night with Jack. Mayrene didn't say anything except, "I'll go over and spend the night at your place, honey. Don't you worry about a thing."

Wanda Nell thanked her and ended the call. She put the cell phone in her purse and set the purse down on the coffee table.

She and Jack sat, looking at each other for a long moment. Jack rose from the couch and held out a hand. Wanda Nell grasped it, and he pulled her up.

Still holding his hand, Wanda Nell followed him to his bedroom.

Wanda Nell stirred a couple of times during the night, and each time she did, she felt the heat of Jack's body next to hers. It sure was different, being in bed with somebody else, because she was so used to sleeping alone.

But she liked it, she decided. The second time she woke, Jack turned over on his stomach, mumbling in his sleep. He put his arm around her and drew her closer to him. She snuggled against him, and soon drifted to sleep again.

When Jack's alarm went off at six, Wanda Nell struggled up out of a deep sleep. The first thing she saw when she opened her eyes was Jack, smiling down at her, his hair tousled.

For a moment she was disoriented, wondering what the heck Jack was doing in her bed. Then the memories came flooding back, and she smiled, too.

"Good morning, love," Jack said. He leaned in to kiss her, pulling her against him.

Wanda Nell kissed him back, her body responding to his. Some time later, both breathless and sweaty, they sat up in bed. Wanda Nell held the sheet around her upper body, feeling suddenly modest.

"What time is it?" she asked.

Jack put on his glasses and consulted his alarm clock.

"Almost six-thirty," he said. "I wish we could stay here all day."

"Me too, honey," Wanda Nell said. "But I've got to get home, make sure Miranda's up and ready for work. And Juliet's going back to school today."

"I know," Jack said. "And I need to go by the hospital and check on Lisa." He sighed. "Talk about coming back to reality."

Wanda Nell reached out and stroked his cheek. "Yeah, and it's hard. But remember, we'll get through this. She'll get the help she needs, and we'll all be able to get on with our lives."

Jack captured her hand in his and held it against his face. Then he turned her palm toward him and kissed it. Wanda Nell could feel the tingling along her spine.

"If I don't leave now," she told him, her voice husky, "well, I've got to go."

Jack released her hand with a smile. He threw back the covers and stood up. Wanda Nell's breath caught in her throat as she looked at him. He bent to pick up his robe from the old cedar chest at the foot of his bed. Slipping it on, his back to her, he tied it closed before turning in her direction.

"I'll go get some coffee on while you get dressed, love," he said.

Wanda Nell nodded. She was grateful he understood her sudden shyness. When he left the room, she got out of bed and gathered up her clothes from where she had dumped them on top of his chest of drawers last night.

A few minutes later, she was dressed. She ran her hands through her hair, trying to get it to look halfway decent. She finally gave up. She definitely had to have a shower when she got home.

Oh Lord, what would the girls think, her coming home this time of the morning? She had never done this before, but she didn't regret it, not for a moment. She smiled at herself in the mirror, feeling like purring, she was so happy. Any last, lingering doubts she might have had about Jack were gone now. They certainly were physically compatible. She blushed again.

In the kitchen the coffee had just finished brewing and Jack poured them both a cup. Wanda Nell took hers black. She needed it strong to help her clear her head and keep it that way.

She was afraid there might be some awkwardness between them this morning, but there wasn't. She hadn't anticipated that their first time together would happen this way, but it had. So be it.

Jack smiled at her. "I think I love you even more, if that's possible."

"I could say the same thing," Wanda Nell said, grinning at him before she sipped at her coffee.

"I'm going to spend the rest of my life showing you just how much I love you," Jack said. "You're an amazing woman, you know that?"

Wanda Nell shook her head. "Thank you, honey, for saying that. But I'm just me. I think you're pretty amazing, too."

Jack came to her and kissed her.

"Don't try to sidetrack me," Wanda Nell said in a teasing voice. "I've got to get moving, and so do you." She set her coffee cup down on the kitchen counter.

Jack laughed. "Yes, we both do." He followed her to the living room, where she retrieved her purse, and then to the front door. "You be careful."

"You too." One last kiss, and she was out the door. Head held high, she walked to her car. Jack watched from just inside his front door. Wanda Nell cranked the car and started backing out of the driveway. She paused long enough to wave one last time at Jack before pointing her car toward home.

She drove a bit more carefully this morning, but traffic was still light. She made it home in about ten minutes. As she drove, all she could think about was her night with Jack. And thank goodness both of them had been prepared, because she certainly didn't want to end up pregnant like Miranda.

Juliet was in the kitchen eating breakfast when Wanda Nell let herself in. "Good morning, honey," Wanda Nell said, dropping her purse on the counter. "How are you feeling this morning?"

"I'm fine, Mama," Juliet said with an impish smile. "How are *you* feeling this morning?"

Wanda Nell did her best not to blush but wasn't sure she succeeded. "I'm fine, too."

"Good," Juliet said. "I'm really glad, Mama."

"Uh, thank you," Wanda Nell said, taken somewhat aback. "I guess Mayrene explained the situation to you."

Juliet nodded. "Yes'm, she said Jack's cousin, Lisa, had tried to hurt herself and was in the hospital." Her face clouded. "Why would she do something like that, Mama?"

"She's very confused, sweetie, and we're going to have to help her get better," Wanda Nell said. "Jack's very worried about her."

"I'm sure he is," Juliet said. She dropped her spoon into the empty bowl. She got up and put both of them in the sink before turning back to face her mother. "Have you told Jack about Miranda yet?"

"What?" Wanda Nell said, surprised. "What about Miranda?"

"Oh, Mama, I know what's going on," Juliet said. "You don't think Miranda can keep something like that from me, do you?" She shook her head. "I feel so sorry for her."

Wanda Nell shrugged. "I guess I shouldn't be so surprised, and I suppose I'm relieved that you know. Is she up and getting ready for work?"

"Yeah, I think she's done throwing up by now," Juliet said, rolling her eyes. "If being pregnant makes you that sick, I don't think I want to ever have any kids."

"It can be pretty awful," Wanda Nell said, laughing, "but believe me, sweetie, the results are worth it."

"Uh-huh," Juliet said, appearing unconvinced.

"I'd better go check on Miranda," Wanda Nell said, wisely deciding not to debate the point any further.

Miranda was putting the finishing touches to her makeup when Wanda Nell found her in the bathroom.

"Morning, Mama," she said. She cut her eyes toward her mother's face before focusing on the image in the mirror again. "And how was your night?"

"It was just fine," Wanda Nell said in a firm tone. She was not about to start answering questions, though she could see Miranda was bursting to ask them. "And Jack is fine, too. He's going to check on Lisa at the hospital this morning."

Miranda put her eyeliner down and turned to face her mother. "That girl is nuts," she said, frowning. "I mean, I've been upset a few times, but I'd never do nothing like that."

"I'm glad to hear it, honey," Wanda Nell said, and she meant it. No matter how much of a trial Miranda could be, she didn't want anything bad to happen to her. "Now, is Lavon ready?"

"Yes, ma'am," Miranda said. "I got him ready before I got sick, and Juliet helped."

"Good," Wanda Nell said. "I'm going to need the car today, so I'm going to take you to work and drop Lavon off at day care. I'll pick you up this afternoon, and I should have just enough time to take you and Lavon home before I have to be at the Kountry Kitchen."

"Okay," Miranda said. "I'll be ready to go in a few minutes."

Wanda Nell went back to the kitchen. She would wait to see Lavon until Miranda brought him out, ready to go. She didn't want to slow them down. She had a quick bowl of cereal while she waited. She was really hungry this morning and would have liked something more substantial, but she didn't have time.

Juliet left to wait for the school bus before Miranda and Lavon appeared. Wanda Nell took her grandson, kissing and hugging him, and he talked a mile a minute. She did her best to respond, but he didn't really require much response. He was quite happy to talk all by himself.

By the time she got Miranda and Lavon in the car, the school bus had come and gone. She drove straight to the day care place, and she waited in the car while Miranda took Lavon inside.

She was back a few minutes later. As she buckled her seat belt, Miranda said, "I sure hate leaving him there, but he really does have fun. He likes playing with the other kids."

Wanda Nell patted her daughter's knee before putting the car into gear again. "I know it's hard, honey. But it's good for him to have other babies to play with. And it's good for you, too, to get out of the house and work. You need to be around other people, too."

"I know, Mama," Miranda said.

Thus far Wanda Nell had avoided bringing up the subject of Teddy. So much had happened since she and Miranda had discussed the situation yesterday morning, and she didn't have time right now to go into it. "Just one thing, Miranda," she said, as her daughter was preparing to get out of the car at Budget Mart.

"Yes, ma'am?"

"Have you talked to Teddy yet?"

Miranda shook her head.

"Okay, well, I think you need to do it tonight, okay? You can't put it off any longer. Promise me you'll tell him tonight."

"I will, Mama," Miranda said, sighing heavily. "Can I go now?"

"Yes. Have a good day, and I'll see you later," Wanda Nell said. She watched Miranda walk into the store, her shoulders hunched. Shaking her head, she drove off.

Wanda Nell glanced at the clock and decided she had time to go through the drive-through at one of the fast food places. She really was hungry, and she might get a headache if she didn't have some more caffeine.

She ordered a sausage biscuit and a large Diet Coke. As she drove toward downtown and Tuck's office, she ate her food, enjoying every bite of it. She had finished by the time she parked her car on the square across from the office building.

It was only about eight-thirty, but Wanda Nell figured the boys were probably in the office by now. She took her drink with her after locking the car.

She rode the elevator up to Tuck's office, and she was pleased to see the lights already on inside. She opened the door and walked in. Tuck's secretary smiled. "Good morning. You go right on back. I know they're expecting you."

"Thanks, Ginger," Wanda Nell said. She opened the

inner office door and stepped through. Tuck's office was just a few steps away down the hall. She knocked on the open door, and Tuck looked up from his desk. T.J. stood nearby, sipping something from a mug.

Tuck stood, and T.J. moved forward to give his mother a hug.

"Good morning, Wanda Nell," Tuck said.

"Morning," she replied. "I'm a little early, I hope that's okay?"

"Of course," Tuck said with a smile. "Have a seat, why don't you?"

T.J. held out the chair for her. "Can I get you something, Mama? We have some muffins, if you want one."

"I'm fine, honey," she said, smiling up at her son. "You sit down and don't worry about me."

He grinned at her and sat down in a chair beside Tuck's desk.

Tuck stood and held out a piece of paper to her. Wanda Nell took it and glanced down at it. It was a list of names.

"This is the list of men who were at the bachelor party," Tuck said, and she nodded. "I thought you could look over it and tell me if anything occurs to you. We're trying to identify all the men on it and figure out what connections they had with Travis Blakeley."

Wanda Nell scanned the list. As before, she recognized several of the names. But now she realized something wasn't right about it.

"There's a name missing," she said, surprised. "I didn't realize it before, but one man's name isn't on here."

"Whose?" Tuck and T.J. said in unison.

"Barnard Roberts," Wanda Nell said, puzzled. "I know he was at the party, because I saw him talking to Gerald Blakeley."

"I wonder why his name wasn't on the list?" Tuck said, frowning. "Surely the police talked to him."

Wanda Nell stared at him. Her mind flashed back to that night, and the aftermath of the party. She called up pictures of what happened after Travis Blakeley collapsed. Finally she shook her head.

"He wasn't there," she said. "He left sometime before Elmer Lee and the others got there."

Twenty-three

The three of them stared at one another, trying to puzzle it out.

"Are you sure about this?" Tuck asked.

"Yes, I am," Wanda Nell said. "I can't remember seeing him after Travis Blakeley collapsed on the floor. He must have left in all the confusion."

"Otherwise he would have still been there when Elmer Lee and his men arrived," T.J. said.

"And Bill Warren," Tuck added.

"It sure looks suspicious," Wanda Nell said.

"It certainly does," Tuck replied. "But what's the connection?"

"What do you know about him?" Wanda Nell asked.

Tuck shrugged. "He's a prominent businessman here in town, and he gives a lot of money to charity. I haven't crossed paths with him more than a couple of times, as far as I can remember."

"Mayrene says he owns a factory out in the industrial park," Wanda Nell said. She told Tuck and T.J. the rest of what Mayrene had told her, about her friend Teresa and spotting Roberts at the casino with a woman.

"Interesting," Tuck said. His fingers steepled, he rested his chin on them while he thought.

"And he was at the casino the same night Mayrene saw Bill Warren there," T.J. said. "That makes it even more interesting."

"But what is the connection in all this? I thought maybe he was a friend of the Blakeley family," Wanda Nell said. "But that's probably wrong."

"I'll go look him up on the Internet," T.J. said, rising from his chair.

Wanda Nell shook her head. "No, hand me the phone. I've got a better idea."

Tuck pushed his phone to the front edge of his desk. Wanda Nell leaned forward and picked up the receiver. She punched in a number.

"Grandmother," T.J. said, grinning as he read the number. He sat back in his chair. "Gossip central."

He and Tuck laughed, and Wanda Nell shushed them.

"Good morning, Belle," she said. "This is Wanda Nell."

"Put it on speaker phone," Tuck said softly. He pointed to a button. Wanda Nell punched it. Tuck motioned for her to put the receiver back in its cradle. Belle's voice was already coming through, loud and clear.

". . . nice that you called this morning, Wanda Nell. I was just saying to Lucretia a few minutes ago how nice it would be to talk to you and find out if you've made any decisions about the wedding yet. I can't tell you how excited Lucretia is. She tried to hide it, but I know she's excited."

"That's really kind of her," Wanda Nell said. "But we really haven't had any time to make plans yet, Belle."

"I understand," Belle said, "and surely you know if there's

anything I can do, all you have to do is ask. I've made a lot of wedding cakes in my day, and I would be so proud to make one for you. And a groom's cake, too. You think about that and let me know. Of course, if you decide you want a professional, I'll understand. I think my cakes are pretty good, but I've never been a professional baker. I thought about it a few times, but I just never could get up the gumption to do anything about it."

Belle paused for a breath, and Wanda Nell seized her chance. "Thank you, Belle, I really appreciate your offer. I promise you I'll think about it. Now, I'm sorry to be abrupt, but I really need to talk to Miz Culpepper about something. Is she where she can come to the phone?"

"Well, bless my soul, Wanda Nell, she's sitting right here, and from the look on her face, she's about ready to have a stroke. I'll give her the phone right now. Here, Lucretia, it's Wanda Nell, and she wants to talk to you."

There was a brief silence, and then Wanda Nell, Tuck, and T.J. heard the strident tones of Lucretia Culpepper. ". . . the most infuriating woman the good Lord ever put on the face of this earth. Don't you ever listen to yourself, Belle? Good grief, I swear they'll have to keep your coffin open for three days after you die until you stop talking."

Tuck and T.J.—and even Wanda Nell—were having a hard time keeping a straight face by this point.

"Wanda Nell! Are you there, girl?"

"Yes, ma'am, I'm right here," Wanda Nell said hastily. "How are you this morning?"

"Other than the fact that Belle is about to send me straight to Whitfield, I guess I'm doing just fine," Mrs. Culpepper snapped. Whitfield was the state mental hospital, and Mrs. Culpepper had begun referring to it on a regular basis, ever since Belle had come to live with her.

"Did you want something?"

"Yes, ma'am," Wanda Nell said. "I wanted to ask you about somebody here in town."

"Who?"

"A Mr. Barnard Roberts," Wanda Nell said. "He owns a factory."

"I know that," Mrs. Culpepper said testily. "I expect I know more about him than you do, Wanda Nell. He used to go to my church." She paused. "That's who I was trying to think of the other day."

"What do you mean?" Wanda Nell exchanged glances with T.J. and Tuck.

"When we were talking about the girl who was supposed to get married," Mrs. Culpepper said. "Can't you remember anything? You were the one who came to me, after all."

"Yes, ma'am, of course I remember," Wanda Nell said, trying not to get irritated. "So what is his connection to Tiffany Farwell?"

"He's her stepfather," Mrs. Culpepper said. "I told you her mother married again, and that's who she married."

"I see," Wanda Nell said, and she did see. A number of things fell into place. She had halfway suspected that this was the connection, but it was good to have Mrs. Culpepper confirm it.

"You could at least say thank you, Wanda Nell," the old lady snapped. "Good gracious, normally you have better manners than that."

"Yes, ma'am, thank you very much," Wanda Nell said in a meek tone. "I really appreciate your help with this. I can't talk about it now, but you've helped a lot."

"That's all right," Mrs. Culpepper said. "I'm sure you're

very welcome. Now when is that scamp of a grandson coming to see me? And Tuck. He'd better come along, too."

"I'm sure they'll be by to see you soon," Wanda Nell said. "Now I really have to go, but thank you again for all your help."

"Good-bye," Mrs. Culpepper said, and the phone clicked off.

Tuck hit the button on his phone as Wanda Nell leaned back in her chair. "You'd better go see her soon," she said.

"We will," T.J. promised. "And you were right, Mama. That was better than the Internet, and a lot more entertaining." He laughed. "Belle is such a hoot."

"She is," Tuck said, grinning, "and listening to the two of them carry on like that, well, it must be what Lucy and Ethel would be like if they were together in a nursing home."

Wanda Nell couldn't help laughing. "You're probably right." She sobered. "But tell me what you think, now that we know what the connection is."

"I'd say it was pretty obvious," Tuck said. "Barnard Roberts had a very strong motive for killing Travis Blakeley. We don't have any idea what his relationship with his stepdaughter is like, but I don't think any man would want to see a young woman he cared about married to a man like that. Roberts may also have been trying to protect his family's financial future given what you heard about Travis Blakeley."

"Exactly," T.J. said. "And the connections to Bill Warren are pretty suspicious, too."

"Yeah," Wanda Nell said. "They sure are. I've been thinking a lot about that. Bill has probably lost a lot of money gambling, and if his bosses find out about it, he's going to be in big trouble."

"And there's a rich man with a problem to solve," Tuck said.

"So Roberts gives Bill Warren money to either botch the investigation or pin it on someone else," T.J. said in tones of disgust. "And Gerald is the most likely, because he used to be in love with Tiffany and hated his brother."

"That's the way I figured it," Wanda Nell said. "But how is anybody going to prove it?"

Tuck turned to T.J. "Why don't you see if you can find out what it is Barnard manufactures at his plant?"

T.J. nodded. "Yeah, I got you. I'll be back in a few minutes." He left the room, headed for his own office nearby.

Tuck picked up his phone and punched in a number as Wanda Nell watched, curious. Tuck spoke into the phone. "This is Hamilton Tucker, calling for Sheriff Johnson. Is he available?"

He put his hand over the mouth of the receiver. "They're putting me through." He removed his hand. "Elmer Lee, good morning. How you doing?"

Wanda Nell could hear only Tuck's part of the conversation, but it was enough.

"Can you spare a few minutes to come to my office, Sheriff?" Tuck listened for a moment. "I assure you, I wouldn't ask you if it weren't really important." He paused again. "Yes, that's right. I think we've got some very important information about that case." He listened a moment longer. "Thanks. We'll see you in a few minutes, then." He put down the phone.

"We need to turn this over to Elmer Lee," Tuck said.

"Yes, I see that," Wanda Nell said. "I guess if anybody can get proof, he will."

T.J. came back then. He sat down in the chair beside his

mother and crossed one leg over the other. He looked at Wanda Nell and Tuck in turn, and said, "Bingo!"

"Tell us," Tuck said.

"Roberts' plant makes different kinds of plastics," T.J. said. "And guess what? They use cyanide in various processes. According to what I read, hydrogen cyanide is very toxic, as a salt or even in gas form. I'm guessing that some form of it was put in Travis Blakeley's drink."

"So Roberts had easy access to cyanide," Wanda Nell said.

"Yes," T.J. replied, "and I did a quick check on him. He has two degrees in chemical engineering, so he would surely know how to handle the cyanide."

"That's it, then," Wanda Nell said.

"Not quite," Tuck said. "It all still has to be proved, and I don't think it's going to be that easy. It will probably be easy enough to prove that Roberts had access to the poison. But of course, there still isn't any official word on how Blakeley died. Not that I'm doubting it was cyanide, you understand, but we still have to keep that in mind."

"I wouldn't take any bets against it at this point," T.J. said.

"Neither would I," Tuck replied. "The hard part is going to be proving some kind of connection between Roberts and Bill Warren. Elmer Lee might be able to make a pretty good case against Roberts, though of course, if what we suspect is true, Bill Warren is going to do his best to derail it."

"They can't be allowed to get away with it," Wanda Nell said. "We can't let poor Gerald Blakeley go to prison, or maybe even death row, for this."

"We won't," Tuck said. "Believe me, I'll do everything I possibly can to free him."

His buzzer sounded, and he answered the intercom. His secretary announced the arrival of the sheriff. "Please send him in," Tuck said. He released the button and stood.

The door opened, and Elmer Lee strode in. The moment he spotted Wanda Nell, he grimaced. "I might have known," he muttered.

T.J. stood. "Here, Sheriff, take my seat, please."

"Thanks," Elmer Lee said. "Morning, Wanda Nell." He nodded before looking straight at Tuck. "So what's so important I had to come over to your office?" He sat down.

Tuck reclaimed his seat, and T.J. pulled another chair close by. "I thought it might be safer if we talked here, in view of what you told us the other day."

"What was that?" Wanda Nell said sharply, responding to the look of annoyance on Elmer Lee's face.

"There's a leak in my office," he said shortly. "Somebody there is feeding stuff to the state police district office. And it's the same person, I'm pretty sure, who's been behind the harassment."

"Do you know who it is?" Wanda Nell asked.

"Not for sure, but I think I have an idea," Elmer Lee said.

"What are you doing about it?" Wanda Nell said, frowning at him.

"You let me take care of that, Wanda Nell," Elmer Lee snapped at her. "I think I know my business better than you."

"Yes, of course you do," Wanda Nell said. "I'm sorry, it's just that I'm so worried."

"I know, and I don't blame you," Elmer Lee said, his tone gruff but not unkind. "I'm doing my best to see that nobody gets hurt. You're just going to have to trust me."

"I do," Wanda Nell said.

Elmer Lee let a brief smile cross his face, but then he was all business. "So what's up?"

Tuck explained everything clearly and succinctly, and Wanda Nell admired the way he laid out the case. If she had been on a jury listening to him, she would certainly have believed him.

"It looks pretty bad," Elmer Lee said when Tuck finished. "But I just don't know."

"Can you think of any other explanation?" Tuck asked.

Elmer Lee shifted in his chair. "No, I can't. I'm not saying you're not right. I guess I'm saying it's going to be harder than hell to prove."

"But you're going to try, aren't you?" Wanda Nell asked.

"Yeah, I am," Elmer Lee said. "But I'm going to have to be mighty careful about it, because I don't want Warren getting wind of what I'm up to."

"Maybe there's some way to force his hand," Wanda Nell said. "Bill's, I mean."

"Now look here," Elmer Lee said, "you just mind your own business. I don't want you getting tangled up in the middle of this. Something bad could happen to you if you do. Do you understand me?"

"Yes, I do," Wanda Nell said, frost in her voice. "And for your information, I wasn't talking about me doing something. I was thinking maybe you, Mr. Sheriff, could do it."

"Like what?" Elmer Lee's eyes narrowed in suspicion as he looked at her.

Wanda Nell shrugged. "I don't know. Something." She thought for a moment. "Maybe you could set some kind of trap. Leak something so that whoever's in your office will make sure Bill hears it."

"You been reading too many mystery books," Elmer Lee said, shaking his head.

"You don't know," Wanda Nell said. "It might work."

Elmer Lee just gave her a disgusted look.

"You do like I said, and stay out of this," Elmer Lee said. "I've got somebody watching Warren at all times, and I've talked to the right people at the MBI—Mississippi Bureau of Investigation. Turns out they were already interested in him."

"Good," Wanda Nell said. "The sooner something's done about him, the better." She stood up. "Now, if you'll excuse me, gentlemen, I'm going home."

All three men stood. T.J. went to open the door for her. "Bye, Mama. Take it easy."

"I will. I'm going home and do some housework and maybe have a nap until it's time to pick up Miranda and Lavon," she said. "Don't you worry about me."

A couple of minutes later, as she was getting into her car, she realized she hadn't had a chance to tell Tuck and T.J. about Lisa. That could wait till later, she decided. Right now, she just wanted to go home and have some time by herself. Before she drove away, she tried reaching Jack on his cell phone to find out how Lisa was doing, but it went right to his voice mail. She left him a message, asking him to call her when he had time.

Ten minutes or so later, as she was pulling her car into its spot, she was surprised to see that Mayrene was still home. She thought about knocking on her door, but she figured if Mayrene hadn't gone to work today, it was probably because she wasn't feeling too good. Guiltily aware that she was probably responsible for that, Wanda Nell decided she would talk to Mayrene later.

She put her purse down on the kitchen table, where she found a note from Mayrene. "Call me later," it read. "I stayed home today to get some sleep, but I'll be up by noon." Wanda Nell dropped the note back on the table. She owed Mayrene a big apology for making her miss work like this.

She was heading for the refrigerator for something to drink when the phone rang. She turned and went to the phone.

"Hello."

"Howdy, Wanda Nell."

Wanda Nell went cold. She recognized Bill Warren's voice.

"What do you want, Bill?" She was surprised her voice came out clear and strong.

"I want to talk to you," Bill said. "We've got some unfinished business, and I think we need to get it settled right away." There was an undertone of urgency in his voice, and that seemed strange to Wanda Nell.

"I don't have anything to say to you," Wanda Nell said as firmly as she could. "You just leave me alone."

"Too late, I'm already on my way," Bill said. "You just sit tight, and I'll be there in a few minutes." The phone clicked in her ear.

Wanda Nell stood staring at the receiver, her mind racing. What was he up to?

Twenty-four

She couldn't afford to panic. What should she do first?

Without really thinking about it, she punched in Mayrene's number. "Answer, answer," she said.

Mayrene picked after two rings. "Hello." She sounded a little sleepy.

"Bill Warren just called. He's on his way here."

"I'll be right there," Mayrene said, instantly alert. "Call Elmer Lee. Now!" Her phone clicked off.

Wanda Nell pressed down on the button to disconnect. She took a deep breath. What was the number for the sheriff's department? She had it memorized. Why couldn't she remember it now?

As she was taking deep breaths, trying to calm herself, the phone rang. She was so startled she almost dropped it.

"Hello."

"Bill Warren is coming your way," Elmer Lee said. "I don't know what he's up to, but I don't think you ought to be there if he's coming to your place. You understand?" His voice practically throbbed with tension.

"He is coming here," Wanda Nell said, her heart beginning to race faster. "He just called me, and he sounded kinda desperate."

"Get out of there," Elmer Lee said.

Wanda Nell's front door burst open, and Mayrene came through it carrying her shotgun. She shut the door behind her and locked it. Seconds later she was in the kitchen with Wanda Nell.

"It's too late," Wanda Nell said. "And Mayrene's here with me."

Elmer Lee swore. "I'm on my way, but I'm going to come as quiet as I can. Be careful, and don't do anything to set him off."

"Okay," Wanda Nell said. She hung up the phone, her hand trembling.

"Elmer Lee?" Mayrene asked.

Wanda Nell nodded. "He's on the way."

"Good," Mayrene said. "Okay, here's what we'll do." She caught hold of Wanda Nell's hand and drew her from the kitchen into the living room.

"I locked the door, but it ain't going to keep him out if he's determined to get in here," she said. "So you try to keep him here in the living room. Try not to let him get close to you, and try to keep him so his back is to the kitchen."

Wanda Nell nodded.

"I'm gonna be in the utility room," Mayrene said. It was the first room down the hall toward Miranda's bedroom. "I should be able to hear him from there, and if he tries anything, I'll come after him. If you hear me or see me coming, you hit the floor. Okay?"

Again, Wanda Nell nodded. All of a sudden, she felt

calm. Mayrene never panicked, and Wanda Nell knew she could count on her friend. Bill might not mean her any harm, but the fact that he insisted on coming to her house worried her. Was he really feeling desperate, or had she only imagined she heard that in his voice?

Mayrene disappeared down the hall just as Wanda Nell heard a car pull up outside. She concentrated on breathing steadily and deeply in order to maintain her calm. She wouldn't show any fear in front of Bill. She was determined about that.

Moments later there came a knock at the door. "Wanda Nell. Let me in."

"I don't want to talk to you, Bill," she called out. "Leave. You're just wasting your time."

"Open the door. I'm warning you," Bill said. He thumped the door hard, and Wanda Nell watched it bulge inward.

"Okay, okay," she said, moving forward. "Don't break down the damn door, you fool."

She unlocked the door and stepped back several feet. "Come in."

Bill Warren pushed the door open hard enough that it rocked back on its hinges. He caught it on the rebound and slammed it shut.

"If you damaged it, you're gonna be paying me for a new door," Wanda Nell said. "What the hell do you want, Bill?"

Wanda Nell had taken up a spot near the couch, and as Bill advanced into the room, she turned slowly so that Bill kept moving in front of her. When he stood with his back toward where Mayrene was hiding, Wanda Nell stopped turning. Thank the Lord he didn't seem to notice what she was doing.

"This is what I want," Bill said. He reached into his jacket pocket and pulled out some folded papers. He held them toward Wanda Nell.

She kept her hands crossed over her chest, refusing to take them. "And what is that, pray tell?"

"It's your statement," he said. "The one in which you say you saw Gerald Blakeley put something into his brother's drink."

Wanda Nell laughed. "I told you I wasn't going to sign any such thing. I didn't see that, and I'm not gonna say I did."

"You're going to," Bill said, staring hard at her. "Just tell me, Wanda Nell. How much do you love your son?"

Her body went ice cold. She struggled to appear nonchalant. "What does that mean?"

"Just what I said," he replied. "You're a good mother, aren't you? You wouldn't want to see your only son, mangled and dead in a car wreck, would you? Just think about that for a minute, and maybe then you'll want to sign this statement."

If she had had a gun in her hand, Wanda Nell would have shot him through the heart right then and there. She was not going to let this cold-blooded bastard do anything to hurt her son or anyone else in her family.

"Why do you hate T.J. and Tuck so much, Bill?" She spoke in a quiet, conversational tone. "Is it because you hate yourself for being like them?"

"That's a damn lie," Bill said. His eyes narrowed in anger, but as she stared into them, Wanda Nell could also see the fear.

"Did you think you could go to gay bars in Memphis and nobody would notice you?" Wanda Nell said. "You're a very attractive man, at least physically, that is. You probably have guys hanging all over you."

Bill's body tensed, and for a moment Wanda Nell was afraid she'd gone too far. He looked like he wanted to hit her.

Then Bill relaxed. He smiled. "You ought to be writing books, you know that? You've sure got an imagination." He stopped smiling. "Now sign this damn statement."

"It's not my imagination," she said, ignoring the hand he had thrust out again. "Somebody saw you, and more than once." She paused, smiling. "And I believe I heard about some pictures, too."

As she watched, he tensed again, and she could see his nostrils flaring. His breathing accelerated. To her surprise, however, he quickly regained control and calmed himself.

"I don't believe you," Bill said, contempt in his voice. "Since I've never been in a gay bar, how could there be any pictures? Somebody may have made some up to make it look like I was there, but it's a damn lie."

For a moment Wanda Nell almost began to believe him. He seemed so sincere and self-righteous, but there was still that little flicker of fear in his eyes.

"Why is it so important to you that I sign this statement?"

"Because Gerald Blakeley killed his brother, and he needs to be put away for it," Bill said. "Don't be stupid, Wanda Nell. I know you're not that dumb. You can make this easier for everybody if you just cooperate."

"Well, I guess you think I am stupid," she said. "But I'm not. And I reckon I know why you're so desperate to get this statement signed."

"What the hell are you talking about?"

Wanda Nell regarded him coolly for a moment. "Now, I don't know for sure how much money you lost gambling, but I figure it has to be a hell of lot. So you're desperate for money." She nodded. "And the man who promised to pay you a lot of money if you got somebody else convicted for the murder isn't gonna pay off until he knows you can get it done." She smiled sweetly.

While she was talking, she watched Bill carefully, alert for any sign of movement on his part. To her satisfaction, however, he appeared too stunned to do anything except stare at her.

"Cat got your tongue, Bill?" She smiled sweetly. "And just in case you're wondering, I'm not the only one who knows about all this. We even know who's got the money you want so bad, and who really killed Travis Blakeley."

From the corner of her eye, Wanda Nell caught a glimpse of Mayrene. She had been so focused on Bill that she hadn't heard a sound as Mayrene left the utility room. She had to hope Bill hadn't either.

A phone started ringing, startling both her and Bill. Wanda Nell went cold again when she realized it was Bill's cell phone. His hand shook a bit as he pulled it from the holster on his belt. He flipped it open. "Warren."

He listened for a moment, and his eyes narrowed as he stared at Wanda Nell.

She had a bad feeling about this. He was looking like he was ready to kill her. He dropped the papers on the floor and started reaching under his jacket. At the same time he flipped his cell phone shut and popped it back into the holster.

Wanda Nell stared at the gun he was now holding.

"What's that for?" she said.

"You bitch," Bill said. "So you think the sheriff's going

to come riding in here to save the day? Well, I got another idea, and I think you're going to help me out with it."

He took a step forward, and Wanda Nell got ready to hit the floor.

"Hold it, buddy," Mayrene said. She cocked her gun.

Bill froze in place.

"Now you just put your hands up in the air, real nice and slow like," Mayrene said. She might have been discussing the weather or what she was going to have for dinner, her voice was so casual.

Bill didn't move for a moment.

"You know, it's been a while since I've had a chance to shoot a jackass, and I reckon that head of yours would look pretty damn good mounted on the wall." Mayrene laughed. "What do you think?"

Bill started moving, and Wanda Nell dove for the floor between the coffee table and the couch. As she went down, she caught a glimpse of Bill spinning around toward Mayrene. Wanda Nell put her head down and waited for the explosion.

The only thing she heard was something hit the floor. Mayrene laughed, and Wanda Nell cautiously peered between the legs of the coffee table.

She saw Bill's gun on the floor.

"Now why don't you just back up against the wall over there," Mayrene said. "Yeah, just like that. Believe me, you give me any excuse to pull the trigger, you sonofabitch, and I'll do it. It'll be worth it."

Wanda Nell heard footsteps, and when they stopped, she slowly got up from the floor. She turned to see Bill, his back against the wall opposite the front door. His hands were up, and Mayrene stood a few feet in front of him, her shotgun aimed right at his gut.

"Kick that gun out of the way, honey," Mayrene said. "And then stick your head out the door and see if Elmer Lee's managed to get his scrawny butt here."

Wanda Nell followed orders. With her foot she nudged the gun well out of the way before going to the door. She opened it, praying that Elmer Lee really was there. She stepped outside onto the small landing.

Elmer Lee was there, just a few feet away near the corner of the trailer, and he had never looked better to her in his life. When he saw Wanda Nell step outside, he motioned with his hands as he moved slowly forward. There were several men in uniform with him, and one man in a suit and tie. He looked to be in his fifties, and Wanda Nell wondered who he was and why he was there.

"It's okay," Wanda Nell said. She realized, with some surprise, that she was cold and trembling. She crossed her arms and rubbed them, trying to warm herself. She walked down the few steps into the yard. She jerked her head toward her door. "Mayrene's got him cornered."

Elmer Lee frowned as he walked past her, followed by his men and the stranger in the suit.

Wanda Nell walked farther out into the yard, letting the heat of the midday sun warm her. She made herself breathe deeply and slowly. She could hear talking going on inside her trailer, but she couldn't make out what they were saying.

She turned around to face her door. Two of Elmer Lee's men came out, Bill Warren in handcuffs between them. Next came the man in the suit, and finally Elmer Lee, a couple more of his men, with Mayrene and Old Reliable bringing up the rear.

Bill Warren shot her a baleful glance as he was escorted past her, but Wanda Nell could only look at him with pity.

She could easily hate him for what he had done and what he could have done, but she felt sorry for him.

Elmer Lee stopped in front of her. He reached out and grasped her shoulder. "Are you okay?"

The concern in his face touched her. "I'm fine," she said. "Really."

"I'd like to read you the riot act," Elmer Lee said, "but I don't think it would do me a damn bit of good."

Wanda Nell grinned. "You oughta know that by now. Besides, I didn't have much choice, did I? He came looking for me."

"Yeah, I guess so," Elmer Lee said. "But you better get down on your knees and thank the Lord that Annie Oakley was home today."

Wanda Nell cast an affectionate glance at Mayrene, still cradling her shotgun in her arms. "Believe me, I will. I don't know what I would've done without her."

"Don't you have some work to do, Elmer Lee?" Mayrene said. "Instead of standing around here bothering Wanda Nell? Get that slimeball out of here."

"I was thinking I might just do that," Elmer Lee said in a wry tone. "But thank you for reminding me."

Wanda Nell had been watching Elmer Lee's men put Bill Warren in the back of a patrol car. The stranger stood at the window, leaning forward, talking to Bill.

"Who's that?" Wanda Nell said. "That man in the suit."

"MBI," Elmer Lee said. "I told you this morning I was talking to them about Warren. It turned out they were already investigating him because of the gambling. He's in some serious trouble."

"You think he'll talk to you and tell you the truth about Roberts?" Wanda Nell asked.

Elmer Lee shrugged. "Who knows? If he's got any

brains, he's not going to sit back and let Roberts walk. And I'm going to do my damnedest to make sure he don't."

"Good," Wanda Nell said. "They probably did that poor girl a favor by getting rid of a monster. But then trying to put an innocent man in jail, and probably on death row . . ." She shook her head.

"It's going to take some time to untangle," Elmer Lee said. "But I think Gerald Blakeley will soon be a free man again."

Wanda Nell nodded. Then she remembered something. "Bill got a call on his cell phone," she said. "Somebody told him you were on the way out here."

Elmer Lee gave her a grim smile. "Yeah, and I know who did it. One of my men caught the little bastard doing it, and now I can take care of him, too. I'm pretty sure he's the one behind all the harassment of Tucker and your son."

Wanda Nell breathed a sigh of relief. "That's very good news."

"Go on, Elmer Lee," Mayrene said. "I think y'all have done talked enough. Wanda Nell needs a little time to get over this. It was pretty scary in there for a while, but let me tell you, she looked that bastard straight in the eye and never backed down." She grinned at Wanda Nell.

"I'll need to get a statement from both of you," Elmer Lee said, scowling at Mayrene. "But it can wait until tomorrow. We'll be busy enough with him for today." He nodded toward the squad car.

"Fine," Wanda Nell said. "I'll be down there tomorrow."

Elmer Lee looked for a moment like he wanted to say something else. Instead he nodded and walked away.

"Come on, honey," Mayrene said. "Let's get you inside and get you something warm and sweet to drink. I think it'll do you good."

Wanda Nell put an arm around her friend, taking care not to get too close to the shotgun. "I bless the day I met you, you know that."

"Of course, honey," Mayrene said, smiling as she led Wanda Nell toward her trailer. "But one of these days I'm just gonna to have to shoot somebody if you keep getting mixed up in murder."

$\mathcal{T}wenty\text{-}five$

Wanda Nell was finishing her second cup of hot, sweet coffee and chatting with Mayrene when her phone rang.

Mayrene was out of her chair and heading for the phone before Wanda Nell could react. "I'm fine, you know," she said. "I can answer the phone."

"I need to move around," Mayrene said, waving a hand at her. "So just you never mind." She answered the phone.

"Yeah, honey, she's right here. Hold on." Mayrene extended the phone to Wanda Nell. "It's Jack." She waggled her eyebrows at Wanda Nell.

Wanda Nell ignored that. "Hi, honey, where are you?"

"I'm just leaving the hospital," Jack said, sounding tired and dispirited. "I'm glad I didn't wake you up. But I really needed to hear your voice."

"I'm glad to hear yours, too, honey," Wanda Nell said. "Do you have to go on to school, or can you come by here?"

"I called in sick to school today," Jack said, "and I want to see you. Thanks, love. I'm on the way. I should be there in about ten minutes."

"Don't drive too fast," Wanda Nell said. Jack chuckled, and she said good-bye.

Wanda Nell got up to put the phone back. She leaned against the counter and stretched. "I think my head is still spinning, so much has happened."

Mayrene grinned. "No kidding, girl. And we ain't had time for you to tell me about last night. What happened?"

Wanda Nell smiled. "Jack was upset when I told him about Lisa, but he handled it real well. He told me a little about her childhood, and he said he wasn't really surprised to find out she had made it up. She's been real insecure all her life, because her parents didn't really want her."

"That's horrible," Mayrene said. "Why do people like that even have a child to begin with?"

"Jack said they hadn't really planned to. It just happened," Wanda Nell said, sighing. "And Lord knows it's easy enough."

"We can talk about Miranda in a minute," Mayrene said wryly, "but before Jack gets here, I want a little detail, honey. You didn't spend the night on his couch, did you?"

Wanda Nell felt herself blushing. "No, I didn't." She sat down again and picked up her coffee cup. It was still warm, and it felt good.

"Well, then?" Mayrene wasn't about to settle for just that.

"I'm not giving you any details," Wanda Nell said, grinning a little, "except to say this. It was worth waiting for, and then some."

Mayrene laughed. "Honey, you are just too demure. But I won't bug you. I can't tell you how happy I am for you." She laughed again. "But now the bull's out in the pasture, so to speak, you can't expect to put him back in the barn."

"Lord, the way you put things sometimes," Wanda Nell said, laughing in spite of herself. "I know what you mean, but there are still some things we've got to get settled."

"Yeah," Mayrene said. "Miranda."

Wanda Nell nodded. "I told her this morning—and it seems like a month ago now—she had to talk to Teddy tonight. I can't let her put it off."

"No, you can't," Mayrene said. "Are you going to tell Jack?"

"Yeah," Wanda Nell said. "I will, but first I've got to tell him about what happened today." She shook her head. "He's going to be upset, I know."

"I reckon," Mayrene said, "but you didn't have much choice, honey. You had to stand and fight, and you did."

"I know that," Wanda Nell said, "but that don't make it any easier." She paused for a moment, taking a deep breath. "I have to tell you something, honey."

Mayrene frowned. "You sound awful serious. What is it?"

"It's about your new boyfriend," Wanda Nell said.

Mayrene drew back slightly. "Don't tell me you don't like him."

"No, it's not that," Wanda Nell said. "Actually, I think he's a really nice guy."

"What, then?" Mayrene stared at her with suspicion. Before Wanda Nell could explain, Mayrene started nodding. "I know what it is. You thought Dixon might have been the killer. Right?"

"Yes," Wanda Nell said. "I'm sorry, but when I found out he's Tiffany's uncle, I thought it gave him a pretty good motive."

"It's okay, honey, I understand that," Mayrene said. "I have to confess that I thought about it for just a teeny-tiny minute myself." She shrugged. "And I couldn't blame him if he was trying to look after his niece. But thank the Lord it wasn't him."

They both heard the sound of a car pulling up outside. Mayrene got up from the table and peered out the kitchen window. "It's Jack," she said. "I better make myself scarce so you two can talk. Holler if you need me."

Wanda Nell nodded. She was thankful Mayrene had taken her shotgun and put it away before they sat down to talk. The last thing she needed was for Jack to see Mayrene come waltzing out of her trailer carrying that gun.

"She's in the kitchen." She heard Mayrene talking to Jack for a moment. By the time she reached the living room, Jack was closing the door behind him.

She held out her arms, and he walked into them, wrapping his own arms around her in a fierce hug. "I missed you," he said, his lips against her hair.

They kissed, and Wanda Nell could feel the tension draining away from him. She led him to the couch and sat down beside him, her body touching his.

"Tell me about it," she said.

Jack took off his glasses and massaged the bridge of his nose. "It was pretty awful, at least at first," he said. "But I talked to the doctor, and I told him what was going on. He was really pretty understanding about the whole thing. Turns out there's a really good therapist in town, and the doctor was able to get her to come out to the hospital this morning while I was there."

"Did you confront Lisa?"

"Yeah." Jack sighed heavily. "I don't know if I can ever forget the way she looked when I told her. For a minute there, I'd swear she hated me. Then she started crying." He put his glasses back on, his hands trembling slightly. "I didn't have a clue what to say to her then, but the therapist was with me. I let her take over."

"How did Lisa react to her?" Wanda Nell took his right hand in both of hers and rubbed it.

"At first she acted like she wasn't even going to talk to her, but this woman is really good. She had Lisa talking to her in about ten minutes. I slipped out of the room and went to get something to eat." He brought Wanda Nell's hands up and kissed them. "You feel so good."

Wanda Nell leaned in and kissed him. She drew back, smiling. "You do, too, honey." She paused. "Did you see Lisa again?"

Jack nodded. "She was still acting distant, but I know the therapist helped. She stayed while I talked to Lisa for a little while. I told her we would see that she got the help she needed." He shook his head. "I think it's going to take a long time before she's really well."

"It might," Wanda Nell said, "but we'll do what we have to do. I'll be right there with you, you know that."

"I know," Jack said, smiling. "Now, enough about Lisa. What have you been doing? Did you go by Tuck's office this morning?"

"I did," Wanda Nell said. "And some things happened here a little while ago. I'm going to tell you about it, but I want you to just listen."

Jack stared at her. "Good Lord, what happened?"

"Don't get all worked up," Wanda Nell said, her voice soft. "It's all over and done with, and everything's fine. Okay?"

Jack didn't say anything. He watched her, waiting for her to go on.

"This is going to take a little while," Wanda Nell said. She held on to his hand as she began to talk. She started with what happened in Tuck's office and went on from there. When she got to the point when Bill Warren arrived, she thought for a minute Jack was going to explode. She could see a pulse beating in his temple, but she squeezed his hand. He didn't speak.

Finally, she was done. She leaned back against the couch, still holding his hand, and waited for his reaction.

"I should have been here," he said. "You needed me, and I wasn't here." He closed his eyes. "I'd like to get my hands on that jerk." He opened his eyes again, and their expression was bleak. "I feel like I'm going to throw up, just thinking about what could have happened. I could have lost you."

"But you didn't," Wanda Nell said. "Don't start beating yourself up because you weren't here. That's nonsense, you hear me?"

Jack shook his head. "No, it's not. You needed me, and I wasn't here. I love Lisa, but you're what's really important to me."

Wanda Nell tugged on his hand. "Now you listen to me, Jack. I love you, and I can't even imagine my life without you now. Yes, I need you, but the way things happened this morning, there was no way you could be here. I know it bothers you, but there was nothing I could do about it. You couldn't either."

"Yeah, but that doesn't make it any easier," Jack said.

"No. You weren't here. Mayrene was," Wanda Nell said. "Thanks to her I didn't have to face Bill alone." She held up a hand, forestalling him. "We may not always be in the right place when one of us needs the other one, but it isn't just you and me. There's Mayrene, and T.J and Tuck, and the girls and Lavon. Heck, even Miz Culpepper and Belle. Lisa, too, when she gets better." She sighed. "The point is, honey, we're a family, and we do what we have to when we need to take care of each other. It doesn't always really matter who does it, just that it gets done."

Jack still didn't say anything. Wanda Nell watched him for a moment. She had one more thing to tell him. "I love you, and I need you. Do you really think I could love you as much as I do if you were the kind of man who didn't care anything about his family?"

Jack offered her a faint smile. "No, I guess not."

Wanda Nell relaxed. She hadn't realized how tense she had been. Thank the Lord he was the kind of man who really listened and thought about what you said to him.

"You make a pretty good case," Jack said, his smile wider now. "You're right, I know. I guess I was letting my Tarzan complex get in the way."

Wanda Nell leaned back and looked at him, her eyes moving up and down.

"What?" he said, his eyes narrowing.

She grinned. "Oh, I was just imagining what you'd look like in one of those skimpy little things like Tarzan always wore."

Jack bared his teeth and beat at his chest, but he didn't try the Tarzan yell. Laughing, Wanda Nell leaned against him, and he wrapped his arms around her.

A little while later, Wanda Nell stood. "I don't know about you, but I could use some lunch," she said, holding out a hand. "What say we go fix something to eat?"

"Sounds good," Jack said. He stood, and hand in hand they walked into the kitchen.

On Saturday, Wanda Nell was in her bathroom, finishing her makeup before going to work, when Miranda came in.

"Teddy's here. He and Jack are talking," she said. "Do you still have time to talk to him?"

"Yes, I do," Wanda Nell said. "I'll be right there."

"Okay," Miranda said. She turned and walked out. Wanda Nell wasn't far behind her.

Teddy stood at respectful attention when Wanda Nell came into the living room. "Good afternoon, Teddy," she said. "Nice to see you." She went up to Jack and gave him a quick kiss. He smiled down at her.

"Afternoon, Miz Culpepper," Teddy said. For a moment Wanda Nell thought he was going to salute her. "Thank you and Mr. Pemberton for taking time to talk to me. I know you need to get on to work, ma'am."

"It's okay," Wanda Nell said. "I've got time to talk, and so does Jack." She sat down on the couch with Jack at her side. "Make yourself comfortable."

"Thank you," he said. He sat down in a chair across from her, his back straight and his attention focused on her.

Miranda hovered in the background until Teddy turned to her. "Randa, why don't you sit down, too?"

Nodding, Miranda sat down in the other chair facing her mother and Jack.

"Miz Culpepper," Teddy began, but Wanda Nell interrupted him.

"Teddy, I really wouldn't mind it if you called me by my name," she said. "Every time I hear you say, 'Miz Culpepper,' I think you're talking to Miranda's grandmother." She smiled.

Teddy nodded. "All right then, Wanda Nell." He smiled briefly. He really was an attractive young man, Wanda Nell thought, but she still couldn't get over all those tattoos.

"And you can call me Jack," Jack said. "I don't think we

need to be so formal under the circumstances." He smiled at Teddy.

Wanda Nell squeezed his hand in gratitude. She had told Jack about Miranda the other day after they had eaten lunch. He had taken it well, and he expressed confidence that Teddy would do the right thing by Miranda.

"He's a good kid," Jack had said, "and I think he's got the kind of strength Miranda needs. And it's time for you to let go."

Wanda Nell nodded. She knew he was right, and in some ways she was eager to do so. She just couldn't help worrying about the outcome.

"Miranda and I been talking," Teddy continued. "It was a shock when she told me about the baby, because I wasn't figuring on us having a baby for another couple of years." He shrugged. "But the good Lord saw otherwise, I guess."

Wanda Nell resisted the urge to look at her daughter. She still wasn't sure whether Miranda had gotten pregnant on purpose, or if it really was an accident.

"Miranda and me's been doing a lot of talking," Teddy said. "And I talked to my mama and daddy about it, too. I can't pretend they wasn't a little upset at first, but they know how I feel about Miranda."

"That's good," Wanda Nell said. Miranda had refused to tell her anything about Teddy's plans, so she was very curious to hear what he had to say.

"Miranda and I want to get married," Teddy said. "I figure we ought to do it real soon."

"Do you have a place to live?" Jack asked.

"Yes, sir," Teddy said. "My daddy said he'd help me and Miranda get a house, and it'll be one we can afford. My boss just gave me a raise, and I think we'll be okay."

"You've really been thinking about this," Wanda Nell said, impressed. "And your daddy's pretty nice to do something like that."

Teddy grinned. "He told me he was gonna do it anyway, whenever Miranda and I were gonna get married. It's just happening a little sooner than anybody planned."

"It certainly is," Wanda Nell said. This time she did look at Miranda, and Miranda gazed blandly back at her.

"So I'm asking your permission for me and Miranda to get married," Teddy said, completely serious again.

Wanda Nell smiled, though she could feel the tears wanting to flow. She looked at Jack, and he nodded, smiling, too. "Teddy, I think Miranda's very lucky, and I know we'll all be proud for you to be a part of our family." Now the tears did start flowing, and Jack smilingly offered her a handkerchief.

Teddy grinned and jumped up. "Thank you, Wanda Nell. I promise I'll be good to her and to Lavon."

"I know you will," Wanda Nell said, drying her eyes. She held on to the handkerchief, though, just in case.

"Looks like we've got a wedding to plan," Jack said. He nodded at Miranda and Teddy as they hugged.

"Two weddings," Wanda Nell said as she kissed him.

Wanda Nell's Favorite Recipes

Faye Cook's Skillet Cookies

1/2 cup margarine (or butter)

1 cup sugar

1 egg, beaten

1 cup dates, chopped

1 cup pecans, chopped

2 cups puffed rice cereal

1 teaspoon vanilla

1 small package grated coconut (approximately 1 cup)

Melt margarine in skillet (iron, preferably), stir in sugar, egg, dates, and pecans. Cook over low heat until thick, about twelve minutes.

Remove from heat, let cool slightly until mixture can be handled. Stir in rice cereal and vanilla. Roll cookies in small balls, then roll in coconut.

Yield: about 4 dozen

Jack Pemberton's Favorite Chili

2 pounds ground beef

1 cup onion, chopped

2 15 ounce cans red kidney beans, drained

2 14½ ounce cans tomatoes, drained

2 tablespoons chili powder (add more for spicier flavor, to taste)

1 teaspoon black pepper

1 teaspoon ground cumin

2 cloves garlic, peeled and crushed

Brown ground beef in skillet along with chopped onion. Then combine beef and onions along with other ingredients in a large crock pot. Cover and cook on low for a minimum of eight hours.

When serving, grated cheese (pick one with a strong flavor) may be sprinkled on top, to taste. Goes great with fresh cornbread.

Yield: about 8 servings